DRAGON LORDS: BOOK TWO

THE
PERFECT
PRINCE

Michelle M. Pillow

Futuristic Romance

New Concepts   Georgia

Be sure to check out our website for the very best in fiction at fantastic prices!

When you visit our webpage, you can:

* Read excerpts of currently available books
* View cover art of upcoming books and current releases
* Find out more about the talented artists who capture the magic of the writer's imagination on the covers
* Order books from our backlist
* Find out the latest NCP and author news--including any upcoming book signings by your favorite NCP author
* Read author bios and reviews of our books
* Get NCP submission guidelines
* And so much more!

We offer a 20% discount on all new Trade Paperback releases ordered from our website!

We also have contests and sales regularly, so be sure to visit our webpage to find the best deals in e-books and paperbacks! To find out about our new releases as soon as they are available, please be sure to sign up for our newsletter (http://www.newconceptspublishing.com/newsletter.htm) or join our reader group (http://groups.yahoo.com/group/new_concepts_pub/join) !

The newsletter is available by double opt in only and our customer information is *never* shared!

Visit our webpage at:
www.newconceptspublishing.com

Dragon Lords: The Perfect Prince is an original publication of NCP. This work has never before appeared in book form. This work is a novel. Any similarity to actual persons or events is purely coincidental.

New Concepts Publishing
5202 Humphreys Rd.
Lake Park, GA 31636

ISBN 1-58608-690-1
© copyright September 2004 Michelle M. Pillow

Cover art (c) copyright 2004 Eliza Black

NCP books are available at special quantity discounts for bulk purchases for sales promotions, premiums, fund raising, or educational use. For details, write, email, or phone New Concepts Publishing, 5202 Humphreys Rd., Lake Park, GA 31636; Ph. 229-257-0367, Fax 229-219-1097; orders@newconceptspublishing.com.

First NCP Paperback Printing: 2005

Other titles by Michelle M. Pillow:

Tribes of the Vampire 1: Redeemer of Shadows (now
available in print)
Tribes of the Vampire 2: The Jaded Hunter
Tribes of the Vampire 3: Eternally Bound
Portrait of His Obsession
M&M Presents: All Hallows' Eve
M&M Presents: Christmas
Dragon Lords 4: The Warrior Prince
Cupid's Enchantment
Dragon Lords 1: The Barbarian Prince (now available in
print)
Dragon Lords 2: The Perfect Prince (now available in print)
Dragon Lords 3: The Dark Prince
Lords of the Var 1: The Savage King
Lords of the Var 2: The Playful Prince
Galaxy Playmates 1: Sapphire
Galaxy Playmates 2: Quartz
Silk (Ultimate Warriors Anthology, now available in print)
The Mists of Midnight
Animal Instinct (Ghost Cats Anthology, now available in
print)
Mountain's Captive

Dedication:
To Mandy Roth
A wonderful Author and Friend

Chapter One

Nadja Aleksander inhaled a troubled breath as she took one last look around her room aboard the medic ship. Silk draped the walls, rich and luxurious. Every modern convenience known to space was at her disposal. She had a beauty bed, maid service, and a personal medic unit that checked her blood levels every morning and automatically wrote out her diet for the day.

Nadja had grown up in spacious rooms just like this one, traveling the galaxy with her surgeon father as he moved from medic assignment to medic assignment. She'd seen many things, discovered many cultures and places. She'd been accepted into the most royal of homes. She'd been given everything she could ever want, except her freedom. It was a prison of gilded bars, but a prison nonetheless.

She looked in the mirror as she wrapped her light brown hair into a bun at the nape of her neck, wishing she could dye the locks a different color to better hide them, and whipped a cape around her shoulders. Her heart thudded nervously as she contemplated what she was going to do. She'd never been on her own before, never been without family or bodyguards close by.

She set a letter on her dresser for her mother and hoped the woman would forgive her, even if Nadja knew she'd never understand her need to leave. The thick folds of the cloak enveloped her completely with its fur lining. Going to the metal door, she slid it open with the push of a button, and then paused to listen.

Below her deck level she heard the celebration that would last late into the morning hours. It was her engagement party and no one noticed that the bride-to-be had been missing for nearly two hours. The engagement wasn't about her anyway. It was about the joining of two men--her father and Hank, his Medical Alliance associate.

She grabbed her bags, flung them over her shoulders and made her way across the ship's hall to the elevator shaft that led down to the docks. With a press of a button, she was whizzed down to the docks. No one appeared to notice her as she rushed from the medic spacecraft, through the hanger darkened with night. When she crawled under the pilot's window, she heard a woman giggling within the cockpit. Irvette would be keeping the pilot occupied for the rest of the night, so Nadja had nothing to worry about. She hurried past the small luxury crafts and the personal units waiting in line for their maintenance the next morning.

Nadja came to a corner but just kept walking, not knowing where she would go. A guard smiled kindly at her as she passed. He glanced at her bags and motioned her to move further down the corridor to a carpeted docking plank reserved for first class. She followed his direction curiously and saw a bunch of women loading into a nearby craft. Above them was a banner that read Galaxy Brides in curving script. She took a deep breath and pulled down the hood of the cape.

A uniformed man with a clipboard looked her over and smiled.

"Are you here for a last minute replacement?" he asked.

Nadja nodded.

"Sign here," he said, handing over the clipboard. "We are several short so they will take care of your health screenings in flight. You'll have room 206 on platform two. It's the room all the way to the back. Ship orientation is tomorrow at 9:00 AM."

Nadja signed her name and handed the clipboard back. Her fingers shook nervously.

"Galactic identification?" he asked. Nadja gave him the card and he barely glanced at it. "Perfect, Miss--ah--Aleksander. Welcome aboard the flight to your future!"

"Excuse me." Nadja's voice was soft and low. The man turned to look at her. "Do I owe you anything for the flight?"

"No, Miss. Galaxy Brides Corporation owes you." He smiled happily.

"I wish to invoke the right of privacy law. If anyone asks, I'm not here," she said. Her voice was soft and demure.

"Police?" the man questioned in surprise, though the idea didn't seem to concern him. He had a quota to fill.

"Stalker," she whispered. The man nodded in understanding. Nadja glanced around and saw a red headed woman standing in line behind her. She lowered her voice, and said, "He won't leave me alone, so I am leaving."

"I'll make a note, Miss. That won't be a problem." He began writing on her file.

"And, by the way, where are we going?" Her voice was again

mild and unwavering.

The man laughed. "Most women ask before they come down here. It must be some maniac you are trying to get away from."

Nadja swallowed nervously but said nothing.

The man reigned in his humor, and answered, "You're heading to Qurilixen, Miss."

Nadja nodded and the man left to check in the redheaded latecomer. She hesitated, looking again at the banner. A droid came forward to grab her bags and began leading them up the plank. This was it. This was her ticket to freedom.

* * * *

One month later...

Nadja smiled, looking nervously around the spacecraft's beauty parlor at the other brides. They hardly seemed like the same women she'd shyly met that first day of orientation. Since then, all of them had been enhanced with beauty machines. Their breasts had been lifted and enlarged using the latest technology in modern genetics. They'd been offered permanent hair removal. The hair on their heads had been made to grow long, which Nadja learned from the Qurilixian uploads was the race's traditional style. The uploads were designed to teach the brides everything they needed to know about their new home, through just a few short hours of brain wave transfer.

When Nadja stepped aboard the ship, she had no idea who the Qurilixian were. She only vaguely remembered learning the planet's name in astronomical geography as a student. Her father had insisted on schooling, though he never actually intended that she would use it.

Since she signed her agreement without even reading it, it hadn't mattered to her where she was going. It was part of her new life of taking chances. She'd decided she was going to take the first ship she saw that would have her and that is exactly what she'd done. Her father and the fiancé he picked for her would never suspect her of such a bold move. She was going to be free.

It appeared that taking chances was going to pay off for Nadja. She didn't miss the irony that she was running away from one arranged marriage into another. But, at least this one would be of her doing and her doing alone. She was the only person who had anything to gain or lose

Nadja couldn't have been more pleased to discover that she was off to the outer edge of the Y quadrant, to a place inhabited by primitive males. It's exactly what she would've asked for. It was perfect. Qurilixen was far away from where her father would think to search for her, and the Y quadrant didn't participate in the extradition act so he couldn't register her name and force her to come back without causing an intergalactic incident.

Qurilixian women were rare since the planet suffered from blue radiation. Over the generations it had altered the men's genetics to produce only strong, large, male, warrior heirs. Only once in a thousand births was a Qurilixian female born. Since they had no women of their own, the services of corporations like Galaxy Brides were invaluable to them. In return, the Qurilixian would mine ore that was only found in their caves. The ore was a great power source for long-voyaging starships, all but useless to the Qurilixian, who were not space explorers.

Nadja smiled, liking that little fact as well. Since she'd been born on a ship that was doing light-speed, she was tired of moving around. She wanted to stay put for once and develop roots. She wanted to make a friend and keep her. It was too hard to develop friendships when the other person realized exactly who her father was. She'd seen more people pale and back away from her at that bit of news than she cared to remember.

As to the grooms, she didn't care what they looked like. She wasn't picky. The best comparison anyone could make was to warriors of Medieval Earth. The Qurilixian worshipped many Gods, favored natural comforts over modern technical conveniences, and actually preferred to raise, grow, and cook their own food. They were classified as a warrior class, though they had been peaceful for nearly a century, aside from petty territorial skirmishes that broke out every fifteen or so years between a few of the rival houses.

Anything was better than the balding pervert her father had tried to force her to marry. She should've known something was up when their ship changed course and headed to another region--one where law would permit her father to choose her husband for her.

Nadja glanced over to her side. Morrigan Blake was looking in her general direction. The woman was quieter than the rest and always seemed to be greatly distracted, as if her mind swam with thoughts that had nothing to do with her surroundings. She'd tried to talk to the woman a few times over the last month and found her to be rather intelligent and polite. Truthfully, Nadja was surprised that an independent woman like Morrigan would choose to go to a place like Qurilixen as a bride.

She held still as six robotic hands flew around her head, putting up her light brown hair into a traditional Qurilixian upsweep. Still looking at Morrigan, curiosity got the better of her, and she asked softly, "What about you, Rigan? Have you finished your Qurilixian etiquette uploads?"

Morrigan blinked in surprise at the sound of her name and Nadja guessed she'd disturbed the woman from her thoughts. It took Morrigan's dark eyes a moment to focus. The woman gave her a light smile.

"Didn't you know?" Nadja carefully looked over to her other side at the sound of trilling laughter. Gena's red hair was finished and her beauty droid was placing the customary short veil over the curly locks. "Rigan finished her Qurilixian uploads first. It would seem she is most eager to please her new husband."

"Or to be pleased by him," Nadja heard someone say. This last comment was followed by nervous giggles. When Nadja looked at Morrigan, she swore she saw the woman's eyes roll in the back of her head.

The brides were being prepared for the Breeding Festival that night on Qurilixen. It was the one night of darkness on the otherwise light planet and considered the only night the men could choose a mate. It was a primitive ceremony to say the least, but Nadja thought it very rooted and straight to the point. Just one night for engagement, wedding, and honeymoon and presto, you were a married couple.

The other women spent the entire trip speaking of marrying Princes and noblemen. The truth be told, Nadja wanted a working man--someone with a small house and a garden. She didn't want a pampered life anymore, where society dictated her actions. She wanted to fade away from the responsibility and spotlight and maybe help people. Marrying a small town family doctor would be ideal. However, she would be happy with a farmer or miner or anyone who could provide a decent enough life so they would never starve.

"I wish I could be so ambitious. I'm afraid I didn't watch a single one of those boring uploads."

Nadja had been so wrapped up in her thoughts, that she didn't see who spoke.

"I tried on my gown this afternoon," Gena announced. Nadja flinched as the woman brazenly started poking at her chest. "They are gorgeous, but I think I am going to go get my breasts enhanced again--just a little bigger--and I'm going to have my nipples enlarged. Those Princes won't be able to resist me. Maybe, I'll marry all four of them just for fun."

"How will you know who the Princes are?" came the cynical reasoning of Pia Korbin. Nadja was intrigued by the woman, who was perhaps the most beautiful on the ship. A large part of the beauty came from her not seeming to realize her own beauty, and that she was the envy of half the passengers. "I've heard that all the men wear disguises. You could end up with a royal guard."

"Or a gardener," a brunette offered with a laugh.

"I hear they wear practically nothing at all," a woman with flaming red hair and sparkling green eyes the color of emeralds added. "Except the mask and some fur."

"You can't miss royalty," Gena announced with a bounce of excitement. "You'll see it in the way they move."

Nadja certainly hoped so. She wanted to avoid them at all costs. Though she really doubted the Princes would be there. Royal matches were hardly made by whim or chance. They were more of a political maneuvering. A royal family would never take a gamble on a stranger. It was more than likely an advertising ploy used by Galaxy Brides Corporation to make the trip more enticing. If so, it was a good one, for it had worked on most of the women.

Morrigan stood as her droid finished, prompting Nadja to try and do the same. Her droid wasn't done placing her short veil and gently pushed her back down. Nadja sighed, resigned to remaining in her chair.

The spacecraft was a nice one, though her suite on the medic ship had been nearly twice the size as her one aboard this ship. Nadja was used to the pampering and thought nothing of it. Some of the women jokingly called their quarters the harem. The service was adequate and the staff completely mechanical, so that none of the women could be compromised. Besides, robot servants were cheaper than human ones. One lifecell battery would keep them running for a century or more.

One by one the women finished their beauty treatments, and went to get dressed. Nadja stood, and saw that Morrigan was already gone. She sighed, guessing that was one mystery she wouldn't be able to solve. Too bad, she would have liked to have the intelligent Morrigan as a friend. She'd been too bashful around the other, bolder women to make too big of an effort. Besides, they would never understand her desire to marry a commoner and not a Prince.

"Miss Korbin," a robotic voice said. "This way, it's time for your last treatment."

Nadja glanced over her shoulder. Pia, who was behind her, frowned in embarrassment. Nadja politely turned away from the woman's hazel stare.

Nadja didn't look around again, slipping down the metallic passageway to her own room. Once inside, she locked the door behind her and took a deep breath. Seeing the wedding gown on her bed, she blushed. Her heart beat erratically inside the walls of her chest and her eyes teared up with nervous fear. Praying she did the right thing, she took a deep breath. It was time to see her future.

* * * *

Nadja's future came in the form of a reddish-brown planet surrounded by a blue-green dusk. Stars were beginning to show overhead, winking down from above as they framed a large spotlight moon. Alien trees grew high with enormous canopied leaves. The trees towered over the planet's surface with trunks nearly a fourth the size of their spacecraft. The forest stretched out around them on one side. A mountain grew high in the distance on the other.

Nadja was near the front of the line of brides. Her wedding gown was of a light green silk and gauze. She never dreamed it would be so revealing before she put it on. Lying on her bed, the dress looked like there was more to it than there actually ended up being. The elegant material waved in the cool evening breeze, clinging to most of her body before flaring out in thin strips over her calves and thighs. Nadja shivered, suddenly feeling like an offering.

The gown pulled low on her chest to reveal an ungodly amount of cleavage. A belt looped across the back, growing from the sides to wrap around her wrists. From there they crossed up and over the arms to lock above the elbows. They effectively held her arms down at her sides and made free movement impossible. Nadja's beauty droid had to dress her or else she never would have figured the straps out.

She had silk shoes of a matching green on her feet, and a short veil of the same that fluttered around her ears, tickling her face. Her head swirled with fear. She felt too exposed as her eyes moved directly before her.

The bachelors of Qurilixen stood lined up like half-naked soldiers. The men were fitted shoulder to shoulder in two lines to form a center aisle. Nadja gulped. They were exquisite.

Music and laughter resounded over the campgrounds. Behind the stoic lines of bachelors, other Qurilixian men cheered and posed. Nadja guessed they weren't part of the actually ceremony. A bonfire burned brightly behind the rowdy men, presided over by couples in throne-like chairs. The couples kissed and petted each other freely and no one but the brides appeared to notice it.

The smell of burning wood and fresh air was stirring intoxicatingly around Nadja on the breeze. Pyramid tents spread out over the field, their colorful banners varying in size and design, with torches intermingled between to light the paths around them.

Nadja swallowed, fighting the urge to run away. What had she done?

Standing like bronzed Gods, the grooms held perfectly still in their lines. The warriors were tall--some seven fcct or more. Their jaws lifted. Pride radiated off of each and every one of them, as they waited for the brides to walk through so they could choose their mates. The men were completely naked except for a fur loincloth wrapped around their thick waists and a black leather mask that hid their faces from view, reaching from upper lip to forehead. They had two pieces of jewelry--a bracelet of intricate gold around their sinewy biceps, and a crystal necklace about their necks.   ·

Dusk quickly turned into night as the brides waited to begin. Nadja had expected warriors--but this? Not a one was overweight, or too short, or disfigured in some way. She saw a few battle scars, but that was it.

Firelight illuminated their oil-glistened flesh. From solid neck to muscular legs, they were perfection. Nadja was horrified. She didn't want perfection. She wanted the middle-aged doctor with the friendly smile and kind eyes. Not a demanding warrior who exercised too much and was assuredly self-absorbed and vain.

But still, through her disappointment, she had to admit that the men did make the blood race in her veins. Perhaps it was the setting that made her heart beat faster and her body quake with unfamiliar sensations. Or maybe it was the erotic smells of fire and food combined with the foreign rhythm of their tribalistic music. Everything around her was so primal and barbaric.

On the journey over the ship conversations had almost always turned to sex, and Nadja learned more than she had cared to from some of the other women. But now, looking at the flesh and bone before her, she saw why the women had been obsessed.

Nadja saw a man in a pilot's uniform returning up the docking plank with his clipboard. He nodded in a businesslike fashion to the brides, his shipment having been made. Soon the line was moving forward and the surrounding campsite became deadly still except for the music. Nadja felt her feet being forced to move with the line. She didn't look around as she kept her eyes on the red earth.

Soon the lustful gazes peeking out from the walls of heated flesh forced her to glance up. The men's mouths were firm lines of deliberation and their eyes shone like the sun reflecting on water, boring forward in golden concentration. Her mind went momentarily numb as a spell was cast over her senses. Her lungs expanded, trying to fill with air. She tried not to stare at them too long. She tried to keep her eyes forward, but then...

Nadja's heart stopped in her chest and her ears were plagued with silence. She was sure she was dying, drowning in the liquid pool of dark green eyes. Somehow her feet kept moving. She was too stiff to do aught else but follow where she was led, and her limbs didn't obey her half-hearted commands.

The warrior who looked at her was one of the tallest in the line. Her mind screamed no, but her body demanded, yes him! The crystal about his neck pulsed white as she stared. Her body lurched in hot physical response. When his lips parted in breath, she felt as if he kissed her. She could feel his mouth's texture, so real against her lips that it stole her breath. Never had lust hit her so powerfully or so swiftly. No, it was all wrong. He wasn't the right type. He wasn't what she was looking for. She had it all planned out on the ship.

The man bowed to her as she walked by. There were promises reflected in his aggressive gaze as it dipped boldly over her form.

When his notice made the slow journey back up, she saw manly possessiveness through the narrow eye slit of the dark mask. In that heated moment, Nadja knew she'd been chosen.

* * * *

Olek of Draig felt his body sing with liquid fire, filling him with a deep longing. The creature before him was tall and slender, a great compliment to his height. She had the perfect coloring of a solarflower--the white porcelain skin of the petals, light blue eyes of the center ring, and light brown hair of the soft velvet stem.

Her figure was slight, begging for a man's protection. Her face was reserved, her eyes confident, yet refined. Olek could imagine putting his arms around her, pulling her into the folds of his chest. His fingers curled, instantly wanting to touch her hips only to glide down her long legs to worship at her feet. His body stirred beneath the fur loincloth. It was going to be a very long night.

To his surprise, she swallowed nervously at his attention and tried to break the contact of their eyes. The crystal pulsed on his neck, holding her to him. He was pleased by her modesty as he sent her a kiss. Her cheeks flamed slightly with a blush and Olek could practically taste her sweetness on his mouth.

Bowing to acknowledge her as she passed, Olek gave his eyes the pleasure of watching her walk away. Her nature was composed, dignified. He grinned happily. She would make him a very fine Princess.

The line of brides filtered through, and soon he could no longer see his future mate on her way to the feast that had been prepared. Turning to follow his fellow bachelors to give thanks, his smile never wavered. The Gods had indeed blessed him.

Chapter Two

What a strange way to pick a life partner, Nadja thought, trying to take a bite of Qurilixian blue bread. Her hands shook too badly, and she was forced to set the slice down. She had thought there would be more to the choosing than an actual line--like maybe a little talking or dancing as they got to know each other. She had to hand it to the Qurilixian men. They knew what they wanted and they obviously just took it.

A large buffet had been prepared, spread over the long, wooden table to which the brides were directed. It was a veritable feast of roasted two horned pigs, cheeses and blue bread, strange fruit, crusted pastries. Nadja even thought she saw white chocolate at the far end. It was too far for her to reach, and she was too nervous to ask one of the servants to get her some.

To her surprise, Morrigan chose to sit beside her. Glancing over, she followed the woman's eyes to where she stared at the married couples feeding each other by the firelight. The brides, nervously eating in isolation, didn't draw notice from the jovial Qurilixian couples.

Nadja picked up a silver goblet of wine, gratefully swallowing the sweet liquid the serving men had poured for her. The servants were fully clothed. Nadja saw that the style was long hair for both sexes. The women wore dresses of flowing material. The men wore simple tunic shirts and breeches, definitely appearing of a Medieval Earth influence.

"Where do you think they went off to?" Morrigan asked quietly.

Nadja, surprised the woman was speaking, quickly swallowed and opened her mouth to answer. She knew that the men went to prepare for the night's events. Her words were cut off by a servant who filled her half-empty goblet.

"They go to make offering to the Gods," the young man answered for her. Nadja lowered her goblet to the table when he'd finished filling it. The servant topped off Morrigan's goblet, urging her to drink with a movement of his hand. The man had a thin scar across the tip of his nose. He scratched absently at it, as he answered, "They ask for blessing this night in finding a wife."

"Oh," Morrigan said. The servant again motioned for Morrigan to drink and she did so with a look of annoyance. The servant smiled and wandered off.

"Are you nervous?" Nadja asked in a hush, not touching her drink. She was too apprehensive about the size of her suitor and the wine was starting to affect her thinking. When Morrigan didn't answer, Nadja giggled in nervousness. "I can barely sit still. I think this drink has a lot of liquor or something in it."

Morrigan still didn't answer, only continued to drink as she helped herself to blue bread.

"Rigan," Nadja began in a hush. This was too much. She couldn't follow that gigantic man back to his tent. It was all wrong. He didn't fit the picture in her head. She wouldn't know what to do with a man like him. He was too big, too warrior like. She had expected someone small--more academic in nature. She had her fill of tough guys while living under her father's rule.

Morrigan quietly looked over at Nadja's pale face.

Nadja's wide, blue eyes glanced around full of fear. Leaning forward, she bit her lips and whispered, "I'm scared. I think I've made a mistake. Do you think they would let me go back to the ship?"

"What's wrong?" Morrigan asked, her eyes narrowing in concern. She leaned forward to hear Nadja's frightened whisper.

"I…" Nadja paused and shook her head. Her eyes teared in anguish as she thought of the invincible body of pure sinew and flesh. Hearing the sexual jokes around her and seeing the couples kissing on the throne chairs, she knew she couldn't go through with it. Gulping, she managed weakly, "They're very big, aren't they?"

"Who, the men?" Morrigan questioned needlessly.

"Yes." Nadja swallowed over her tensely thudding heart. The more she thought about it, the more terrified she became. Surely a man his size would injure her. Her head spun. "Do you think they will … will hurt us? They seem bigger than most Earth men."

Morrigan looked at the woman in surprise. "Nadja, have you been with a man before?"

Nadja shook her head, embarrassed. Her father was a doctor. Every morning up until a month ago she had been given medical checks. If her virginity had been compromised he would've known and would've been livid. Whoever took it would've ended up at the wrong end of her father's scalpel and she'd have been locked in punishment for the rest of her life. She'd barely even been kissed, too afraid the medic unit would report the foreign germs on her mouth.

"Not even a droid?" Morrigan insisted.

"No," Nadja said. She let her eyes roam over the fluttering tents in the distance, unable to meet the woman's probing gaze. Morrigan seemed very adept at reading people. Shivering, she lied, "I was always too embarrassed to go to the clubs and try one. But I've seen pictures. Do you think that these guys are ... shaped differently?"

"I haven't given it much thought," Morrigan admitted. "I think that galaxy law requires the species to be, uh, physically compatible before they are matched up. Otherwise, the marriage would do no good. Besides, I hate to sound crass, but the whole point of this is so they can propagate their species."

"I suppose," Nadja answered, not relaxing one bit at Morrigan's cold view of their situation. She gripped her goblet and swallowed more of her wine. Without having to be asked, a servant was right there to refill it for her. She gulped that cup too, much to the man's obvious pleasure.

"Did you ask any of the others?" Morrigan inquired when the servant had retreated down the table. "Have any of them said anything about not being with a man before? Or maybe having been with a man?"

Nadja was confused and shook her head in denial. "We've never discussed it."

"It's really not that big of a deal," Morrigan insisted with a smile. Nadja barely saw it. "I hear several of the women have had their virginity replaced. So it can't be that bad, can it? It hurts for a second, but no more than the series of shots we got on the way here."

"I suppose you're right, though I hadn't heard that." Nodding her head in agreement, Nadja tried to calm down. It wasn't working. She was too scared. She had to go back to the ship before it was too late. She had money in her bag and could easily pay for a return trip. Once there she could find another ship to take her somewhere else--anywhere but here.

"Oh!" Nadja gasped and stiffened. She was too late. The men had arrived. Instantly, she picked the green-eyed barbarian out from the crowd. It was as if he sensed her, finding her along the table and coming for her directly. The wine swirled in her head and she again swore she was going deaf.

Where there had been silence over the festival grounds, music again filled the air. Its low rhythm was as sweet as a warm spring sun and as gentle as the wind's caressing kisses. One by one, the prospective brides fell silent. As they watched the Qurilixian bachelors in wonder, the handsome warriors made their way to stand below the tables. Their eyes scanned and quickly fixed upon the woman of their choice.

Nadja gasped, her heart fluttering, as the green-eyed giant of a man came before her. The crystal pulsed, doing something to her will. It was like a fog descended on her brain, consuming her with liquid and fire, tearing down her inhibitions and resolve. She tried to fight it. She tried to turn away from those probing green orbs. It was no use. He was there and he was looking at her as if she already belonged to him.

The man leaned forward and her breath caught. When he smiled, a light-hearted ardor that drew her in, she nearly swooned. Her fingers began reaching for a drink, anything to keep her from jumping up and discovering if his lips were anything like she imagined. Her hand never made it. His mouth parted to speak and her hand fell down to the table.

"I am Olek, bride." He made sure there was no mistake about why he was there. He'd come to claim her. "Come."

Nadja didn't refuse. How could she? Those eyes, they commanded her with a soft magic. She saw kindness in them and relaxed. Maybe his build meant he worked hard for a living. He could be a carpenter or a farmer. He might not be a warrior at all. The thought helped to calm her fear. When he smiled his seductive smile, her fear returned tenfold.

Olek took her hand in his. His warmth seeped into her suddenly chilled fingers, shooting sparks of snapping fire up her arm. She let him lead her around the edge of the table. Magic filled the air with a spellbinding force, controlling her as she dutifully followed Olek's command. She shivered in anticipation, but the feeling was overshadowed by an intense fear of not being able to live up to his expectations. Surely a man like this would be used to women in his bed. Would he expect her to know what to do? Would he be ashamed of his choice when she didn't even know how to return his kiss?

She walked silently behind him. Given ample view of his strong backside, her mouth went dry and she couldn't look away. The muscles in his hard thighs pumped with each of his graceful steps. Her eyes followed them up as his flesh dipped beneath the loincloth. She had seen naked men before when she watched her father perform surgeries. She knew that men's privates came in all different shapes and sizes. She hoped this one came small. Looking at his broad shoulders, so intimidating, she swallowed. Very, very small.

He took her through the campsite, past a row of pyramids. Nadja could see the other women ducking into the various tents with hardly a protest. She heard laughter drifting about on the breeze from the married couples in their own celebration. The fire still burned brilliantly. Music played faster, encouraging the couples to dance in joyous celebration.

Suddenly, Olek stopped next to a green tent and Nadja almost bumped into him. He turned, giving her troubled expression a laughing grin. He tilted his head to the inside of the tent. Softly, the burr of his accent rolling over her in a wave, he urged, "Come, bride."

Again, she couldn't deny him, moving to dip under the tent's green flap, which he kindly held up for her. However, as she drew near him, she smelled the warm oil on his glistening skin, mixing with the natural scent of man. Nadja was sure this was as close as she had ever been to a conscious man before--especially one so inadequately dressed.

Weakly, she faltered, glancing up into his eyes. Before she knew what was happening, a strong hand was coming up to her face, gently cupping her cheek. The touch was fire to her flushed features. Her lips parted with a ragged, scared gasp. Olek took it as an invitation he wouldn't dare to refuse.

Nadja almost screamed in fright when he tried to kiss her. Dodging under his arm, she darted inside the tent. Olek grinned, though his eyes were baffled. His look resembled that of a stalking beast readying to go after his prey, relishing the anticipation of the hunt. He absently let the tent flap fall shut behind him as he followed her inside.

Nadja froze mid-step as she looked around. The red earth floor was covered completely in soft furs. It cushioned her feet beneath her slippers. Below the center point of the pyramid was a high platform bed, which required a step to climb onto it. Silk hung down around the sides, stirring delicately in the torchlight like soft white clouds.

Nadja recoiled from it as if it was covered in poison. It hit her how intimate this night really could be. Stumbling back, she bumped into a wickedly hard chest.

She jolted in fright, scurrying away from the solid, warm muscles. Her eyes spun, taking in the three corners. In the first, there was a bath drawn, the steaming water coming out of the basin. A sweet perfumed scent rose with it. Folded towels, bath oils, and rinses were neatly arranged at the side.

The next corner had a table full of chocolates, fruits, and cream sauces. One long bench with cushioned seats went along the side, resembling a couch. An earthen wine jug was set in the center. Feeling the heady consequences of the liquor she drank too much of at the feast, she turned her head away.

The third corner, behind the bed, was harder to see at her angle so she ignored it. Feeling rather than hearing Olek coming up behind her, she panicked. Swirling on him, she held up her arms and backed away.

Merriment poured from his eyes and she blushed profusely to see it. He held back, standing tall as Nadja's eyes moved to study him. Before she realized it, her gaze was traveling a seductive journey of discovery over his taut chest. Already his small nipples were hard buds of desire. His flesh dipped in all the right places only to raise and swell with each of his shallow breaths. There was no fat on his chiseled form. She bit her lips, absently chewing at it as she looked.

His broad shoulders carried his thick arms with ease. They were arms that could crush her if he so choose. The metal band on his bicep would have fit on top of her head like a crown. Looking closer, she saw that it was the shape of a dragon that wound around his arm.

Blinking, she looked at his covered face. He did indeed appear bold and strong like a dragon.

"Are you pleased?" he asked when she didn't move. Again, his smile was elegant and light. This was a man who laughed often.

Nadja blinked. To his delight, she colored even more. He took a step forward, moving as if to touch her. Her words stopped him.

"No," she shot, her eyes narrowing in fright. Her breath deepened, as she ordered anxiously, "Just stay back a moment."

His head tilted to the side, waiting for her command.

Nadja took a deep breath, trying to control her undisciplined heartbeat.

"I don't think there is a need to do any of..." She gulped looking around to the bath and then to the bed. Shivering, she took hold of her thoughts. She tried to lift her hand and grew frustrated by the binding straps. With a frown, she began tugging the belt off her arms. "I mean to say, I know the tradition of this night is to prove yourself a worthy mate by a display of your..."

His brow lifted, she saw it shifting beneath his mask. He watched her free herself from the arm ties, liking the way her breasts bounced with her jerking movements. She left the ties to hang at her waist.

Swallowing over her embarrassment, she croaked, "...prowess."

A grin spread wide over his amazingly firm lips. Those lips weren't fair. No man should look that delectably tasty. Nadja made a small sound of distress before continuing.

"I am telling you, there is no need for that. I am not concerned with...." Nadja felt like kicking herself. Her words sounded weak and trembly. Her voice was coming out in hot, breathless pants. What was he doing to her? She felt on fire, like she needed to take off her clothes. Her skin was flushed, starting to sweat. Absently, she fanned her face, trying to concentrate.

Olek watched his lovely bride carefully, enjoying the way her lips sucked in between her teeth, as she tried to get out whatever it was she was trying to say. Her eyes kept dipping to his fur loincloth, as if trying to see through it. Yet, her fingers threaded in front of her, as if ready to strike him if he were to try and pounce on her.

Forgetting where she had left off, she repeated, "I am not concerned with your prowess ... ah!"

Olek whipped his loincloth boldly from his hips and dropped it to the fur-lined floor. He stood naked and proud before her. His feet parted. His arms fell to the side as he held still, inviting her to look her fill of him.

Nadja inhaled a chestful of air, cutting off her words. She rounded her eyes into large spheres. She couldn't look away. Her face paled to see that the size of his mild erection was very much in proportion to the rest of his oversized anatomy. She stretched her fingers, insanely eager to touch it, to have it touch her. The center of all her aching and wonder began to throb, getting scorchingly hot at the idea. She'd dreamt of such things, on those lonely nights far away from any spaceport.

To her mortification, an extremely playful grin spread over his mouth when she didn't turn away. He found hold on his naked hips and tapped his fingers lightly against his flesh.

Nadja gasped, panted, gasped again. He lifted his hand and she thought he would touch himself. She waited to see what would happen when he did. She'd read once that men could harden themselves at will. She was disappointed for he only scratched his stomach and lowered his fingers back to his hip to wait.

Olek couldn't help himself. He let loose a very arrogant, low masculine chuckle. Her round blue eyes stared at him as if he were a striking serpent coming for her. He didn't move, letting her eyes look their fill. And she was looking. In fact, she was doing nothing else. If he wasn't careful, this flushing innocent in front of him would faint dead away. Already he could see she'd stopped breathing altogether.

Nadja stared. The muscles moved up his hair-roughened legs to form rock hard thighs and hips. Nestled beneath a treasure trail of hair, which climbed down from his flat navel, his blatant arousal slowly grew in size and strength.

"Are you pleased?" Olek asked, a deep growl forming in the tone. The words held much more meaning than before. They were a testament to his mounting desire. If she kept looking at him so intently, sucking at her bottom lip with such concentration, he would defy all the Gods and take her right here and now.

Nadja snapped her mouth shut and spun away. Her body swam in dizzying waves and she had to catch herself to keep from falling. Olek looked nothing like the men on her father's operating table. They'd been floppy. He was solid, massive ... oh. Keeping her rounded eyes from looking at him again, she flung her hand frantically behind her. Feebly, she commanded, "Get dressed. I told you I don't have any interest in ... that ... thing."

"You are not pleased?"

Nadja didn't see his spreading grin and didn't know that he was teasing her. A sound of distress left her throat and she had to close her eyes to keep her world from spinning. Hugging her arms to her chest, she bit her fist.

"Do I not please you?" he insisted when she didn't answer right away.

Thinking she had hurt her future husband's feelings somehow and knowing it wasn't a great way to start off their possible life together, she said, "No, you're built fine ... ah, finely built, Olek, really you are. It's just ... I don't put much stock in these things. I think we have more important ... oh!"

Olek couldn't stop himself. He moved to nuzzle her delectably slender throat with his parted lips, licked at her sensitive flesh, and tried to nibble her ear. He was determined to prove her shy words wrong.

She shivered to feel him. Olek grinned along her neck. The little ornery devil inside him made him do it. When she fluttered so nervously, he couldn't resist teasing her. With her body so close, he couldn't stop from touching her. Many grand and wicked ideas filled his head.

Nadja belatedly jumped away, rubbing her neck to try and remove the feel of his moist kiss. It didn't work. He knew it. She tried to deny it.

"Stop that, you one-track barbarian." Her harsh words masked her anxiety.

That stopped him short.

Nadja glanced back at him, unable to help taking another peek. Forcing her eyes to roll in her head, her words were stunted, as she ordered, "Get dressed."

"Choose," Olek said instead. The one word was hard.

"I ... I can't choose, Olek," Nadja answered, knowing he wanted her to choose him for her husband. It wasn't fair. He couldn't really speak until she granted him permission. The only way to grant him permission was to accept him as a husband. "Not yet."

Nadja backed further away from him when he moved. Olek stepped with her, not bothering to cover himself from view. His naked body flexed as he stalked forward, powerful like a beast.

Nadja backed into near the side of the tent. She couldn't escape. To her surprise, Olek didn't jump her, but instead lifted his hand to gently stroke the backs of his fingers over her cheek and neck. His touch paused below her ear, near her racing pulse.

Continuing to caress her, he soothed tenderly, "Your name."

Nadja blinked. The feel of him was too much. What was her name anyway? She couldn't remember.

Leaning over, he lightly kissed the corner of her lips. Nadja stiffened, not returning the embrace. She stared at him. He closed his eyes to her as he smoothly brushed his dry lips over the length of her mouth in a tender probing.

The pulse leapt beneath his gauging fingers. Olek could smell the beginnings of longing in the intoxicating perfume of her body. His arousal lurched, dying to answer the call of her loins. The heat from her breasts beckoned his hand lower to them.

He moved the backs of his fingers to slowly trail over her collarbone, dancing along her quivering flesh. She shivered, panting for breath. Nadja slowly lowered her gaze, her lids suddenly too hard to hold up. Olek drew his fingers over her porcelain flesh, dipping over one breast, deep into the valley, and then over the second. He didn't grab or caress, letting her get used to his closeness. She shivered anew, goose bumps rising along her skin.

He trailed his fingers over her skin another time, passing over one mound and then the other. When her breathing deepened and he heard the heart hammering in her chest as if it was his own, he grew bolder. His finger slipped between her flesh and the silk of her gown. Starting at the side, he drew along the edge, dipping deeper with each passing second. As he reached the center, her nipple was already half erect, awaiting him.

Olek took a deep, agonizing breath as he curled his finger around the nub and pulled it up to set over the top edge of the gown. Then, continuing on, he did the same with the other side.

Nadja's eyes flitted up to him as his finger continued to curl in an aimless pattern, not touching the liberated centers again. When he had her eyes steadily caught in his, he deliberately looked down, letting her see that he watched her body's reaction to him. His mouth parted, blowing hot breath onto her skin. Goosebumps rose on her flesh, her nipples budded to hard erection.

Gasping, Nadja pulled her head back from him to break the torturous contact, and closed her eyes. She knew that he would expect her to be a wife in all ways--especially in these ways--but she wasn't ready. She had to have some questions answered first. She wouldn't be choosing him blindly, not when the outcome was the rest of her life.

"Choose," he urged her. To his disappointment, she hid the round gems of her nipples from his view, pulling her gown up with a fidgety jerk.

Nadja firmly put a hand to his chest, all too aware that he was still completely naked. He'd kept distance between their bodies when he touched her, but she had a feeling that if she asked him he would close the space, giving her what every screaming nerve in her body wanted from him. It was as if her body recognized him completely and wanted him to fulfill it in every way.

"Put your clothes on first," she said, her throat working in nervousness. "Please."

Olek smiled softly at her, seeing the seriousness to her eyes. He slowly nodded. Nadja saw two braids were wound into his hair from temples to ends. The silken locks dipped to his shoulders, brushing back when he moved.

Nadja stood next to the tent wall and allowed herself one peek of his naked backside as he bent over, before forcing her gaze away. Her whole being shivered with the remnants of his fiery touch, heated to a level she'd never thought capable. She held rigid, her eyes trying to focus on anything but him.

Gasping in astonishment, her gaze found the third corner. Nadja closed her eyes in trepidation. It was a low chair, much like an examination table, with stirrups for the feet and straps to hold them into place. A pillow sat on the floor, as if for kneeling. An open trunk of feathers and oils was behind it. She couldn't see much else within the trunk but those two things were enough.

Looking at Olek, she saw he watched her. He was again dressed as she had asked. He tilted his head to the chair in offering. She violently shook her head with a vehement, "No!"

Olek was playing with her. He couldn't help it. This little creature fluttered so nervously that he imagined she might try to take flight and dart away from him.

"Your name," he said.

Nadja took a deep breath. This was more like it. Now that he was more fully clothed they could have a civilized conversation. That is, if her head quit spinning, and her breasts stopped their dreadful aching, and her eyes stopped trying to undress him from his loincloth.

Wishing her words held more force, she said, "My name is Nadja Aleksander."

Chapter Three

Nadja.

The name rolled pleasantly in his brain. It was a good name, a pretty name, a respectable name, and it suited the dignified beauty before him exceedingly well. As her voice gained control, he was pleased to find her naturally soft spoken. Her unpretentious tone was low and sensual and coiled around him in feminine influence. It was a fine contrast to the harsher voices of his fellow Qurilixian. It was a voice he would gladly spend his days and nights listening to. It was a voice he would love hearing shout out his name in passion. He found he wanted to ask her questions just to hear her answer them in her sultry siren's tone.

He didn't have to ask. Her lips parted and she spoke to him freely with a question of her own.

"Are you a farmer, or perhaps a miner?" Nadja asked, looking over his physique.

Nadja had met many Princes and his body wasn't of a pampered Prince or nobleman. For that she was glad. Olek was confused by the relevance of her question. He shook his head, prompting her to say, "Then, what do you do for a living?"

Olek smiled, staying quiet. He thought it was a sensible question, and admired it while still wishing her thinking wasn't so logical. Closing his eyes, he imagined his tongue bathing in wine as he drank from her flushed, pale skin. He almost groaned with the idea of it.

"Oh, sorry, I forgot you can't converse yet," Nadja said with a frustrated sigh. "That makes this rather difficult, doesn't it?"

Olek merely smiled. It wasn't supposed to be a light decision and he was glad she didn't take it as such. Maybe she would drink from his flesh. He wondered how those lips would feel wrapping around his arousal, sucking liquor from him with her hot mouth.

Nadja sighed louder. She was completely unaware of his erotic thoughts. Biting her lips, she said, "All right, let's try this another way. Are you a working man?"

Again an irritatingly beautiful smile met her question. His teeth were straight and white. Seeing her attention to his mouth, Olek let his tongue slide over the edge. Oh, but the distance between their flesh was driving him mad. He tensed, his stomach muscles contracting. Maybe after she drank from him, he could get her to ride him hard like she was breaking in a new ceffyl. He'd even let her tie him up if she wanted, completing the fantasy. He'd bet his crown those long legs of hers could restrain him.

Nadja shivered and shook herself. His look only heated more intensely.

"I'll tell you right now, I want a working man. Are you one?" she insisted. Relief overwhelmed her when he nodded his head. At least he wasn't a Prince.

Olek stepped forward watching the subtle curving of her body. If his mind didn't stop drawing pictures of her, he'd attack. She moved to look at him, holding him back with the force of her gaze. She wasn't finished.

Swallowing, Nadja said, "I won't lie to you or try to trick you. I'll work hard--by your side if I have to. I don't have girlish notions of what this marriage is to be about. I don't expect us to be in love and I don't expect you to tell me you love me. In fact, I would prefer it if you respected me enough not to try and placate me with such sentiments."

Olek watched her quietly, not showing any emotion as he took in every word. His gaze remained as sizzling as molten lava.

"I do expect loyalty and honesty," Nadja continued, heartened by his silence and patient listening. "And I'll give you the same courtesy in return. I believe this could be a great partnership."

When she paused to look at him, Olek nodded once, urging her to finish. His eyes bore into her with a piercing fire that curled her toes and made her stomach ache in an all too unusual way.

"I suppose you'll want children?"

Olek didn't like the practical, uniform way the words came out of her mouth. He nodded in answer anyway. His eyes dipped to her slender hips and to the unfairly seductive pose they were in. Her legs were spread just enough that he could run his finger between her thighs to test her softness, her wetness, her feminine heat. He tried not to groan.

"Fine," Nadja agreed, unnerved with his continued staring. He eyed her like he wanted to procreate at that very moment. "I shouldn't mind children ... in time. But, not right away."

Again, Olek nodded. What did he care? He wasn't thinking of

children, just practicing the making of them. He knew that nothing could come of them tonight. Because of their laws, climax couldn't be reached. However, he was a glutton for punishment and he would gladly spend the night torturing them both.

"As to," Nadja paused unable to hide her blush, as she motioned to the bed. "As to us being together, I think we should wait until we are better acquainted."

Olek frowned, his jaw lifting in surprise. Subtly sniffing the air, he smelled the lingering hints of her desire for him. If he was forced to smell that every day, there was no way he was going to wait to claim her. He would go mad. His loins tightened in instant protest to the idea of denial. He was a man of refinement and infinite patience, but even a saint would crumble under such torture.

"I'm not saying I won't marry you. I just don't want to … to … to copulate just yet," Nadja explained, proud of her diplomatic choice of words. "Besides, if we are to have children later, then there is no need to do it now."

Olek's frown deepened. His arms crossed boldly over his chest. He hoped she was finished. He couldn't take much more of her nervous logic. Already, he could tell she was inexperienced in the ways of men and assumed that was why her words were so frustratingly clinical.

"So, those are my terms. If you agree to them, step forward and I'll remove the mask. If not, stay there and I'll be happy to leave," Nadja finished. She didn't have to wait long before he took a confident step forward and then another. His arms stayed crossed, but his eyes devoured her face with their fervor. It was the same as having a thousand fingers touching her skin at once.

Olek didn't like her last stipulation. But, as he saw the glaring loophole in her demands, he decided to accept it. He would just have to make it torture for her until she begged him for his … copulation.

"Oh," Nadja breathed when he stopped before her. He stood proud and unmoving. Breathlessly, she said, "All right, you've decided already."

"Choose." The words came out like a command.

Nadja bit her lip. She studied his face. Her fingers shook as she reached out to touch the leather of his mask. Nervous, she untied the straps at the side. She brushed his braided hair aside and paused. "You're sure then?"

Olek's dark eyes glistened like the surface of glassy water, deceptively hiding a deep undercurrent below. Only then did she see the soft glow of the crystal about his neck. It got brighter the closer he came to her. His mouth pressed together in a harsh line, as he again said, "Choose."

"All right, Olek," Nadja said. Finishing the task, she pulled the string. The glow of the crystal reflected off her hands with its white light. The mask slid to the side unveiling a face more handsome than she could have pictured in her mind. His nose was strong and straight. His brow the sculptured perfection of a man well made. He had the high, proud cheekbones of his people, but his deep-set eyes were what held her. They didn't change from their green depths, as she looked into them. "I choose you."

Olek's mouth curled with mischievous humor. The mask dropped from her fingers at the look before she could even draw them away. It fell against his shoulder before sliding to the floor.

"Hi," Nadja murmured weakly. She tried to smile and failed miserably.

"Hello, Nadja," Olek returned, lifting to cup her cheek. His voice was strong and so confident in his rolling Qurilixian accent. It sent shivers over her skin.

"I think tradition says we have to talk," she said, trying to act cool. She attempted to pull away but her body refused to move from him. Her treacherous flesh wanted to stay and find out more about his touches and heated looks. Inside her stomach swam with the knowledge of what she had done. In one little act, she had married herself to a complete--albeit incredibly handsome--stranger.

"No," Olek corrected. "Tradition is that we must discover each other."

"Yeah," she agreed with a nod. "Talk."

"No, discover," he corrected.

"So we talk," Nadja wasn't sure she liked the suddenly dominant way his brow rose on his forehead. "As in converse."

"It's my people's tradition, Nadja." Olek smiled. It was a wicked look, full of masculine determination and authority. He leaned forward to tower over her. "I think I know what it is. We are to discover each other. We are to learn each other. We are to reveal ourselves completely."

Nadja, tall for a woman, wasn't used to being towered over. Olek's eyes dipped purposefully over her dress, consuming her with his heated gaze. Nadja stiffened in fear. She was in for a long night of trouble.

* * * *

"My King," a blond haired soldier said, as he came through the forest of colossal trees. The torches didn't reach this part of grounds, but the moon shone bright to light the way in a blue glow. The man stuck his hand over his heart and bowed. He was dressed as a servant, but his eyes looked around with cunning. "All the Princes have found brides."

The man he addressed stepped forward into the light, his eyes giving chills to those who obeyed him. By looking at his face, it was impossible to determine his age. His body was young and healthy. His eyes appeared as old as the stars.

"Very good," the blond King said, smiling a cruel smile. "Let us wait until they are bonded completely. Only then can we assure the end of their line. Once those Draigs lose their mates they will be done. The new Princesses will die, starting with the oldest son's bride. The line of the Draig rule will be ended and the Var will once more be the only force in this land."

The warrior smiled. As he watched, the King rolled his neck on his shoulders as he shifted into a more natural form. Hair grew to cover his face and body, claws formed on his hands. His mouth elongated, gnashing with sharpened fangs. When he looked back it was through the eyes of a wild cat. His voice crackled in low, deliberate tones in the back of his throat. Growling, he ordered, "Go."

The King watched the spy take off before turning to run swiftly into the forest, disappearing completely as he blurred into the trees.

* * * *

"Stay back!" Nadja held out her hand. "You don't have to do this, Olek. I am pleased by you, very pleased."

"I'm glad to hear it," Olek smirked, his face radiating with confidence.

Now that the mask was off, Nadja could see that his green gaze held much humor in its depths. Was he laughing at her?

Olek let his eyes travel her uninhibited. "But I wish to see if I am as pleased by you. Take off that gown. I want to look at you."

Nadja glanced at the mask, wishing she could put it back on. This man was too much for her. Whatever had possessed her to consider him? She wanted a fat, short, old doctor with a sweet temperament and little sexual prowess. Why had she suddenly raised her standards? She must've been temporarily insane!

It's all that wine I drank at dinner, she thought suddenly. The crystal pulsed, causing a wave of emotion to flood her system. And that damned rock!

"No, you agreed," Nadja sputtered, clutching the gown to her chest.

"I agreed no copulation, wife," Olek answered with a grin that heated her cheeks to flaming. "I didn't say I wouldn't finish this night as it was meant to be finished. Or do you wish for me to call the council elders for clarification?"

Nadja considered that. What was her other alternative? She didn't want to have to go back. She couldn't risk her father finding her. She was well aware of what he was capable of. Swallowing, she asked apprehensively, "You just want to look? That's all?"

Olek's nostrils flared in excitement. "Yes, let me look, for now."

"You … you won't touch me?" Nadja tried to take a calming breath. She didn't believe she was considering doing it. She thought of her father and steeled her nerves. She had to do it.

Oh, but this is going to be sweet torment, Olek thought, part in anticipation and part in agony.

"Not until you touch me first," he promised.

Nadja swallowed in relief. That wouldn't be so hard. She had no intention of going to him. But, as his eyes lit with challenge and mischief, she grew worried. What did this barbarian have in mind?

"No tricks?" Nadja persisted, trying to stall.

"Would you like me to help you undress?" he offered, smirking with an arrogance that made her knees weak.

Nadja's mouth opened, but no sound came out. Instead, she furiously shook her head. Swallowing, she looked around.

"Where?" she asked, beginning to shake terribly. "Here?"

"Anywhere you wish." Olek didn't relent and he didn't back away. It would be good to get this shyness out of the way. He didn't want his wife afraid of him. He would just have to prove to her that he could be trusted with her body, as well as her spirit.

Nadja took a step back, looking around. Seeing the table, she said, "Can … I need a drink."

Olek's body almost exploded in disappointment, as Nadja skirted past him. He took a deep breath, trying to be patient. They had all night for this and a lifetime for the other.

"Would you like some?" Nadja asked.

"Trying to get me drunk?" Olek mused, coming slowly to follow her.

Nadja instantly blushed, proving she had in fact thought of it.

"Qurilixian males don't get intoxicated with this wine." Olek lifted a finger as if he would touch her neck, but then drew back, remembering his promise not to touch her until she touched him. By the look on her face, he might be waiting a very, very long time. "We are immune."

"So you just get the girls drunk." Nadja tried to laugh. His darkening look made it come out in a short, soundless chuckle. "Sorry."

"Why are you so nervous? I am your husband. You have no reason for this embarrassment. The whole purpose of our customs is to do away with doubt. We trust in the powers around us to know our path."

Nadja gulped down a goblet of wine before coughing. Taking a shaky breath, she said, "Yes, but you are also a stranger. I only saw you for the first time a few hours ago."

Olek lifted the crystal about his neck. He twirled the glowing orb in his fingers. "But this proves we were meant to be. That is why we have these ceremonies, so there will be no walls. We trust in the power of it to guide us."

Nadja swallowed nervously. "So, is it true you have always had those? Since the day you were born?"

"It is," Olek answered, pleased by the relaxing note he detected in her tone. It was good she showed an interest and knowledge in his people's ways for they were now her ways too.

"And has it always pulsed like that?" Nadja took another drink. As if to prove her point, the crystal pulsed brightly sending tormented agony sweetly through her limbs, creating a mad rush of ache and need inside of her.

"No, only tonight, when I first saw you come to me," Olek said. Taking the crystal, he touched it lightly to her skin. A fire ignited on her flesh where he drew it softly in lazy circles about the base of her neck. "That is when the crystal first came to life."

"So, it reacts to the moonlight?" Nadja probed, her lashes fluttering weakly. She felt the crystal pulling her towards Olek's body, numbing her mind to everything but this handsome warrior man.

"It reacts to what is between us naturally. It shows us the will of our hearts," he answered. Her reaction to his admission wasn't what he would have expected.

Nadja stiffened and pulled away from him. A frown marred her features. "I told you. I don't love you and I don't expect you to love me. I will be practical about this."

Olek was hurt. How could she know the many years he had waited for her? He'd had blurred dreams of her since he was a boy. It wasn't just fate that brought her to him. It was destiny. Even if she didn't believe it, he did. And he knew it to be true, as did all his people.

"Nadja," he whispered tenderly. "Why are you afraid?"

"I'm not afraid--"

"You promised honesty," Olek interrupted. "I can smell your lie on you."

"I..." She took another drink, stopping only to glance at him. For good measure, she turned away and took another.

Olek frowned, lifting his hand to stop her. With his fingers, he tilted the edge of her goblet down and drew it from her without touching her hand. She jerked in alarm.

"It's time, Nadja."

"Time?"

Olek's eyes dipped down over her form clad in the traditional silk. He overwhelmed her as they leisurely consumed her with his hunger. After his heated inspection was finished and she was trembling uncontrollably, he didn't need to answer her.

"Can you get the lights at least?" Nadja twisted her hands.

"There is no point, little solarflower. I can see in the dark. Now, come."

Olek stepped back, his eyes drawing her forward with his will as he led her to the center of the room onto the soft fur rugs. When he stopped, Nadja stepped to him. He took his hand and held it above her hair, drawing it over her face without touching. She closed her eyes, feeling his heat but not his touch. Olek moved over her neck and chest, down over her stomach and back up again. When he stopped, she opened her eyes, amazed that she could feel so much without even being touched.

In a low murmur that sent chills over her, Olek said, "You are beautiful. There is no need for shame. Take off your gown for me."

Seeing the look in his eyes, a passionate spark that was all for her, she couldn't refuse him. First, she kicked off her slippers. Her toes dug into the softness of the fur. Next, she slowly lifted her hand to her side. Nadja studied his eyes as she moved. Tugging at the silk bodice, she pulled the strapless top down. Instantly a breast was freed. His nostrils flared slightly, but he didn't look down. The crystal pulsated its spell around them.

Freeing the other breast, she slowly pulled the gown down to her waist. She hesitated. The tent was warm, but the heat radiating off her new husband was all she felt and her back became chilled without Olek's fire. His eyes lightened, coloring with a golden hue. She blinked and the look was gone. Surely, it had been the reflection of torchlight.

"Finish," Olek said. The word sent a breath over her skin.

Nadja swallowed nervously. Leaning over, she pulled down the gown. Soon she was standing, clad in only her lace panties.

Olek, keeping his gaze steady, took a step back from her. As he put distance between them, he let his eyes travel down. He couldn't speak. The breath caught in his throat. She was in perfect feminine shape. Her body was toned with muscle, yet with just enough female softness to the curves as not to make her look hard. Her flat stomach pulled against her hip bones, creating a delight for the eyes as the lace clung to her hips. He already had seen her slender arms and most of her legs, but they too added to the wistful, wood sprite image before him.

Observing the long length of her legs, leading from her small ankles all the way to her hips, his body quaked. These were legs that would easily wrap around a man and hold him inside her.

"Am...?" Nadja couldn't finish. When Olek looked up, he saw her face was down and turned from him. Her pale cheeks were colored to the brightest of embarrassed pinks. The cascading curls of her soft brown hair spilled over her shoulders, coming forward to hide a delectable breast from view.

"You're lovely, solarflower." His voice was hoarse with his rampant desire. "Now, take off the rest."

Nadja couldn't make herself look at him. Uneasily, she pulled her panties off her hips and kicked them to the side, baring herself completely. No one had ever seen her naked, save for the beauty droids who had pampered her--and they never cared.

Olek sucked in a breath. Beneath his fur he was hard, pulsating fiercely with his arousal. Her mound was covered in a thin trail of hair. His lips parted, wanting a taste.

Nadja froze as he moved around her, careful to keep a wide distance between them as he looked. Olek stopped. He saw a mark on her firm backside.

"What is this?" he mused, leaning slightly closer to get a better look of the black symbol. He didn't recognize the meaning of the marking.

"Oh," Nadja turned, stretching around to look at the swirling design. She'd had it for so long that she had forgotten it was there. She hated it. It was the brand of the Medical Alliance, essentially marking her as their property. "It's just a tattoo. I got it a long time ago."

Olek frowned. She wasn't lying, but he could tell there was more to it than she let on. He continued forward, but she was still distractedly looking at her back hip.

"Nadja, look at me."

She did, peeking through the veil of her lashes.

"Look," Olek insisted. She turned her face more fully to study him, though her head was still dipped. "I want you to see what you do to me."

Nadja gulped. She was too stunned to move. Did all men speak this boldly? Where all men as confident with women? Or was it just husbands to their wives?

Until the night her father announced her engagement at a dinner party, she had never even been approached by a man. The announcement had come as a surprise and a horror. Hank had given her an engagement ring with a very inappropriate gift. She had been horrified and ran away--much to the disgusting pig's pleasure. Standing here now, looking at Olek's perfect form, she couldn't imagine a life with Hank.

Olek took the fur from his waist. There was still distance between their bodies, so even if he wanted to he couldn't reach her with his arms without going to her. Dropping the loincloth to the floor, he stood proudly before her.

Without flinching, he said, "See what looking at you does to my body?"

Nadja did see and it terrified her as much as it fascinated her. The long length of him was sprung to full attention. Veins grew out on the sides, forcing his erection still and tall. She was a doctor's daughter, so the technical part of how they fit together she had known about for years. As to the reality, she didn't see how it could possibly work.

"Olek," Nadja said, shaking her head. "Please, don't--"

"Shhh." Olek didn't allow her to finish her plea. "You are mine. That is the end of it."

Nadja looked into his passionate eyes and was lost. Yes, she was definitely his.

Chapter Four

Nadja stared at his arousal, an arousal he claimed was all for her, for an abnormally long time. Slowly, she blinked, looking up into the harsh expression on his face. He was fighting for control. She had to admire his restraint. But, seeing his expression, she grew worried.

"You said you wouldn't touch me until I touched you," Nadja said softly. It was odd standing so before a man. But Olek's gaze only held molten approval and she didn't shy away. His look empowered her on a baser level, giving her a confidence she had never felt. Wine swam warmly in her veins, causing her to relax as she let her husband and his mystical crystal work their magic over her.

"I am not going to touch you," Olek said with a roguish smirk growing on his masculine mouth. He licked his lips in anticipation. "You are going to touch yourself for me."

Nadja swallowed in fear, already out of her league. Sure, she had tried a few hesitant things while alone in the dark, but she was always too scared the medic unit would discover what she had done and report it to her father. That damned unit reported everything to her father--even a small piece of chocolate she once ate. It had been delicious and almost worth the three days of punishment she had received for it. She had never tried one again.

"I," Nadja could hardly breathe. Her cheeks flamed, but she couldn't look away from his magnetic eyes. "Olek, I can't do that. I'm not--"

"Yes," he broke into her words. "You can."

"No, I..." To his amazement, her cheeks deepened in color. He wouldn't have thought it possible. With a deep breath, she said, "I don't know how."

That brought him up short. Tilting his head to better study her, he sniffed the air. She wasn't lying.

"How is that possible? You are no child." Olek waited a long time for her to answer.

"My father," Nadja began, not really wanting to think of the man at such a moment. "He--we had this medic unit. I would measure my … ah, levels each morning. I couldn't even eat chocolate without him finding out. And, well, if I was to … ah, you know, it would tell him that in my daily report."

Olek frowned. He knew he would likely never have daughters, but he didn't imagine he would control them in such a way. His people believed that children were part of the group, to be guided and molded by the extended family unit, allowed explore and discover, allowed to make mistakes. How else would they learn?

"They were very thorough machines," she said, humiliated. She closed her eyes, wishing the ground would open and suck her in. Her fists clenched at her sides.

Olek said nothing. He was too busy thinking of ways he could pay back her father for treating her so callously. He knew by the look on her face that there was much more she wasn't telling him.

"I'm sorry," Nadja said softly, when he didn't speak. "I should have said something about this before. I really don't know anything when it comes to … and I understand if you want to put your mask back on. I won't tell anyone I took it off."

Olek didn't move, save for his chest.

"You are no longer under his tyranny, solarflower," Olek said. The pet name washed over her, doing something to her already melting insides. "If you wish to know something of your body or mine, ask. I'll freely tell you or show you everything I know. Every passion you feel is normal and very right. I feel the same for you."

Nadja swallowed. Her voice wouldn't work if she tried. Being married to a simple man was looking better and better each passing moment.

"Now, it would give me much pleasure if you would touch yourself," Olek said. His eyes bore heatedly into her flesh. "And it will give me even greater pleasure when you touch me."

Nadja shivered despite herself.

"Like this," he urged in a tender hush. Taking himself in hand, he stroked his hard manhood several times. Nadja bit her lip, wishing she could get the courage to go to him. She followed the movements of his fingers. The crystal pulsed and glowed from his chest. Of their own accord, her fingers found her stomach. They scratched lightly at her flesh, absently mimicking his wicked movements on his own shaft.

Olek nodded in approval, urging her silently to caress herself for him. With a weak pant, she slid her finger to reach into her wetness. The nub of her passion tweaked in pleasurable anguish. Watching him, she timidly stroked herself. Her legs twitched. Her hips jerked in a little circle. Her finger spread her own opening.

Olek growled. He stroked faster as his eyes devoured her hand. If he wasn't careful, he would explode.

Soon her hand wasn't enough. Nadja wanted his experienced hand to be on her flesh. She wanted it to be his finger dipping next to her center fire. With a moan, she went to him--ready and unmindful of anything else.

Olek grinned, a naughtily dominant look that drove her to distraction. It hadn't taken her long at all to come around. The fact pleased him very much.

Nadja hesitated only briefly as she looked down at his hand wrapped around his erection. Letting go, he moved it to the side. Nadja licked her lips, glancing up at him for approval before she touched him. Olek nodded weakly. He was sure he would go mad at any moment. Her fingers had stirred her natural scent into the air to torment him.

She was giddy with excitement, her chest heaving as she took him in her hand. He was solid and firm beneath her palm. Olek's hips jolted at the tender assault. Nadja pulled back, worried that she may have done him harm. His features did look pulled back in pain. Putting his hand over hers, he brought her hand once more to him and showed her she could squeeze and not hurt him.

The moment she stroked his manhood with her fingers, Olek turned her and drove her back towards the bed. He instantly explored her back, her arms, her neck and hair. He lowered his mouth to claim hers in a mind-searing kiss that left them both breathless and faint. He tasted her, as his lips sucked her tongue into his mouth.

A moment of panic overtook her as his dangerous erection sought to be closer to her depths. She had little time to protest as he brought himself next to her. He crushed into her, causing a new wave to flood her heated flesh. She achingly rubbed her breast against his sturdy chest, budding to attest her newfound desires. She clutched her legs, fearful of the scalding heat his searching manhood was spreading, as it burrowed naturally into the fold of her hip.

She let him go, desperate to explore the rest of him. Her touch was timid in its innocence, which only drove him to greater distraction. Olek's hands were not so unsure and they ventured over her, stroking and teasing every tender piece of flesh he could reach.

"Olek," Nadja groaned, not understanding what was happening. She felt on fire. She felt as if she were drowning, overwhelmed by this man and his passions. She couldn't keep up, couldn't process what he was doing, what she should be doing.

"Shh," Olek knew he had to slow his touch. If he took in too much more he would become a rutting beast. She followed his lead, coming to lie on his chest as he absently stroked the flesh of her back. His heartbeat raced beneath her hand, matching her own frantic rhythm.

"Did I do something wrong?" she asked, wondering why he stopped.

"No, you did everything very right. But, we cannot finish it this night. It's forbidden."

She blinked, not sure if it was relief or anguish overcoming her at the words.

"Tonight is for discovery only--discovery of self, of passion." His breathing was hard. She stiffened slightly when he moved to stroke her breast. Knowing she couldn't help it, he smiled. "Lay back on the bed."

"But, you said--"

"We cannot finish this, little solarflower, but I'm not finished exploring you. Lay down." Olek tilted his jaw to the mattress.

Nadja, whose legs were feeling suspiciously like jelly, nodded and stepped up the raised platform before crawling on the bed. Lying down, she placed her hands on her stomach and waited. Olek sighed as he stepped away.

Grabbing a bottle of oil, he didn't bother to dress. Nadja stiffened.

"What are you doing?" she asked.

"I am going to let you get used to my touch, solarflower," Olek answered with a playful wink.

Nadja was breathless as he rubbed oil between his fingers. Starting at her feet, he began massaging the arch. Nadja tensed, giggling. Her foot jerked.

"Hold still."

"I ... I can't," she giggled louder, jerking again. "I'm ticklish."

Olek smiled and deepened his touch. Soon, her foot got used to the attention and her laughing expression turned more serious.

"There," he soothed, "just relax."

She jolted when he touched the other foot, but soon the intoxicatingly erotic scent of oil flooded her senses and his hands worked magic on her feet. He worked a calf then the other, taking his time as he touched her. Nadja didn't move, closing her eyes and just feeling. He slid his gentle hands over her knees with aching tenderness. She tensed as he came up her thigh, but soon the power of him relaxed her once more.

Olek groaned. His eyes bore into her center fire. He saw the oil glistening on her skin. His fingers flowed over soft, smooth flesh, itching to slide higher, right into her. He held back, moving to massage her other thigh. To his pleasure, she didn't tense again.

Skipping her middle, he massaged her hands and arms in turn. Then, he ordered her to turn onto her stomach. She didn't see his look of intense pleasure as his eyes laid claim to her pert buttocks. He treated the backs of her legs to the same treatment he had given the front, before going on to her shoulders, neck and back. As he worked his way lower, he moved to straddle her. His mouth opened, wanting to take a playful bite out of her flesh. He denied his mouth, but not his hands.

With a staggered breath, he cupped her buttocks. A moan escaped Nadja, weak in her relaxed state. His thumbs dipped to edge closer to her aroused center.

"Turn," he said huskily. Olek lifted himself up, still straddling her as she moved.

Nadja was weak, but she obeyed.

He renewed his hand's journey at her neck, sliding between her breasts to her stomach. He touched her hips, her sides, working his way to the center peaks of her breasts. She arched her back and he took the soft globes fully into his palms. The oil made his caresses all the more pleasurable. Unable to deny his mouth again, he leaned over and sucked a nipple between his lips.

Nadja bucked off the bed as lightening struck her soul. Olek growled in pleasure, tasting her, biting gently, reveling in her natural response. The other breast received the same treatment from his hand, pinching and caressing.

"Ah-h," Nadja gasped for breath. She grasped weakly at his

hair. Before he knew what was happening, his legs were parting hers. Oil slid between them, helping him glide forward between her thighs. His solid erection came to her, insistent that it get its fair share of her pleasure. Her heat beckoned him with its moist offering.

"Olek," Nadja called out, trembling. Her body stiffened to feel such a hard mass by her tender opening. She tensed, unsure what she was waiting for.

Olek stopped, hearing her cry. Taking a deep breath, he knew he couldn't take her. If the others sensed their fulfillment tomorrow, as they went to crush the crystal before the council, all would be lost. Their marriage wouldn't be approved and he would have to spend the rest of his days alone.

"I'm sorry, solarflower," Olek grunted as he withdrew. "We mustn't."

"I know," she said, aching for the unknown.

"Just give me a moment." Olek gasped to catch his breath. He turned from her, running his fingers into his hair as he waited out the worst of his denied passions. When he could again move, he looked over. Nadja had fallen asleep. He almost laughed.

With a sigh, he lifted her up into his arms. She blinked, trying to wake up and he shushed her back to sleep. He knew it had been a long night for her. Easing her under the covers, he couldn't help taking one last look of her flushed body in the gentle torchlight.

He dimmed the torches, putting some of them out to darken the tent. Then, shaking his head, he went to bed on top of the covers next to her, careful not to touch her body with his overheated one. Sleep wasn't even close to claiming him. This was going to be an extremely long night.

* * * *

Nadja blinked awake, a cold sweat beading her flesh. She shot up in bed. All around her was darkness. She reached out, jolting to awareness as her arms met with the fur coverlet. She was naked underneath.

Blinking, she tried to clear her vision and see through the dark. Her horrified, sleep-hazed eyes looked around, frantically searching for her father or his men in the dark shadows of the tent. Her mind screamed at her, yelling that he would know what she'd done, that she let this barbarian touch her, that it had given her pleasure to have him touch her. He'd put her in punishment for a month this time. She'd never survive a whole month, deprived of sleep, of light and fresh air, of food. This time, he might actually kill her.

Her eyes adjusted to the dimness. Her heart was the only sound she heard as it beat dangerously and wild in her ears. Slowly, as the fog of sleep lifted, she realized he couldn't have possibly found her. She took a deep breath, looking over to where Olek slept near her side. She was safe.

A strange comfort came over her fear. Here was a simple, giving man. She told herself she could trust him to take care of her. He would take her to his little cottage somewhere, where they could live a life away from the limelight. She didn't have to live in fear anymore. There was no way her father would find her--not like if she had married a nobleman whose picture could be published in any number of ways, whose name would be carried in connection with hers across the galaxy.

On a planet like Qurilixen they would never have heard of her father's name, or known his untouchable reputation. She would have changed her name before now, but there hadn't been enough time to fake her Galactic Identification. She would change it now, she decided. She would take Olek's name as her own, whatever it was. She would never have to utter the word Aleksander again.

With Olek she had done well. He would never know who she was. Her past ended at this very moment. She wouldn't spend her life looking over her shoulder, waiting for her father's men to come for her. Olek was strong. He would keep her safe. He was perfect.

Nestling down next to him on the bed, she pulled the covers over her body and gently moved to touch his cheek. Olek didn't move, merely sighed. Nadja drew her hand away from him. As she closed her eyes, she thought, *Yes, we will have that simple life. Nadja Aleksander will vanish--forever.*

* * * *

Olek felt his wife sit up as she jolted awake. He didn't move as she looked around the room. His tired mind kept with her, relaxing as she snuggled back down. It was only a nightmare that disturbed her slumber. He tried not to smile as she touched his cheek in a gentle caress. Soon, he detected her breath to deepen, as she drifted into a more peaceful sleep. Whatever it had been, he hoped her nightmares were over.

* * * *

Nadja yawned, smiling slightly as she refused to open her eyes. It had been a good night, her best since discovering her father's engagement plans for her. Stretching her arms, she met with the empty bed.

The tent was bright, lit up from the outside. Taking a deep breath, she tried to tell herself that it was real. She was safe and she was free. A smile graced her lips as she sat up. Olek was gone. It didn't matter. She had studied their tradition and knew that he would honor their marriage no matter what. Guiltily, she thought of her father.

No, she told herself. Olek will never have to deal with him. It's all in the past and we will make our own future. He'll never have to know what I have done. I am not Nadja Aleksander anymore. I am simply Nadja ... I am a solarflower.

She smiled, liking his pet name for her.

Glancing around, she saw a stack of neatly folded clothes at the end of the bed. She yawned for good measure before reaching out to grab them. With a flush, she realized she was still naked. The long dress was more formal and definitely more concealing than her crumpled wedding tunic on the floor. It had an undertunic that fitted tighter to her skin as she slipped the soft cream-colored linen over her head. It fit her perfectly, as if it had been made for her.

Next, she grabbed the overtunic. It was more like a long green jacket, sliding over her arms and latching in the front with a little silver clasp at her waist. The front skirt fell open, revealing the cream underneath. The undertunic peaked out at her neck and wrists. Looking down, she wished she had a mirror. The dress was absolutely the most beautiful thing that she had ever owned--better than all the diamonds and jewels her father had given her. She hoped it didn't cost her husband too much. She wouldn't want to drain their expenses by being frivolous. But, twirling, she grinned. She loved it.

Spying the table set with chocolate, she bit her lip and glanced around. No one was there to stop her. There was no medic unit to climb into. And surely Olek had meant them for her. Just one wouldn't hurt anything.

Excited, Nadja went to the table and picked up a chocolate. She swallowed, almost nervously, before biting into it. The taste exploded in her mouth and she was hooked. Chewing furiously, she swallowed, and then grabbed another. Before she thought to stop, she had eaten her way through the entire plate.

She smacked her lips in embarrassment, but couldn't help the contented grin that spread her features. She licked her fingers in a very unladylike fashion.

Leaning back, she looked closely at her wrist. She saw that silver embroidery edged the gown with little flowers. On the side of her chest, right above her heart was the emblem of a dragon. She grinned as she thought of how Olek's eyes looked like a dragon's the night before.

"I did indeed marry a dragon," she mused quietly.

"Sorry?"

Nadja turned, blushing at Olek who stood in the tent flap. Her breath caught in her throat. He too was more dressed, in black breeches that molded perfectly to his calves and thighs. He wore black boots. His tunic was green, matching hers, though the silver dragon on his chest was much larger. Nadja, who couldn't help thinking it was because his chest was so much larger, blushed.

"It's nothing," she said shyly. Not wanting to admit what she said. He would think her a foolish romantic if she repeated it. She stood up from the table, sheepishly wiping her mouth on the back of her hand. "I was just talking to myself."

Olek grinned. Nadja's chest leapt at the expression. At that moment, she could see herself being truly happy with Olek. There was such goodness to him, a kindness that radiated from his easy smile.

Coming forward, Olek glanced at his wife's pretty face, seeing a telltale smudge of chocolate on the corner of her lips. He looked down at the empty tray and smiled.

"Hungry?" he mused.

Nadja flushed. "I couldn't resist. I've only had chocolate one time and that was this tiniest little piece. I promise I won't overdo it again."

"Do it as often and as much as you wish," Olek murmured benevolently. "I'll just have to keep you busy enough so that you don't grow fat and bloated from the indulgence."

Nadja could guess what he meant by 'busy'. It was there in his molten green eyes that were shining with the clear shimmering of sun reflecting on water.

He bent over her, leaning to lick the smudge from the corner of her mouth. Nadja shivered, momentarily closing her eyes at the warm contact. Whispering against her mouth, Olek said, "Mmm, delicious."

Nadja exhaled loudly.

"So," she began with a flush. "You still want to stay married?"

"Silly solarflower," Olek murmured in response. His fingers smoothed her hair. Nadja stood, contented to let him. Her locks were still a bit tousled from sleep. He took the crystal from his neck and held it up for her to see. It glowed softly. He handed it over to her. "I give this to you. Come, we must take it to the council and declare that it is our will to remain together. Once you break the crystal, it can never be undone, not in death or separation. We will be one being."

Nadja swallowed.

"Are you ready?" he asked.

Blushing, she asked the very feminine question, "How do I look?"

"Like a solarflower," he responded, unable to help kissing the tip of her nose. Once he got her back to their home, he would see to it that they weren't disturbed until evening--perhaps the rest of the week. He had plans for his little solarflower.

Nadja smiled. "All right, Olek, what exactly do I need to do?"

Chapter Five

Qurilixen had three suns, two yellow and one blue, which produced an abnormally bright planet. Nadja blinked in the sunlight, trying her best to keep from grinning like a fool. Looking at Olek, she blushed prettily when he winked at her.

Only fifteen minutes had passed from the time he came to the tent to get her until she found herself standing on the edge of a stage, before the Qurilixian council. In the center of the standing councilmen sat one very regal lady in purple, next to a man in the same shade. Nadja noticed they both wore crowns signifying royalty.

Nadja felt her stomach tighten, a bit queasy. Surely, it was just nerves. She tried to ignore it.

Let them have their thrones, she thought, looking at the King and Queen. She leaned naturally closer to where Olek stood. He felt her move and took her hand in his. I want my simple life.

Nadja drew strength from his strong palm, almost too exited to stop and wonder that such a man as this was willing to declare to his whole race that he chose her--that she was his alone. She felt so wanted, so worthy. The new rush of feelings made her confident.

"Queen Mede, King Llyr. May I present Lady Nadja Aleksander of the Earthen people," Olek introduced Nadja, dropping her hand as he gave a formal bow. Nadja curtsied as Olek had shown her. The royal couple's smiles widened as they saw Olek take back her hand. They nodded in pleasure. Nadja shivered, noticing how the light from the suns made everyone's gaze look as if they shifted with gold.

Olek turned to Nadja, nodding down to where his crystal was clutched in her hand. She smiled. Dropping it to the ground, she stomped it with her heel. Instantly, she felt a little dizzy. Her head spun as if coming out from a spell. A fog lifted from her senses. Her head began to ache and her stomach churned violently.

Behind them, the cheering crowd resounded over the grounds. Not wanting to embarrass Olek, Nadja forced the sudden nausea down her throat and smiled tightly.

Queen Mede stood, joined by her husband. Loudly, the Queen said, "Welcome to the family of Draig, Lady Nadja. I hope you will enjoy your new home."

Nadja's smile wavered slightly. Why did the Queen just call her Lady? She glanced at Olek. He merely winked at her and she tried to dismiss it as a polite address to a new bride.

Nadja curtsied, "I am sure I will."

The Queen and King stepped forward, both to kiss her cheek in turn, pleased to see she had spoken and carried herself so well. Her eyes swam a little in her head, but no one noticed.

Olek glanced down at her, knowing it was normal to feel a bit light as the power of the crystal was forever secured. He too felt the effects, but he was used to the crystal's influence and it didn't bother him to such an extent.

"Nadja," he murmured quietly so the gathered crowd couldn't hear him. "I would also like the honor of introducing you to my parents."

Nadja smiled expectantly. Her eyes lifted to him, bright and wide. When he didn't move, she blinked and said, "Of course. I would like that very much. Where are they?"

The Queen and King both chuckled. She blinked again, looking at them in confusion. Why were they still standing there? And why were they looking at her like that?

Nadja turned back to Olck in confusion, not wanting to believe the curling suspicions whispering in her head. She studied his face. He smiled, looking incredibly pleased with himself.

"Nadja," Olek said with a smirk. His eyes danced with laughter as he motioned to the royal couple. "These are my parents."

Nadja gulped. Her heart screeched to a deadly stop in her chest and she was sure she was having a heart attack. The smile froze on her face. Her whole body went numb. No, he didn't just say that.

"Nadja?" he questioned when she didn't move, only continued to stare at him like she was about to strangle him or drop dead, whichever came to her first.

Nadja turned. Her eyes were hard as she looked at the royal couple.

"You," she said softly, her voice refusing to come out any louder. "You are his parents?"

"Yes," Queen Mede answered. Nadja saw that the woman's

smile appeared kind. But, her eyes were as liquid in color as her husband's. "Welcome daughter. We are most pleased to have you as part of our family."

Nadja stiffened as the Queen gave her another kiss. She nodded at her, her movements rigid as if her neck might break from the effort.

"Thank you," she said through tightly clenched teeth. She blinked hard, biting back her outrage.

The King leaned over and asked his wife in their Qurilixian tongue, "What's wrong with her?"

The Queen answered in kind, "Just smile. The poor girl is stunned. She just found out she is a Princess."

"I'll never understand these Earth women," he said, but he smiled at the frozen girl nonetheless. Changing his words so she could understand him, he said, "Welcome daughter. It is as my wife says. We are most pleased to have you in our family."

"Thanks," Nadja ground out again. At his wife's gentle urging, he kissed her cheek once more. Her eyes rounded a bit wider, but she couldn't force herself to return the affection.

"Maybe you should take her home now, son," the Queen said so the woman couldn't understand. Nadja looked as if she barely breathed. Her porcelain skin was starting to dramatically pale to gray.

Olek smiled at his parents, nodding in agreement. A slight smile graced his lips as he took Nadja's stiff arm. Happiness building in his chest, he led her away.

"Let us hope the other Princesses have their wits about them," the King whispered with a playful smirk.

The Queen shot him a heated glance, and hit him in his arm as she allowed him to lead her back to her seat. Trying not to laugh at his handsome face, she murmured, "Behave!"

* * * *

As soon as they were away from earshot, a very livid Nadja yanked her arm from Olek's grasp. He glanced at her in surprise, not expecting it from the obviously stunned woman.

"Your parents, barbarian?" was the only thing she could manage to get out.

Olek frowned, not understanding. Slowly, he nodded his head in confirmation.

"Your father is the King? Tell me you are a bastard son and not a Prince," she demanded hotly. She didn't see the forest around them, or the red dirt path he had been leading her up. She swallowed back her bile, trying to keep her voice down, trying not to tear him apart by his limbs, trying not to disembowel.... "Tell me that calling them your parents is just another word for King, as in the father of us all. Tell me he isn't really my new father-by-marriage. Tell me this is all a joke."

"No, Nadja, he is the King. Which makes me a Prince and you, as my wife, a Princess," Olek said laboriously. Her attitude was way past shock. Her eyes were shooting daggers. If looks could kill, he and everyone he'd ever met would have been evaporated in that very instant.

"A Princess," she repeated with a stiff nod. "Oh, a Princess. Why not?"

"Yes." Was his wife going crazy?

"Are you crazy, barbarian!" she hissed under her breath.

Olek was amazed to see she never once yelled in her anger, but said everything with a deadly, frightening calm. It was much worse than someone who threw a loud tirade and tossed their arms about. It was the quiet ones who could think and control their anger that you had to look out for.

"I can't be a Princess!" Nadja argued. "I married a farmer, or a miner, or a blacksmith, or a country doctor. I am going to live in a small cottage in the middle of the forest. I am going to have a little garden. I am going to have a peaceful, non-important life. Do you understand me, barbarian? I didn't marry royalty. I couldn't have. You said you were a working man."

"As a Prince, I do work," he defended.

Olek scratched his head, not understanding what the big deal was. Most women would be ecstatic by the discovery. She was titled, would have servants. She was rich. But Nadja wasn't ecstatic. She was downright infuriated.

"Right, doing what? Kissing babies? Shaking hands?" Nadja said with a darkening glare. She put her hands on her hips. "Being a pampered barbarian Prince isn't work! You lied to me!"

Olek gulped. By all that was sacred, she was beautiful.

"You obviously haven't negotiated peace with the Var," he mumbled under his breath. Lowering his lids to give her a smoldering sweep of his eyes, he murmured seductively, "And you didn't think me such a barbarian last night."

Nadja blushed in mortification. "Last night I didn't realize I had bound myself to a liar."

"I never lied," Olek defended, his voice growing.

Her tone stayed deadly calm. It was eerie how she could hold in her anger, letting it churn. "You never told the truth. If you had told me you were royalty, I would never have agreed to this. I could have saved us both the trouble."

Olek didn't answer. He believed her.

Nadja stared him down, all hopes of a simple life fading. If she was a Princess, then her name would be widely known. Her father would come for her. She couldn't let that happen, not after she tasted a night of freedom. She thought of the chocolate churning in her stomach. Obviously, freedom wasn't the only thing she had tasted too much of.

Nadja turned a sickening green. Grabbing her stomach, she ran to the forest, trampling the yellow ferns that spread out beneath the colossal trees, before falling to the ground. Nadja instantly found out that chocolate wasn't as good coming up as it had been going down. Her body jerked as she threw up. Olek was beside her immediately, holding back her hair and tenderly murmuring soothing sounds.

"I think you overdid it," he said compassionately when she finished. He tried to draw her into his arms to hold her.

Nadja jerked her shoulders away, spitting onto the ground. She wouldn't draw comfort from him, not now, not ever. Looking at him with all the betrayal she felt, she gasped for breath. "I take it back. I want a divorce."

Olek was stunned. She was still pale and swaying slightly on her feet from the sudden illness. Frowning, he said, "Don't you think you are overreacting?"

Nadja didn't answer, trying to take deep gulps of air to calm her stomach. She was never eating chocolate again.

"I told you, solarflower, once you broke the crystal, it can never be undone, not in death or separation. We are one being, like it or not. I'll not let you go. There is no divorce for our people."

"The only thing we will ever be, barbarian, is an unhappily wed couple." Fear made her voice waspish and hard. She trembled, having seen firsthand what her father was capable of. He wouldn't need the help of the extradition act to come for her. She had no idea how long it would take the news to reach his ears. It could be a week, a year, five years. She would never feel safe and no amount of barbarian warriors would be able to help her when he did come. Swallowing, she commanded, "Now take me to our new home. I let your lying barbarian hands touch me and I need a bath."

* * * *

Nadja looked around the bathroom, eyeing her new prison of gilded bars and cried. The nightmare hadn't ended. She was truly a Princess and she despised Olek for it.

Olek had been silent as he led her into the entry of the castle palace. Wrought iron gates lifted high over the entrance leading into the side of a large mountain. From the distance, the mountain looked like any other, so Nadja was amazed to find a palace camouflaged within it. Wide domes allowed light inside the tunneled path of red rock. Then, entering a front door of thick oak, they had come to a series of passageways.

The mountain castle was as picturesque as she would have expected a castle to be. It was clean and decorated with tasteful paintings and sculptures. Tapestries hung on the walls, alongside banners with the emblem of the royal dragon. Nadja was quiet as Olek led her to his wing of the palace, the part he called his home.

When he opened the front door with a short voice command, Nadja had stepped inside one of the most gorgeous homes she had ever seen. The richness of it only dejected her more. She was supposed to have a modest five-room cottage, not a large wing of a palace.

Olek's home was decorated with the dark green of his royal colors combined with a cream marble that bespoke of refinement and elegance. There was a giant water fountain in the front hall. The water trickled down the natural rocks, creating a pleasant background noise to the place, and plants grew in its crevices.

Next to the fountain was a circular living area, surrounded by high-backed, comfortable chairs. A large dome glass ceiling allowed light in. With the push of a button, a giant curtain would swirl around the dome to darken the home. A large marble fireplace was carved into an inlet in the stone wall.

Between the living room and the kitchen was an exotic fish tank wall that you could see through. The little bug-eyed blue fish swam in absent circles, blinking their eyelids and picking at an underwater lettuce that grew in their tank. A huge red sucker fish adhered its oversized mouth on the side. Gradually, it changed color to pink and then to yellow. Nadja could see its teeth working against the glass as it ate.

Lush plant life hung tastefully from the ceiling and grew in the corner of the living room, vining its way to a sun room off to the side. Nadja sighed, wryly thinking that she had indeed gotten her little garden. It brought her little pleasure.

Another fish tank, one with dark blue waters that was hard to see through, separated the bathroom from the main living area. From her vantage point in the natural hot spring tub, she watched the tank. Occasionally, she would see the fin of what looked like a two-headed shark swim by.

The bathroom was red, carved from the mountain. The tub came up in the center of the bathroom floor, rising from the ground and bubbling constant warm water. Nadja couldn't find a drain in the bath, but did find a button on the wall that showered water down from the ceiling into the center of the bath.

There was the normal toilet and sink, and a vanity counter that curved around the circular walls with a long mirror over it. Beneath the countertop were numerous cabinets, some with towels and others with toiletries. With a turn of a knob, the outside light directed throughout holes in the ceiling would dim and brighten.

Nadja had seen her bags from the Galaxy Bride's ship in the front hall. She'd just have to unpack later and settle in. She wanted to see how Olek liked her rearrangement of his things. If she was going to be forced to stay as his wife, then she was going to make things exactly how she wanted them.

Well, she thought bitterly. Not like she wanted them at all. She'd rather he led her to a little shack with a hole in the roof and made her peel potatoes all day. That would have made her happier than she felt now.

Her tears began anew.

* * * *

Olek sat miserably on one of his high-backed chairs. He drew his fingers in absent lines along the sides. He sensed the strange sadness coming from the bathroom, radiating off his wife. She refused to speak to him, but he could see the outrage in her every step as he brought her into the castle. When he opened the front door to his home, he hoped for a small smile or a gasp of pleasure. He'd worked hard decorating his house in hopes of pleasing his someday bride, as did all the Princes. She didn't even glance around. It was as if she didn't care.

A deep ache filled his chest and he sunk lower into his chair. This wasn't how he envisioned married life. He wanted peace in his home. As the ambassador of the Draig, he had battles and negations and threats of war to deal with nearly everyday. It was stressful. The peace of his people depended on him.

To his surprise, Nadja came out of the bathroom. Her hair was wet around her shoulders but brushed back from her face. She was swimming in the folds of his robe. Her eyes and nose were red and Olek frowned to see it. She had been crying. He hadn't heard her though, only felt her pain.

"Where's my room?" she asked. Her voice was nearly as hollow as her eyes, as she looked past him. She waited patiently, not hurrying him along to answer.

Olek saw her shiver.

"Fire," he said. The fireplace lit. Nadja barely blinked as she glanced at the flames.

"Does everything work on voice command?" she asked, listlessly.

"All but the overhead lights."

"My room?" Nadja asked again, breaking off any conversation he might start.

"Our room is this way," Olek stood to grab her bags for her and led the way.

Nadja said nothing. She silently followed him down a short side hall near the front entryway. She kept her eyes averted, refusing to remember anything that happened the night before in the tent. Truth be told, her wanton actions mortified her. And that she had acted such to an obvious stranger humiliated her even more.

Taking two steps up, he led her into a massive oval room. A large bed was in the middle, lowered down so that it was only a short step up from the floor. Like the bathroom, this room had light tunnels carved and scattered throughout the ceiling.

There was another fireplace carved into the wall. A fur rug lay out in front of it. On one side of the room, down two steps, was a large circular closet with a balcony window that showed out over the countryside. It was gorgeous.

If Nadja was moved, she didn't show it.

The bed had a green coverlet embroidered with the royal emblem of the fierce dragon. Nadja barely blinked as she crossed over to the bed. With a stiff hand, she drew back the covers.

"I'm taking a nap," Nadja said, laying down and turning her back to him.

Olek swallowed. There wasn't anything welcoming about that declaration. There wasn't anything to it at all. Her words to him were dead.

"I'll be working in my office if you need me," Olek said quietly. "It's right next to the kitchen."

"I won't need you," she said softly in return. Nadja stared at the fireplace. Her whole body wanted to fight, to scream at him, but her life had taught her it wasn't wise to yell at the man who held the power over you. Anger was best dealt with quietly and bottled in. Then, and only then, could Nadja render a dignified response, and avoid being put into punishment.

Her words tore at Olek. He dimmed the overhead lights to let her sleep. As he walked away, he heard her say, "Fire."

The orange of flames lit over the walls of the short hall. He took a deep breath and left her alone.

Chapter Six

"Open!"

Olek looked up from his stacks of documents and frowned. He pushed his hands through his hair in frustration and quickly smoothed the locks down, brushing the side plaits over his shoulders.

"Let me out, you…"

The muffling of Nadja's words was lost as they tapered off into an angry growl. He stood and moved around the haphazard pile of papers on his desk to see what she was up to. Hearing her continued outrage, he'd guess her short nap was over.

Nadja stood before the large front door. Her hair was pulled back into a large bun at the nape of her slender neck. She wore a silk blouse and slacks, both her own clothing from her bags. Her short boots tapped impatiently on the marble floor as she stood, hands on hips, glaring at his front door.

"Sneaking out?" he asked, unable to hide his amusement at the scene.

Nadja blushed to hear his voice, but kept her back to him so he couldn't see it. To her horror, her dreams had been of him, naked, touching himself and touching her. They still burned in her mind and body.

When she felt she was controlled, she looked at Olek. He was still dressed as he had been that morning in his formal green tunic. His long hair was braided down the sides though the locks looked as if they had been slightly tousled. He was achingly handsome to look at and her heart fluttered in a trill of excitement.

Olek saw the red tint to her face and took it as anger. He had hoped that by letting her sleep, she would wake in a more reasonable mood. It didn't seem that was going to be the case.

Nadja, who in fact had been planning on sneaking out until the door refused to budge, replied, "I didn't realize I was a prisoner. I wanted to get out of this house and go for a walk."

"You're not a prisoner, solarflower," Olek murmured softly, coming forward. Oh, how he wanted to touch her. "Is that what you think it means to be royalty?"

She didn't answer.

"Nadja," he continued, emboldened by her silence, but not her stern look. "We are not prisoners here. You are as free as any other. I know the stories from other cultures where royalty isn't allowed certain privileges, but we are not so strict. You can have a life. We do have to live by example and we do live to serve our people, but we are not prisoners to them."

"So I have a job," Nadja concluded darkly. "What is it? Holding your crown at ceremonies or wearing an outfit to match yours and smiling pretty for the cameras?"

Olek grimaced.

"I don't want that life, Prince Olek," Nadja said, wishing desperately that he could understand. But, being who he was, she was even more afraid of telling him who her father was. If word got out, he and his family could be embarrassed and scandalized. They could ship her back in hopes of avoiding public dishonor. They could ship her back to avoid attracting her father's certain kind of wrath. Gripping onto her dream with both hands, she said, "I wanted a simple life. I want a garden."

"We can live simply." Lifting his hand to the sunroom, he said, "And there is your garden, solarflower. I'll build you a hundred of them if it makes you happy. I'll turn our whole home into a garden. If you want a cottage home, I will build you one in the forest. If you want the mountains, I'll build you one there too. We can vacation there. I want you to be happy, Nadja."

"You think you have all the answers." Her eyes were hard. "You really have no idea."

Olek was confused by the low words. He stepped forward, studying her face. What was she trying to hide?

"Nadja, what is this really about? Are you trying to disappear from someone or something? Are you in trouble?"

Nadja tensed at his perceptiveness. She hadn't expected him to guess her secret so soon. How else could she answer, but to lie? "No."

Olek detected the falsehood instantly. She really was a bad liar and refused to meet his eye.

"If you were, you could tell me," Olek persisted quietly. "I would stand by you, help you. My family would stand by you. You are one of us now."

His words caused her to tremble, but she hid her vulnerability and gave him a dark smile. She was sure when he knew the truth that he wouldn't be so willing. "I told you no. Don't make me repeat myself."

"Fine," he said softly. "Keep your secret for now. But I hope one day soon you will come to know that you can trust me with it."

Nadja turned back around, effectively cutting off the conversation. Enunciating her words, she demanded, "Open this door."

"It's not a good idea to wander about without an escort," he began.

"You mean a prison guard?"

"Open," Olek instantly commanded. The door pulled up to let her pass. "It's easy to…"

Nadja strode out without a backwards glance.

"…to get lost," he finished faintly.

Olek sighed. He was at a loss. He felt helpless. Nothing he told her seemed to make her happy. Sighing, he fought the urge to follow her. He turned back to his office and the pile of work he had started on his desk. He knew the first step of reaching any negotiation between two troubled people was a show of trust. And that is exactly what he would do. He would show Nadja he trusted her, even if she didn't trust him.

* * * *

Nadja was lost. Not that she really cared. She was sure if she kept wandering around the red stone halls someone would run across her and force her to go back to Prince Olek.

At the end of each hall were little carved squares with markings on them. Nadja guessed they were encoded directions. She couldn't read them and couldn't begin to figure them out, so she ignored them. She turned aimless corners, stopping to look at the sculptures and paintings before moving on. The palace was almost as decorative as an art museum. It was exquisite, though Nadja would never have admitted it, as she snarled at the lovely pieces.

"Princess Nadja?"

Nadja froze, the title irritating her to no end. When she turned, she saw the Queen and moved to curtsey.

"No, no," the Queen said lightly, with a pleasant smile coming to her features. "Do stand, Nadja. We only save such things for public ceremonies. Our people like to watch our old customs, but it doesn't mean we have to live with all of them everyday."

Queen Mede glanced back over her shoulder to the hall she had just left. It was most distressing. Ualan's wife Morrigan had indentured herself as a slave and her other son's wives were being just as stubborn. Except for Nadja, who knew the truth of what she had become and was hopefully accepting it, the other Princesses had no clue who they had married.

It was just as well. Queen Mede understood that it was hard to see past the crown and her son's wanted to be sure their wives chose for themselves without the added attraction of money and power. This morning, before her shock, Nadja had appeared quite taken with Olek and that gave Mede hope.

"Is Olek with you?"

As Nadja opened her mouth, the Queen realized she couldn't have been more wrong. Nadja was most discontent, just as the others.

"No," Nadja answered flatly, turning stiffly back to the painting. Her tone hardened, as she said with a private laugh of irony, "He's working."

Working man my-- Nadja fumed silently, unable to finish the thought with the earnest queen staring at her.

"Working? Again?" The Queen sighed. "I hoped he would take a few days off now that he was married."

Nadja said nothing. She was uncomfortable discussing anything with Olek's mother.

"It doesn't matter to me," Nadja said, before she could stop herself. "I would rather he kept himself busy and away from me."

"Away from…." the Queen repeated only to stop in confusion. "Nadja, are you…?"

"I'm fine." Giving another curtsey, she murmured, "If you would excuse me."

"Wait," the Queen said. She desperately wanted to get to know her daughters and Nadja was the only one her sons would allow her to see just yet, as she was the only one who knew the truth of her station. "What are you doing just now?"

"Getting myself lost," Nadja answered honestly.

"May I keep you company?" Mede asked, hesitant. "I could take you shopping in the village. We could get whatever you wanted. You still need to be fitted for new gowns, shoes."

Nadja took a deep breath. The Queen was eyeing her silk

blouse and slacks without malevolence. What else was she going to do? She was tired of looking at paintings. Slowly, she nodded, "All right. I wouldn't mind some fresh air."

* * * *

Later that evening when Nadja arrived home from her shopping spree with the Queen, Olek was still in his office. He had gotten nothing done, thinking about Nadja instead of work. Absently he had drawn endless sketches of her naked body, her face, her smile on the corners of his documents. He ached for her in a way he could barely contain. Even when she was gone, her scent stayed with him, teasing his already overheated desire.

"Just put the plants in the sun room," Olek heard his wife say. "I'll arrange them how I need to later."

He heard voices join hers and the footsteps coming across the marble entryway. He knew where Nadja had been, as the Queen had secretly sent a servant to tell him. He smiled, having to remember to thank his mother for the consideration.

"Olek?"

Olek flinched. That was the voice of his mother. Almost like a nervous schoolboy, he began stacking his papers on his desk to hide the naughty sketches he had done of his wife. When they were put away, he stood to cross over to the hall.

Nadja bit her lip as the Queen called out to her son. All day the woman had done nothing but list Olek's good qualities for her. He was such a brave fighter, a good man, an expert negotiator, a hard worker, would make a good father--wink, wink.

"Mother, Nadja," he acknowledged with a smile. Quizzically, he turned to the mass of servants who were following Nadja's directions and putting things away.

"Your wife is quite the shopper," the Queen mused with a grin.

Olek didn't care. He could well afford her anything she wanted and was pleased to see that she was making herself comfortable in his home. He wanted her to arrange things exactly as she would have them.

"I needed some things," Nadja said a bit defensively. "This house is decorated for a man, not a woman."

Olek crossed over to where some plants lay on a table, their dirty roots spread out beneath them as if they had been dug out of the forest. He looked at Nadja, lifting his brow.

"You can't eat these," Olek said. They were ugly little plants so she couldn't have picked them for beauty.

"That's what I told her," Mede said. "But, she insisted."

"Wait," Nadja said, pointing at a man with a long box. "That one goes over there in the bathroom."

Olek shared a grin with his mother. Quietly, he moved to sit before the fireplace as Nadja continued to give instructions. She handled herself with politeness and knew exactly what she wanted. The men showed her respect, their eyes smiling at her in instant adoration. He watched carefully, as she charmed each and every man in the room with her reserved nature--every man including him. She was truly a Princess.

An older man, wearing the sturdy tunic of a craftsman came to the door. He looked around. Then, seeing the Princess, he smiled and came forward. Olek watched as Nadja pointed to the sun room and motioned with her hands. The carpenter nodded his wrinkled face, bit his lip, calculated his thoughts, and then answered her. Nadja smiled, motioning him to go ahead with whatever it was she was planning. The man began measuring the entryway into the sunroom.

"I should get going," the Queen said. Turning to her new daughter, she smiled, "Nadja, I'll see you tomorrow for those dress fittings. The seamstress said she would be here by nine."

"Fine," Nadja answered, smiling at the woman. Olek wished the smile was for him. "Don't forget you also promised to show me the family library tomorrow."

"Maybe Olek could take you," Mede suggested, eyeing her son meaningfully.

"I would love to," Olek murmured. He watched as Nadja's back stiffened. He could just see the frown darkening her features.

Mede waved at her son, who in turn lazily motioned back to her in kind. He shot her a disobedient grin. His eyes once again strayed to Nadja's back.

Olek waited. His brow rose quizzically, as the delivery men left, leaving boxes and packages spread about in their wake. Nadja didn't look at him directly. He couldn't help but stare at her.

"My lady, I can start tomorrow morning if you like," the carpenter said in his stilting accent, putting his measuring tape away.

"That would be wonderful," Nadja said, walking the older gentleman to the door. "Come whenever you're ready."

"Yes, my lady," the man agreed. Then turning to Olek, he bowed, "My lord."

Olek waved his hand at the man and smiled, vastly amused by the whole scene.

When the door shut on his command, Nadja turned. The pleasant light faded from her features as she studied him wryly. Without saying a word, she picked up her uprooted plants and began moving to the sunroom.

"Did you buy out the entire village?" he asked, teasingly.

Nadja frowned and moved to look at him. Her lips tightly pressed, she said, "I needed a few things."

She turned and walked to the sunroom. Olek wasn't so willing to let the conversation die, even if he was the one who had to carry all of it.

"What was the carpenter for?" he asked, keeping his tone light.

Her eyes got defensive, and again he was surprised when her voice didn't rise to a yell. She looked angry enough. "I need a door. I am making this room my office. You get your private space, I get mine."

Olek followed her into the large atrium. Boxes blocked the pathways and he stepped around them. Nadja was holding the plants in her hand with a light grip, and she was looking around.

"What is all this stuff?" he asked, bending over to pick through the boxes.

All he saw was a glass container before she demanded, "Leave my stuff alone. I'm not going to search through your personal belongings. The least you could do is stay out of mine."

Olek lifted his hand back and retreated from his curious exploration.

"So, you're planning a bigger garden?"

"Don't you have some work you could be doing, Prince?" she asked, ignoring him as she drew a rectangle pot from the box already filled with dirt. Setting it down, she crouched, repotting the plants from the forest.

"Those really aren't used for anything," Olek said, still doing his best to ignore her ire. "They won't bud with flowers."

She turned to give him the 'you're still here?' look and said nothing. Quickly, she finished and stood, moving to go to the kitchen. Olek blocked the path.

"Do you mind?" she asked, softly. He looked at her with a charged electrical need she could feel all the way down to her toes. No matter how hard she tried to pretend she hated him, she knew it wasn't entirely true. She hated her situation, she hated her fear, but she could never hate him. Her body quivered with fiery longing at that look, eager to pick up where he had left off the night before.

Nadja tried to shuffle past him, but he moved to block her way. He took a step forward, forcing her to retreat.

"I need to get water for the plants," she said weakly.

Nadja tried again to move past him again. He blocked her. She swallowed apprehensively, not sure what he was up to.

Olek's eyes lit with dangerous intentions, as they began the journey down her throat. His body stirred, smelling the fragrance of her desire for him. The sunroom dome was on a timer and Nadja jumped as the curtains clicked and began to close overhead.

"What are you doing, Olek?" She grew worried by his silence. Suddenly, her legs hit a low carved shelf and she realized that her back was surrounded by plants and flowers.

Olek didn't stop. He came forward until his body was pressed next to hers, trapping her with his solid heat. Every hard inch of him burned into her body, sending needles of pleasure over her traitorous nerves. Her eyes dipped at the contact and she took a deep, steadying breath.

"I'm going to tend to my little solarflower," he murmured, moving forward to kiss her parted lips.

Nadja didn't even try to pull away. As his lips touched hers, she moaned. Her body weakened. She found a ledge and clutched it for support. He boldly laid claim to her mouth with a scorchingly hot kiss, searing her senses with liquid desire.

"Olek," she tried to say against his mouth, though she didn't draw her parted lips away from his. "I don't want--"

He deepened the kiss to cut off her words while stealing her breath. Nadja moaned, panted, whimpered. His body ignited and he pressed the center of his torment into her hips so she could feel all of him.

"Take off your clothes, Nadja," he urged against her mouth. "Strip for me again. Let me see your exquisite body."

Nadja shivered. When she didn't comply, his hands were at her slacks, unbuttoning them.

"Tell me you want me to take you right here," he demanded confidently against her mouth.

Olek held so much power in his tone that Nadja shuddered to hear it. She could never be that bold, could she? She held still, letting him do what he will, unable to fight or deny him.

"Tell me you're hot for me. Tell me you want me to turn you around and ride you right here and now."

Nadja moaned into his mouth. She couldn't speak for he was stealing her breath with his wicked words and head-spinning kisses.

"Tell me you want me inside of you." Olek broke the kiss, not giving her anymore of his mouth until he had her plea. He slipped his hand into her underwear, moving to touch her. "Tell me you want me thrusting myself right here."

Nadja was moist with desire and his finger took full advantage as it lightly stroked her. Shockwaves of pleasure shot through her from his touch. A whimper left her lips, soft and pleading. She opened her mouth, staying back from his. She did want him. It was treacherous agony. How could she fight her own body as well as his?

"Say it solarflower," he commanded. He grew urgent, his searching hands touching deeper, rubbing against her center nub, stroking a dangerously hot fire. "Say you want to be my Princess. Say you're happy here with me. Say you want me to take you here and now. Say you want me to end your torment as well as mine. I'll make you happy, I promise. Please, solarflower, let me make you happy."

Nadja couldn't say it. She knew she was his wife and she took her obligations and her word seriously. Besides, where else could she go? Galaxy Brides would try to find her for breach of contract. Olek would look for his runaway bride and her father would be sure to get wind of it all the faster. Her position here was as much her doing as his. She chose to take off the mask, knowing full well what she was doing, knowing she was marrying a complete stranger. But, to say the words out loud? She couldn't do it. It would make them too real.

"No," Nadja breathed to his amazement and to hers as well. She would never understand how the word was shoved past her tightened throat. Her body instantly stiffened, trying to rebel against the logic of her mind.

Olek's body jerked in pain as she denied it. He was hard, ready for her, ready to claim her completely. Never had lust bit him so wretched and hard. However, he wouldn't prove her words true and act the barbarian for her. He didn't need her holding that against him as well.

To her everlasting torment, he pulled his hand from her eager body and stepped back. His shoulders rose and fell as he tried to catch his breath. The temptingly soft feel of her was still against his fingers.

"Ah!" The sound came weakly from Nadja throat as he withdrew. She wished he hadn't stopped. She quivered, ready to demand him back.

"Go tend your garden, wife," Olek said quietly, backing away, his eyes piercing into her as he left her alone. Angrily, he stormed from the room and Nadja heard him leaving the house. Her knees weakened and she fell to the floor.

Trembling, she groaned. Her stomach throbbed and ached with what he did to her. Nadja had no clue how to end the torment herself and was too afraid to try. Forcing herself to stand, she went to the kitchen for a glass of water. But, instead of watering the plants, she poured the glass on her white silk shirt to cool her flaming skin. Olek's denial was definitely worse than any punishment her father had put her through.

* * * *

Olek stormed through the passageways. He didn't care where he went as long as it wasn't back home. His eyes flashed a dangerous gold, threatening a full shift into the beast he could become. His teeth gnashed angrily. His fists needed a good fight.

Taking a deep breath, he knew his aching body needed to cool. He saw his brother Ualan, covered in mud from a day of mock battle out in the swamps. He growled darkly. Ualan's eyes flashed as he returned the sentiment with one of his own. The brothers passed each other, not stopping to speak.

Chapter Seven

Olek didn't come home that night. Nadja hated to admit that she waited up, listening for him from their bed. Judging by the state he left her in, she wondered if he sought out someone more agreeable to tend to his masculine needs. The idea tore bitterly at her, raising her chest in anger to hide the pain. She dozed lightly, but didn't get much rest. She considered sleeping on the couch, but wouldn't give up the satisfaction of snubbing him if he tried to touch her.

By the time morning came around and she dragged herself out of bed, she was mixed between outrage and worry. Worry that something had happened to him, and anger that someone else might have happened to him. Regardless of her mood, she didn't try to leave. The door had yet to be programmed to her voice so she couldn't, even if she wanted to.

The Queen came promptly at nine as promised. Mede could open the door with her command. The dressmaker was right behind her followed by a half-dozen dutiful helpers--all men. They carried swatches of material for her to choose from. The woman was kind, speaking to the Queen in the Qurilixian tongue. Queen Mede would in turn translate for Nadja.

Lifting her arms up, she held still as the dressmaker measured her chest. Nadja asked the Queen, "So, you just have the four sons?"

"Just?" The Queen laughed, looking up from where she had moved a high-backed chair to better see. "There is nothing just about being plagued with four sons."

Nadja smiled despite herself.

"All the women on the trip over were abuzz with them. The Princes were all they could talk about," Nadja admitted. "I thought it was an advertising ploy by the company to get women to sign on."

"And you, Nadja? Were you abuzz with the idea?" the Queen asked thoughtfully.

Before stopping to think, she answered honestly, "No. I wanted a simple man like a fat, country doctor."

Nadja blinked, realizing what she had revealed. Her mouth opened in instant apology. This battle really was between Olek and herself. She liked Mede too much to say anything to offend her.

The Queen shook her head to stop her apology and grinned.

"And your other sons?" Nadja prompted, lowering her arms as the dressmaker finished. "Did they all find brides?"

"Yes," the Queen answered, but Nadja could tell she was troubled. "They have."

"Can I ask their names?" Nadja inquired, curious at to which of the women had also won the notice of royalty.

"Ah, Ualan is married to Morrigan Blake. Zoran married a woman named Pia and," Mede paused and chuckled. "To tell the truth, Yusef's bride won't give him a name so we don't know."

Nadja's giggle joined Mede's.

The door suddenly slid open and Olek came walking in, wearing the same tunic he had left in the night before, only it was a little more wrinkled. Nadja's carpenter was with him. Her smile faded when he looked at her and she affected an indifferent air.

Olek's heart slowed in his chest when he saw he was the cause of her sudden displeasure. He'd heard her and his mother's laughter outside in the hall and hoped to find her in a better mood. She looked beautiful, standing tall on her stool, wearing the soft cotton top and pants of his people.

As Nadja watched, Olek spoke to the carpenter in their shared language, pointing at the sun room and giving him commands. The man nodded at her attention, but listened to her husband.

Nadja jumped off the stool, much to the dressmaker's ire, and ran after the men as they studied the sun room's entryway.

"Hey, what do you think you're doing?" Nadja asked quietly, pulling Olek's arm.

She studied him suspiciously trying to ascertain if he had been with anyone the night before. His face was shadowed with a beard and his eyes were darkened as if he hadn't slept. Her heart leapt in her throat and she couldn't speak. Then, his mouth curled quizzically at her silence and it was as if they were the only two in the room

The spell was interrupted as the dressmaker came to tug on Nadja's arm, intent on dragging her back to her post on the stool. Nadja couldn't understand what the woman was saying, but she knew she was being scolded. Olek's smile deepened, his eyes still holding her in their depths.

Hearing Mede's chuckle, Nadja blinked. Then, frowning at Olek as she came back to her senses, she demanded in her soft tone, "You better not tell him to change anything I ordered."

Olek turned back around, ignoring her. Nadja's heart still fluttered in her chest from his piercing gaze. Her limbs were weak as she again lifted her arms for the dressmaker. The woman forced her to look forward, so she couldn't longer see what Olek was up to. She was too proud to turn around to peek.

Mede smiled a secret smile, having witnessed the look between her son and his new wife. They may be at odds, but the passion was definitely there. King Llyr would be happy to know that all was going to be just fine on this front, even if the couple didn't realize it yet for themselves.

* * * *

To Nadja's delight, the carpenter did get to work on the doorframe. As the dressmaker finished her many measurements, it was time to pick out the patterns. Mede was a great help, as she chose most of the appropriate gowns for each of a Princess' occasions. When it came down to material, Olek's closet was consulted and matching designs were laid out for Nadja's formal wear.

By the time she had finished, Nadja was exhausted. The Queen left with the dressmaker, winking at Nadja as she passed through the door. Nadja gave her a tired smile in return. Leaving the carpenter to his work, she began walking to the kitchen. The Queen had offered to let her dine in the common hall with the rest of the castle, but Nadja had refused. Eating at home suited her just fine.

Crossing by Olek's door, she couldn't help peeking in. The night before she had explored the home while putting away all her purchases and unpacking her suitcases. His office was neatly organized, except for his desk, which was cluttered with electronic organizers and stacks of paper written in several different languages she couldn't read.

Before she realized what she was doing, Nadja was stepping into the office instead of the kitchen. Olek blinked, looking up in surprise to see her. He had taken a shower and shaved. His dark cotton shirt brought out his eyes. His hair was still a little wet, combed back from his face to hang about his shoulders.

"All finished?" Olek asked, leaning back in his chair and stretching his hands behind his head.

A slight, humorous smile found its way naturally to his lips and Nadja realized he just couldn't help himself. She nodded, scrunching up her mouth. "I told your mother to make sure the dressmaker shows you the list first. Mede ordered a lot and I wasn't sure what my budget was."

"You don't have one." He kept his hands threaded behind his head, but they itched to reach forward and pull her to his lap. He would love to kiss her lush lips as he had his way with her on the desktop. He'd even settle for just holding her next to him.

"Oh." Nadja blinked. "Mede said I could put everything on our account. I'm sorry I should have asked before going shopping. I'll pay you back for everything--wait here."

Olek frowned as Nadja left his office. Her face had been beautifully distracted as she ran from room. He stood to follow her and made it as far as the living room when she came back. The carpenter had disappeared into the sun room.

Nadja held a gold box overflowing with the jewelry that her father had given her. She fingered it lightly. Lifting a diamond necklace so he could see it, she dropped it indifferently back onto the pile.

"I planned on getting rid of this stuff anyway," Nadja said, with a shrug. "I'm not sure who to take it to. I didn't see any brokers when I was in the village. Maybe you know someone who'd buy it. Then, you could just take whatever cash I owe you for your trouble plus what I owe for yesterday and give me the rest."

"Nadja--"

"No, it's all right. I trust you to be fair about it," she broke in. She held out the box to him and when he didn't readily take it, she shoved it into his chest.

Olek reluctantly held onto it instead of letting it drop. Looking down, he saw her name engraved on a few of the top pieces. It didn't look as if the stuff was stolen.

Carefully, Nadja added, "Maybe a jeweler could melt it down before reselling it."

"This isn't necessary. I don't expect you to sell your belongings--" he began. Again she interrupted before he could finish.

"No, really," Nadja said a little too eagerly. "I don't want any of it and the cash would help me out until I can find a job."

"You have a job."

"Being a Princess?" Nadja snorted, shaking her head. Her eyes turned sad. "No thanks. I'm sure I can find something that pays decent enough. I can earn my own way. It's what I planned on doing anyway."

"When I said you didn't have a budget, I simply meant you could buy whatever you needed. I won't leave you." Olek set the box aside and moved to stand before her. "I can well afford it."

Nadja glanced down, seeing he wore the simple Qurilixian cotton drawstring pants. Mede had told her it was the casual style of the evening and of day's off. She took a step back, her body all too willing to remember what his had felt like next to hers and how she had ached for hours afterwards.

"Just the same," she answered. "I would have you get rid of that stuff. I don't want any of it and I won't change my mind. Just make sure you tell the jeweler to take my name off of everything before he sells it."

Olek conceded with a nod. Nadja seemed to relax.

"We need groceries," she said, changing the subject with refined ease as she walked to the kitchen.

"I usually dine in the hall. My brother Ualan is the cook in the family."

"Is that where you ate last night?" Nadja queried, feigning indifference. "With your brother?"

She missed Olek's smile behind her back. He wondered if she was going to ask him where he had been.

"I ate at the royal office."

"With your brothers?" she probed. Even though she made a great show of rummaging through his refrigerator, she listened with her whole brain to his answer.

"No." Olek watched her shoulders stiffen slightly. She might still be upset with him, but she obviously cared enough to be jealous. To his disappointment, she didn't inquire further, so he offered, "I was with my father."

The King suspected that someone tried to break into the royal office and they had been pouring over possibilities. They didn't want to alarm anyone else in the family until they knew for sure, but it was possible a spy was in their midst. As far as they could tell, nothing was missing.

"I don't really care what you do," Nadja lied with a shrug. Frowning, she slammed the door shut and sighed. There wasn't anything that tempted her. She went to the cupboard and repeated the same procedure, rummaging through, finding nothing, and shutting the door.

After her third unsuccessful try, Olek stepped forward, offering, "We could stop and get something on the way to the library. Or I could have something delivered there if you like. I promised to take you."

"Oh," Nadja said. She thought that maybe he had forgotten. He tried to move closer to her and she artfully avoided contact with him as she went to the living room. Olek followed behind her. "If it's not too much trouble … that would be fine. You don't have to stay there with me if you have work to tend to. I just need to know where it is."

"I have time," he offered, disappointed that she seemed so eager to get rid of him.

"Let me just grab my translator," Nadja said, walking into their bedroom.

Olek eyed the gold jewelry box and frowned. Picking it up, he took it to the safe hidden in his office floor. Even though she said she didn't want it, he would hold if for her just in case she changed her mind, or until she told him the real reason for wanting to get rid of it. As his fingers lightly dug through the top layer of jewelry, he couldn't help but wonder who had given her so many expensive gifts.

Grabbing some of the papers off his desk, he put them into a long, narrow case encrusted with his royal seal. Nadja was ready for him when he came back. He couldn't help but smile as he saw her. However, his smile was becoming less and less frequent as of late.

Nadja glanced down at his case and, despite her natural curiosity as to what he really did all day, she didn't ask about it. Olek stopped her at the door, speaking to it in a random succession of Qurilixian words, before murmuring, "State a command so it can record you."

"Open," Nadja stated, very pleased that she would be able to get out on her own. Olek confirmed her voice command, and motioned for her to speak.

"Open," she repeated and the door slid open. Repeating the same procedure, he had her order the door to close. She smiled slightly. Olek said nothing as he led her out into the hall.

The palace library was much larger than Nadja could have

imagined. Books, giant old tomes of the written word, lined the high wall shelving. Nothing was on computer and the musty smell of dust and age was thick on the air. Nadja was instantly taken with the room.

Though she found a few books written in English, they were mostly old novels from Earth. She was glad she had brought her book translator with her. The books she was interested in reading were only in the Qurilixian script.

Olek stayed patiently out of her way as she figured out their filing system. Sitting on one of the low red chairs, he took out a pencil and began to work. His eyes strayed to her backside, as she lifted up on her toes to scan a book's binding and then read the title on her little screen. She was lovely, and his body ached just to hold her. She stubbornly refused to ask him for help, though it would have sped the process along for her.

A servant brought lunch, a simple fare of meat, cheese and bread. Nadja made a sandwich and ate standing up while she searched, refusing to sit with Olek. Olek merely picked at the plate, lounging back in his chair as he made the pretense of not watching her.

Finally, several thick volumes and a few hours later, she was ready to go. Olek eyed her load, glancing over the titles. There were several medical texts, an encyclopedia of the planet's herb and plant life, gardening, and at least one scientific journal. The other bindings were blocked by her arms.

"Do I need to tell someone that I am taking these?" Nadja asked. It was the first thing she had said to him in hours and her voice was husky from little use.

It had been very disconcerting to have him so near, watching her. His sultry eyes left her weak without even knowing it. So many times she wanted to cross over to him and just start kissing his perfect mouth, touching his perfect body. Nadja had never been so bold and she didn't easily forget his denial of her the day before.

Olek blinked, surprised to hear her finally speak to him. He had tried at conversation a few times only to be shushed by her silence.

"No, it is the family library. You may take what you like," he answered. "Only when you're done, bring them back for the others."

Nadja nodded, surprised at how readily they accepted a

stranger into their midst as part of their family. She hadn't been denied a single thing. Olek sighed, going to lift the heavy load from her arms into his. Nadja almost refused, but they were heavy so she let him take them.

When they got back to their house, the carpenter was finishing up. Nadja was very pleased with what the man accomplished in one day. She was even more amazed that he built her new shelving in the sun room for the additional plants she had bought. He'd also made her a potting table with places to hang spades and hand rakes. To her surprise, she realized that Olek ordered not only the additional construction on her behalf, but he bought her a cushioned stool.

She smiled and thanked the carpenter as he left. Olek walked the older man outside, murmuring to him in their shared tongue. When he came back, Nadja managed a weak nod of thanks as she left to explore her room. Olek smiled sadly, leaving her to unpack her boxes and leaf through her books.

Chapter Eight

Olek couldn't get anything done. Nadja was in his head. Everywhere he looked in his home, she was there. In the throw pillows she added to his couch, in the tablecloth and vase of flowers on his dining room table, in the endless assault of feminine toiletries lining his bathroom counters and cabinets. He never realized a woman would have need of so much stuff.

The rest of the evening, he stayed in his office, listening for movement from the other side of his office wall. He wanted her so badly, longed for her with every fiber of his being and she wouldn't have him. He'd seen her desire that night in the tent. What had happened? Why was being a Princess such a big deal to her? Would she really have been happier with a poor farmer?

It didn't make sense, especially in light of her expensive jewels. It wasn't as if this refined beauty grew up poor on a farm and was used to such a life. In fact, he would bet she would go crazy in the first month of constant, hard, manual labor. Everything about her screamed that she came from money and affluence. It was in the way she carried herself, the way she instructed servants with ease and kindness, the way she commanded respect without even knowing it. These were traits bred into a person from birth, not mimicked or learned.

Unable to stay his curiosity any longer, Olek stood and moved to her door. It was cracked open and he saw the light coming from inside. The evening dusk was leaving a chill and he quietly murmured for fire.

Knocking softly, he urged the sun room door to fall open. It wasn't the garden he expected. Instead, her potting table was filled with glass jars bubbling with strange liquids. A stack of writing paper carried strange symbols and notations. Books were scattered on a clean bench, several opened to different pages. In the middle of it all was his wife.

Nadja's brow was furrowed in concentration as she lifted her translator to the book. She mumbled something under her breath, made a notation, and turned to lift one of the jars of green liquid. Still muttering to herself, she wrote her observations down on the paper.

"Nadja?" Olek asked, realizing she didn't hear him come in.

Nadja jumped, nearly spilling the green liquid down her shirt. Her body froze and she took several deep breaths. Her heart hammered in her chest. She'd just discovered that the combination of roots she'd blended made a very effective chemical acid. It could have taken her skin off.

Setting the glass down carefully, she demanded, "What are you doing sneaking up on me like that? Didn't you ever hear of knocking?"

"I did knock," Olek defended, seeing that she was shaken. He ignored her usual ire, and stepped into her new office.

Nadja's fingers trembled as she twisted them together. Looking down at her notes, she quickly covered them to hide them from view. It was pointless because he couldn't read them anyway.

"What exactly are you doing?" Olek asked, his voice rolling out soft and low. "This doesn't look like gardening."

"I'm…" She hesitated, a frown marring her brow. "It's none of your business. I don't bug you about what you do all day, or last night for that matter. You could afford me the same courtesy."

"All day I work on matters of the House of Draig--rather boring but important stuff. Last night, I was in the royal office going over papers with the King and I fell asleep on the couch," he said lightly. To his surprise, the admission actually seemed to relieve her.

Nadja gulped. She had almost convinced herself he was with another woman. Different scenarios had played endlessly in her head. But, looking at him, she saw the truth in his eyes. Suddenly, it was as if she felt him inside of her. If she closed her eyes she could almost detect his heart beating next to her chest.

Olek lifted the green jar. "Is this a kind of fertilizer?"

Nadja tensed as he recklessly swirled it. "Don't!"

A splash of liquid came out over the edge and dotted onto one of the plants. Instantly, the leaf bubbled and melted. Olek frowned, his eyes turning to her suspiciously.

"It's not what you think," Nadja said, holding up her hands in defense of any unspoken words. When he didn't lower the jar, she eased it out of his fingers and set it on the table.

"How do you know what I am thinking?" he asked, still wary.

"It was a simple mistake. The translator was reading your word for poison as potion and I just now figured it out what it was trying to say. The combination of these elements make acid, not…" Nadja paused looking at him. "I'm sorry. It's all really very boring."

"No, please, go on," Olek murmured, liking the sound of her low, siren's voice. He could listen to it forever, it didn't matter what it said.

"No, it gets really … scientific. You couldn't possibly be interested." Nadja began slowly urging him back to the door. When she got him outside, she shut the laboratory door and followed him to the couch. "I would just appreciate if you didn't touch anything in there until I can figure out how to write Qurilixian on my labels."

"I can easily read seven languages and speak nearly thirty fluently," he mused. "Label them however you like."

Nadja blinked at the admission. "You have an uploader unit here?"

"No," he chuckled. He stopped walking, standing with her near the fireplace. It glowed over her skin, contrasting her features. "We don't use uploads. Sometimes the material doesn't stick when you need it to."

"Too bad. It would really help the brides learn the basics of your language. The phonetics alone can give you a headache…"

Nadja swallowed, not planning on revealing so much.

Too late, Olek caught it. Smiling in pleasure, he asked, "You're trying to learn my language?"

"I…" Nadja hesitated and looked away. "It would only be prudent. Since I am stuck here, I should be able to speak to people."

"Why didn't you ask me for help?" His voice deepened, as he closed the distance between them. He reached to stroke her cheek, casting a spell between them as his touch moved over her throat to brush over her collarbone. "I will gladly teach you."

"I don't need your help," she denied, her eyes drifting closed as his mouth hovered near. The masculine smell of him overwhelmed her and she leaned naturally into him, ready for his kiss. Olek was surprised at how sincerely she softened into his arms. For all her refined defiance, her defenses crumbled easily.

"I would give it," he said, leaning in to close the distance between their lips.

No matter how much Nadja convinced herself that she would deny him when this moment came, she couldn't. His warmth drew her in and caused the stirring of emotions she couldn't control or fight. Her body sought the feel of his, just as it sought air and food for survival.

His mouth conquered her lips with tenderness before trailing to her neck. His movements became urgent as his hand found hold on her breast. He began backing her up to the water fountain in the front hall.

"Tell me you want me," Olek murmured hoarsely to her throat.

Nadja couldn't speak. Her cheeks flushed red with the very idea.

Olek growled at her silence. Her body said everything her lips refused to. Her hands found his shoulders, his back. Her fingers tangled into his hair, urging him onward.

Olek suddenly lifted her to standing on the edge of the fountain. Coming up beside her, he forced her back into the water. Her feet splashed as she landed. Water pooled over her shoulders, wetting her tight cotton shirt and budding her dark nipples to straining.

Olek didn't ask her permission as he tore the shirt from her body. His gaze burned into hers, daring her to deny him, as the water tickled and caressed her naked flesh. He stepped close to her, causing her to lean against the hollow of the rocks. Ripping a long strip from her shirt, he studied her face for a reaction and grabbed one of her wrists in his large palm. Lifting her arm with deliberate slowness, he raised it above her head. He looped the shirt around the peak and easily tied her to the fountain. His eyes dark and serious, he lifted her other hand and tied it up in the same fashion.

Nadja was too far gone to resist him. She parted her lips, but it wasn't a sound of protest that whispered past her throat.

Olek eyed his handiwork, very pleased. He glided his hands over her flesh in the water. Lightly, he touched the sides of her breasts, denying their straining centers. Pleasure coursed through her racing blood, heating her even as the water cooled. Her mind followed the delectable movements of his fingers.

Kneeling before her in the water, he moved his hands over her slender hips. He pulled at the waistband of her soaked pants and pooled them into the water, unveiling her naked body to his hungry eyes.

Nadja trembled before him. He glided his hands everywhere, touching everything but her most heated parts. It was pure torture. Her arms strained weakly to be free, to be able to touch him in return. The fountain sprayed over his body, dampening his shirt and hair, soaking into his cotton pants. The material molded to his solid, firm body. She gasped, jerking harder against her restraints.

Olek worked his way up her flesh, massaging and caressing. Her hips jerked, searching desperately for his fingers. Her breasts arched for him. She was beautiful, writhing in her innocent passion for him. With her restrained, it would be so easy to claim her. But Olek needed answers first and this might be the only way he could get them. This was the only time she let down her guard, mindlessly responding to him in her honesty purity.

He drew near to her, letting her wet body feel his warmth. Her breasts vaulted towards him, only able to rub the aching tips lightly to his shirt.

"Olek," Nadja gasped mindlessly, trying to catch her breath. "Please."

Olek grinned, a devilishly masculine look of dominate pleasure. He put his hand over her head, towering over her.

"Oh, please," she moaned, her eyes closing in her aching need.

"Please?" Olek urged her, whispering his word against her skin. Her body jerked in response.

"Yes, please," she begged, her leg lifted to touch his as she hung helplessly before him. Her calf rubbed insistently against his hip, trying to free him of his clothes. She managed to work her leg to the flesh of his waist. Nadja groaned loudly in gratification of the small triumph.

"What do you want?" he asked softly against her ear.

"Olek, please, don't, just, oh!"

"Tell me," he commanded hotly. "Tell me what you want, Nadja."

"I want you," Nadja said softly, her cheeks flaming slightly, though her body didn't stop its aching search for him.

"What do you want from me? Tell me what you want."

"I want ... this," she moaned, thinking she felt him shift a little closer. Her leg pulled at him, wrapping around his firm buttocks as she tried to force him to her burning center. Every nerve in her was screaming his name. Her blood raced, pumped faster by a heart that nearly leapt from her chest.

"Who do you want, Nadja?" Olek asked, his strong voice dipping low, almost a growl.

"You," she said, growing terribly desperate. This was a torturous game, but she wouldn't have stopped it for anything. "I want you, Olek."

"Who am I to you?" Olek persisted. Her body called out to him, causing his loins to tighten with their delectably sinful desires.

"You're my husband," she said, confused.

"And who is your husband?"

"A Prince," she said, even more so. Why was he talking when he should be kissing her? She strained for the feel of his mouth to hers, as her lips throbbed with need. Her body yearned for him to end his torture of her.

"That's right, and you are my Princess, aren't you?"

"Yes," she moaned before begging, "I'm your Princess. Please, no more, Olek."

Olek couldn't deny the soft request. Dropping his questioning for the moment, he let her pull him into her body. The rough material of his pants separated their heat as he fitted his arousal next to her.

Nadja gasped in the pleasure of it, moaning and squealing with delight as he moved himself against her. "Oh, yes."

"Do you want me inside of you, Nadja?" Olek's words were bold, uninhibited. "Do you want me to claim you?"

"Yes, oh, yes, Olek," she cried, growing louder. "Claim me. Come inside me. Please end it."

Her arms tightened, wrenching delightfully against her restraints as she tried to force him closer.

He leaned over to kiss her breast, sucking the water from the delicate bud, lapping into it with his rough tongue. She gasped with pleasure at the sensations his mouth caused. Her body felt like it was falling off the side of a mountain. He moved his hand down her flat stomach, stopping to test her wetness for him as he dipped a finger inside her tight holding.

"Olek, yes!" she breathed. She jerked, convulsing violently as he stroked. She was so close. He felt so good, knew just the right way to touch her. The rough rocks ground into the tender flesh of her back. She didn't care. Pleading, she moaned, "Ah, there, right there, mmm, don't stop. Please, don't stop."

"Tell me why you are so unhappy being my Princess?" he murmured against her throat. He licked her racing pulse firmly with his caressing tongue as he drank the sweetness from her skin. "What are you running from?"

"I am not running from anything," Nadja lied, breathless. Olek froze.

Nadja was too mindless to notice at first. Her body kept moving against his, rubbing herself to his hand. A moan came from his lips. Slowly, as she realized Olek no longer kissed her, she opened her eyes to look at him. To her utter horror and disappointment, he deliberately pulled his body away.

"A-ah, no," she gasped.

Setting his hand over her head once more, he leaned so that her leg slid off his hip, her foot splashing in the water. Staring deep into her troubled gaze, he frowned. Her chest was heaving. The scent of her desire was in his head, trying to fog his brain. "You said you would be honest and loyal."

"Olek," Nadja pleaded. "Come back. Don't do this now. Please, just kiss me."

"You said you would be honest," he repeated, harder, fighting to gain his control. It would be so easy to just finish his game. The fire in his denied body raged, making his words harsh, hollow.

Her body writhed in anguish. Nadja's features snapped in anger. Wrinkling her face, she growled in warning, "Olek!"

"Honesty," Olek yelled, knowing that his tactics weren't fair. But, in battle and in desire, nothing was fair. Her unreasonable feelings about his station weren't fair.

"You said you were a working man!" Nadja stated in return, her tone deadly in its softness. Her arms struggled to be free, though this time it was to punch him. She tried to kick her leg out to strike him. Her voice never rising to a yell, she proclaimed, "You lie, I lie. I think it's only just."

"I didn't lie," Olek said in mounting frustration. His voice rose, daring her to do the same. He wanted to see her explode, to show anything but this frighteningly emotionless calm that was reclaiming her eyes. Even her passion was being swallowed up into her hardening gaze.

"Untie me, Royal Highness," Nadja said evenly. Only the puffing breaths lifting her chest in rapid succession gave away that she still desired him. Her blue eyes shot daggers at him from the porcelain depths of her face. "I am through talking to you. I'm going back to work."

"Untie yourself." He tossed his hands into the air. His body hurt too badly at the moment to stop and think. "You said you didn't need my help."

Olek left her there, alone, afraid that if he touched her again, it would be to strangle her.

Nadja watched him storm off to the bathroom in amazement. The door slammed shut behind him. She waited a long moment for him to come back and say he was kidding. He didn't. He really wasn't going to help her down.

Nadja's face hardened in outrage, but she kept silent, swallowing her angry words deep inside until they burned as hotly as her passion. Her body aching, she braced her feet on the wet rocks. Their coarse surface gave her hold as she inched up. Flinging her wrist several times, she managed to loosen one hand from the bonds. It came flying forward at the jerking movement. The second was much easier as she got herself down. She glared bitterly at the bathroom door as she crawled out of the fountain.

Nadja left her clothes behind as she stumbled naked to their bedroom. Her thoughts were black as she cursed him in every way she knew how. She even invented a few new curses when she ran out.

"That is the last time you will ever touch me, Prince," she swore, using one of his best tunics as a towel and trampling it to the closet floor beneath her feet. All the time she wished it was his face she smashed. She dressed quickly, hissing and cursing in displeasure the entire time.

Eyeing the bed, she knew there was no way she could spend the night in it with him. So instead, she threw his pillow out the open doorway into the hall and slammed the door shut, locking it firmly behind her.

* * * *

Olek stormed the length of his bathroom in frustration. His little bride was more than he had ever bargained for. Oh, but she was a stubborn little vixen! The image of her wet, restrained body stayed with him, making his arousal painfully hard when he would have it lessen.

Bitter, he shrugged out of his clothes and climbed into the natural hot spring that was his tub. Closing his eyes, Nadja's naked form danced before him, taunting him with what he couldn't claim. His jaw hardened resentfully. Olek lessened his manly torment by stroking himself to a resentful release. When he was finished, the tension might have been gone from his hips, but the aching was still there in his body.

Drying off, he wrapped himself in a robe. His eyes sought the fountain. He hated to admit that part of him hoped she would still be there, trapped, needing him. She wasn't. Olek decided it was a good thing, as he would more than likely not be able to control his actions.

Going to the bedroom, he stepped over his pillow lying in the hall with a suspicious frown marring his already furrowed brow. Testing the door, he realized she had locked him out of his own room. His nostrils flared in irritation.

Nadja listened to his angry footsteps. He banged on the door, but didn't break through it. He growled out a bunch of multi-lingual curses, much more effective than her earlier efforts had been. She just shivered and kept quiet, her body trembling violently to hear his powerful voice. A traitorous part of her wanted him to break down the door and demand his husband rights from her more than willing body. Instead, she heard Olek stomp away.

* * * *

The next day Nadja awoke way before the dawn. She quickly dressed and snuck from the bedroom. Olek was sleeping on the couch. His robe was parted over his chest, mocking her with the deep folds of his muscles, which she couldn't touch. Tilting her head, she curiously tried to see up his thigh, but the robe hid his more private area from view.

Nadja didn't wait around for him to wake up, but instead went into her laboratory, grabbed a book on herbs, her translator, paper, and a pencil. Crossing silently over the marble hall, she ignored the water fountain, her pants and shredded shirt still floating in its moving waters.

Silently, she slipped out the front door with a whispered command and left him.

* * * *

Olek's eyes opened with a weary sigh. He blinked, looking automatically at the front door. It was closed. Thinking he must have been dreaming, he stretched his tight arms over his head as he stood. He needed to exercise. Zoran would undoubtedly get on him for missing practice for the last couple of days. His brother wouldn't favor a new marriage as a reasonable excuse to slack.

More than likely, Zoran was out on the field every morning with the dawn, leaving his little bride abed while he went to drill the soldiers in battle exercises. From what his father said about the unlucky state of all the Princes' marriages, Olek almost felt bad for the soldiers.

Zoran was a hard taskmaster on his good days. If he was angry, he would be a monster to be under the command of. He chuckled, remembering Ualan covered in swamp muck the other night as he passed him in the hall.

Seeing that Nadja wasn't in the bedroom, he assumed she was in the sun room. Quickly, he dressed, frowning to see his war council tunic damp and crumpled on the floor. Picking it up, he knew he would have to get it laundered immediately. The war council could meet at any time on the shortest of notice. Theirs was a land troubled by an uneasy peace. He should know. He had negotiated the peace.

Grabbing his sword, he strapped it over his shoulder to let it fall to his waist. Maybe a sour Zoran was just what his body needed. A day of that man's workouts was enough to purge the foul temper out of even the most dedicated of soldiers.

Slipping out of the house without alerting Nadja, he tossed the tunic to the first servant he saw on his way to the practice field. The man nodded and took it straightway to laundry without having to be asked.

Olek strode through the passageways and out the front gate. A courtyard surrounded the palace fortress, close to the surrounding valley, near where the breeding festival grounds were. In the valley sat a small village under the protection of the House of Draig. The roads were of the rocky earth, smoothed flat and even. The village was kept immaculately clean, built with almost a military perfection of angles.

Olek loved his people almost as much as he loved his family. It was his duty to protect them the best he could. It was hard work and he took his duty very seriously, as did all the Draig Princes. Sighing wearily, the burden seemed particularly heavy that morning.

The villagers' homes were constructed of rock and wood, so that even the poorest of families looked to be prosperous. No one was left wanting for food or clothing and everyone was expected to pull their own weight the best they could. The Draig population wore light linen tunics during the day much like the royal family, but minus the dragon crest and finer embroidery. They were a happy people, hard working and honest.

From the ground, because of the carefully planned angle of the castle's design, the mountain palace looked like a solid mountain with a gate in the side leading to a village. In times of war, even the iron gate could be camouflaged with rock to hide its exact location from the enemy. It was impenetrable. At such a time, the castle could fit all of the villagers within it.

Olek found Zoran exactly where he thought he would be, standing, arms crossed, before the young soldiers, shouting commands. Olek nodded solemnly at his brother. Zoran smiled a devilish older-brother grin, nodded back, and shouted the command for an attack. Olek blinked in surprise, but quickly swung his sword from his waist, as the whole of Zoran's sparring battalion came to tackle him to the ground.

Chapter Nine

Nadja spent her afternoon in the forest, crawling around the ground, as she looked up plant roots in her book and taught herself their Qurilixian names and properties. By the time she headed back home, her hands and knees were covered with red dirt. Her hair was frizzed out of her bun and a small smile of accomplishment lined her lips.

When a few of the young boys had stumbled upon her while she gathered, she invited them to help her search for plants. They made a great game of it, instantly trying to outdo the other for her attention by bringing her the most. One boy even cut his arm on a branch trying to climb up to a high peak to fetch her a bit of moss for her collection. She used a piece of the moss along with other herbs to make him a salve. He wore the makeshift bandage she'd fashioned for him out of a leaf with pride--much to the envy of the others that had then tried to hurt themselves in similar ways.

As she walked, even married men stopped to look at her, instantly as enamored as the young boys had been. The men smiled to themselves, as the dignified beauty absently nodded her head at them. Not even her dirty clothing could detract from her charm.

The boys ran ahead of her an hour before, spreading their tales of the strange new Princess and displaying the war wounds they had bravely received in her service. So far, she was the only Princess they had seen out on the grounds and they were all curious about her and the others.

Her arms loaded with a bag full of plant roots, her book, and translator, Nadja made her way to Olek's wing of the castle. The door opened on her command and she stepped in. She ordered it closed behind her, trying not to make any noise as she crept to the laboratory. Everything was as she left it that morning.

A half hour later, everything transplanted and labeled to her liking, she went to the kitchen. To her surprise, she saw Olek wasn't in his office. Curious, she searched the house. He was gone.

She washed her hands in the kitchen sink. Not bothering to change, she grabbed a plateful of fruit. Seeing a red foil bag in the back of the refrigerator with her name on it, she opened it and frowned. It was chocolate. It smelled temptingly sweet, but she remembered all too well what it had felt like coming up. She wouldn't be trying that again any time soon. She pushed the bag back to its corner.

* * * *

That evening when Olek stumbled in, worn from fighting off wave after wave of attacks from Zoran's men, Nadja was still with her plants. A few of her books were spread out over the dining table next to the kitchen wall along with papers filled with her tight handwriting. He saw that she had been writing in his language and smiled to see a few misspelled words and grammatical errors.

Wearily, he dropped some food into his fish tanks. The blue fish came to watch him, blinked at him, and then followed the wave of his hand as if he was a friend. Almost too tired to move, Olek made his way to take a bath. Nadja was still inside her room when he finished, the door shut to him. The books were gone and the table was cleared off.

Olek was almost sorry he had allowed the door built on the sun room, since he could think of no excuse for going in there. It wasn't likely she would want him anywhere near her after what happened the night before. He couldn't rightly blame her.

To his everlasting shame, he remembered leaving her tied up and helpless on the fountain. He had been so angry, his body past the point of the most virtuous man's tolerance. Her begging voice echoed in his head. His body's suffering was his own fault. She had asked him to fulfill their needs, had urged him to kiss her. But, Olek knew that if he wanted a happy marriage, she needed to accept him fully.

Grabbing a glass of wine and some of his papers, he sat on his couch before the fire. His pillow was still there from that morning and he knew that he would more than likely spend the night where he was.

He was scratching the back of his head, reading a particularly frustrating document from the Lithor Republic from across the star system--it took twelve pages of scrambled wording before he figured out they were merely requesting the exports of ore and wilddeor meat--when he heard an excited yell from within

Nadja's sanctuary. Blinking, he looked up in surprise.

Nadja came rushing out. Her clothes were covered in dried, red mud and her hair was frizzed eccentrically around her dirt-smudge face. She found him instantly, as she proclaimed, "I need a guinea pig."

"A what kind of pig?" Olek frowned. Boy, she was even lovely covered in dirt. His body leapt with the need to kiss her smiling face.

"A test dummy," she said in distraction, coming for him.

"A what?" he asked, growing weary at her determined look. He couldn't so easily forget the green acid she made the day before because she mistranslated a word.

"Just hold still," Nadja said coming to sit beside him. "This won't hurt a bit. I'd use it on myself, but I couldn't wake myself up."

Olek saw her reaching for him and jerked back in dismay. Glancing down, he saw she held a green plant with a yellow center. The plants were found in abundance on the forest floor around the village. One smell and he'd…

Olek reacted too late. Nadja rubbed the plant beneath his nose and he dropped instantly onto her lap. She jolted, feeling the weight of his head buried in-between her thighs, face down. His breath heated her flesh as he slept.

"Huh," she said softly in amazement. Her body jolted wickedly at his weight. The image of his dark hair against her was shooting vivid sparks of pleasure all over her limbs. Weakly, she sighed, "It really does work fast."

Pushing him up, she trembled at the rush in her veins. She had tried to keep herself busy to ignore her feelings for him. For a moment, in her excitement to try her discovery, she had forgotten she was mad at him. Now she looked at him, she studied his handsome, motionless face. According to her notes, the size of the flower would only knock a man of his size out for about ten minutes.

Olek's lips were parted in silent breath and she couldn't resist. Lightly, she kissed him, letting her mouth feel his. She found hold on his sturdy neck, resting over his pulse. Her tongue hesitantly edged out to try and discover more of him. Slowly, she let her fingers trail down his chest only to stop nervously on his hip. He tasted like wine and she nearly swooned.

Shaking herself, she pulled her lips away. Her heart beat

erratically in her chest. It wouldn't do to get caught molesting him while he slept. Gingerly, she took the jar of antidote cream clutched in her fingers and smeared some beneath his nose.

Olek blinked, jerking as he became aware. Angrily, he glared at her. Feeling the cream under his nose, he swiped at it.

"What did you do?" he asked, furious. Instantly, he darted forward to grab her hand. Her pulse raced erratically beneath his curling fingers.

Nadja blinked in surprise at the suddenness of his movements. "What? You're not hurt."

"What did you do to me?" Olek demanded, suspiciously tasting his lips.

"I just needed to try this cream," Nadja began. His hard glare cut her off and he shook her.

"I am not your … guine-a pig," Olek said, remembering her word for it. "You won't experiment on me! What did you do?"

"It's harmless," she said, lifting up the small jar. "Look, it's just an herbal cream. You could practically eat it and be fine. It would taste bad, but it won't kill you."

He eyed the cream and then her. Again, he tasted his lips. As his heart slowed, he could definitely taste her on his mouth. Nadja colored slightly, but admitted to nothing.

"Your books," she began weakly. "It said that soldiers who fall in battle in a patch of this stuff often are rendered helpless. The enemy can … you know … get them in their sleep."

Olek's brow rose on his face, but he was listening. In the past it had been a problem, but they had learned to get around it. Often, forest battles were avoided unless necessary.

Sounding very scientific, she stated, "To kill the plant off completely would be disastrous to the ecological stability of the … well, here, come see, I drew a chart."

Nadja tried to stand, but his grip tightened on her hands. Nadja blinked in surprise at the fury in him. She didn't think he would be that mad. Her father used his new concoctions on her all the time ever since she was small and she'd never been hurt. All right, he had given her an annoying case of warts once, but he did fix it.

"First, I'll have your promise you will never do anything like that again," he growled.

"Why?" she blinked, thoroughly confused. "Do you think that I would do anything that would hurt you?"

"Maybe not intentionally," he shot, his voice dark. "But you don't know what you are dabbling with. Remember the green acid? What if you had killed me?"

Nadja gasped. The green acid had been an honest mistake and she had been testing for poisonous properties in one of the plants. He didn't trust her at all. He thought her stupid. It was worse than a slap on the face.

A knock on the door stopped her heated reply. It was getting late in the evening and Olek frowned, going to answer it. Turning to her, he said, "This conversation isn't finished."

She paled, seeing that he was extremely irate.

Olek opened the door. A man stood there, hat in hand. Nadja came around the side of the fountain and smiled at their visitor. He nodded to the Prince, and acknowledged politely, "Draea Anwealda."

Olek nodded back, wondering what the man wanted. He didn't have to wait long. The man limped forward and bowed at Nadja.

"Princess Nadja," the man said, his English words strongly accented. She stood, smiling curiously at him.

"Hello, welcome," she said, waving him forward. She purposefully ignored Olek. The man smiled in relief, limping over to her.

Olek frowned, following slowly behind. He couldn't hear what all the man said to his wife, but he heard the words 'foot' and 'hurt'. Suddenly, Nadja glanced over to him and frowned. Leading the man back to the sun room, she shut the door firmly behind her.

Olek scowled, scratching the back of his head in confusion. If the man hadn't been so old, he would have barged in after her. However, he didn't want to start anymore rumors about his and his brothers' married lives than already were circulating throughout the village.

Sitting on the couch, he waited. Not fifteen minutes later, Nadja led the man out of the sun room. He was no longer limping and he had a wide grin of appreciation on his face. He took her hand enthusiastically in his and shook it. Nadja leaned over and kissed his cheek. The man almost jumped out of his skin in embarrassment, looking to see what her husband would do to him for the breech.

Olek merely smiled at him, though it was a hard, tight smile.

The man bowed happily to Olek and murmured, "Many

thanks, Draea Anwealda, many thanks."

Olek stood, letting the man out. When he returned, he asked, "Mind telling me what that was all about?"

"Yes, I do mind," she said. "It's none of your business."

"Nadja," he warned.

"Weren't you just yelling at me a minute ago? Something about you not trusting me? Or was it you thought that I'm too stupid and would kill you by accident?"

"What are you up to?" Olek asked, suddenly realizing that he may have intense feelings for his wife, but the crystal didn't make him know her. There was a wealth of secrets behind her eyes that he needed to discover. The passion was there. The connection was shaky at best.

"Come sit on the couch and I'll tell you," she purred with mock sweetness.

Olek grew wary, seeing her expression. There was an impending scheme lurking within her. He moved to sit by her side.

Nadja purposefully licked her lips, coming closer to his mouth with hers. He tensed. She slowly worked her hand up his strong bicep. He froze in anticipation. He felt her light touch all over his body. His manhood lurched in excitement, becoming full.

"I was working," she said, blinking innocently. "And I just earned five hafoe eggs for my breakfast."

Nadja wasn't sure what a hafoe was, but it didn't really matter.

Olek blinked, confused. She hovered her lips closer, working her hand to the side of his face. He tensed, waiting.

"As for you and your distrust, I have two words," she murmured softly. His eyes lit with anticipation. "Sweet dreams."

"Sweet…?" Too late he saw the large plant in her hands as she crushed it before his nose. With a curse dying on his lips, he was out again. This time, Nadja pushed him over. Taking his papers out from underneath him, she stacked them neatly on the floor, grabbed his glass of wine for herself and went to bed, leaving him fast asleep on the couch.

* * * *

Nadja was missing when Olek awoke, but he was in too foul of a mood to go and look for her. He was dejected, confused. There was so much she wouldn't tell him about herself and he didn't know where exactly he had gone wrong with her. That night in the tent had held so much promise for their future and it had all just come spiraling down since.

He was sore from Zoran's thorough workout and he decided to skip his exercise yet again. Let his brother take his foul temper out on someone else for awhile, Olek had his own demons to deal with.

Grinning wearily, he saw he wasn't the only one hiding out. Ualan was staring out from the shores of Crystal Lake. Olek followed his gaze and glanced out over the waters. The surface shimmered like glass, reflecting the light in waving patterns.

Beneath the surface, low on the lakebed's floor was where their crystals formed and grew. Whenever a son was born, the father would dive, grab the first piece he could find, and give it to the baby. From then until marriage, the crystal protected the son and gave him power. When they married, the crystal transferred some of that power to their wives and secured their joined fates when it was crushed. Once destroyed, their lives were only whole with their other halves. Without their wives, they would feel hollow.

"You missed practice again, brother," Olek said, looking down at where Ualan sat against a giant tree.

Ualan smiled, having assuredly sensed his presence. He lifted his hand in greeting, not bothering to explain his absence. He didn't need to. It was written on his face. Like Olek, his other half was fractured and his life wasn't whole.

Ualan looked much like Olek, with the same build and same brown hair. His solid blue eyes were as troubled as his brother's green ones. Olek, always the most amiable natured, managed a wry laugh.

The soft, murmuring rhythm of the lake's water lapped nearby. The green skies were light and blew stirrings of clouds over the distance. The trilling call of a sofliar could be heard as the bird nested overhead. Taking a seat beside his brother, Olek lifted a weed from a patch of nearby grass and thoughtfully plucked it into his mouth.

"I see we are both cursed," Olek grumbled, content to join in Ualan's sulk. "Lest you wouldn't be avoiding your duty or me mine."

Ualan didn't even try to deny it. "My wife has proclaimed herself a slave. Since she's the one to indenture herself, I cannot release her."

"Yes," Olek agreed. "I cannot help you there. The law states clearly that only she can seek the royal pardon."

"She won't," Ualan responded to the unasked question in his brother's eyes. "And I have no idea how to persuade her."

"Does she know who you are? Does she know it's you who can clear her?"

"No, I have no wish for her to know, not before she admits she is my wife," said Ualan. His shoulders lifted with a tired sigh and he rubbed his eyes. "I won't have her considering my royal birth. It would defeat the purpose of the masks. Gardener or King, it's the same to the crystal bearers."

"I think our King is considering never doing business with Galaxy Brides again," said Olek, giving a smirk. "For they have sent all his sons mor-forwyns."

"That they have."

"Is it true she announced she was leaving you right after breaking your crystal?" asked Olek. Ualan nodded.

"Woe that Morrigan should find a spaceport," grumbled Ualan, the burden of his frown deepening.

"Woe that she found a spaceport of our enemy," Olek added with a meaningful nod. He had spoken with his father and it would seem that someone had been looking over the palace's blueprints. When Ualan glanced over in surprise, he continued, "There have been rumors that our brides have not been seen within the castle."

"And who would dare to spread such a rumor?" Ualan asked, his eyes narrowing.

"Supporters of the Var would be my guess," Olek said. "Our father has decreed a festival in honor of his new daughters to coronate them. We have a week to convince them."

"I don't relish the idea of our brides meeting. I shouldn't like to see them banded," the blue-eyed Ualan grumbled somberly. He was the future King and felt the weight of that world on his shoulders. Olek didn't envy him, though his job was just as troublesome. Despairingly, Ualan added, "I can't hide the fact that she is a slave. I can't bring her out."

"Ah," Olek mused, letting a soft smile come to him. "Our mother has started the rumor amongst her maids that she does it out of embarrassment for how she acted after binding you with the crystal. Soon it will be common news. She will be respected for purging her honor."

Queen Mede's diplomatic ways were a great compliment to his

bold warrior father and reminded Ualan a lot of Olek.

"The King fears that the Vars have spies within our walls," Olek answered, turning serious once more.

"And you?"

"I was to head to the shadowed marshes before the festival began. They were uncommonly bold," Olek admitted. He thought of Nadja and wondered how he could convince her to pretend she was in love with him for one evening. He wasn't sure it could be done. "I could sense it on them. They plan something."

"Hmm."

"I know something that will cheer you, brother." Olek suddenly chuckled, brightening with merriment for a moment. "Yusef's bride turned his own blade against his manhood. He was honor bound to put her in chastisement."

Both brothers shared a hearty laugh and breathtakingly handsome smiles. Their mirth echoed around them in the trees.

"Did she...?" Ualan snorted.

"No," Olek chuckled, unable to help himself, "just a nick."

"I hear Zoran's screams like a tree witch every time he's tried to touch her," Ualan said. "It is glad I am that he lives in the far side of the palace."

Olek nodded, taking the grass from his mouth and throwing it to the water. He watched it float away. "Mother is quite upset by it. It seems Zoran felt compelled to disfigure his wife and cut off all her hair. The castle is abuzz with the rumor and no one has seen her about."

"That makes no sense." Ualan was obviously confused. "Zoran would not shame his wife."

"Our father says he saw it," Olek answered with a shrug. "He's upset because of the celebration. My wife has these contraptions, I'll see if one won't grow the poor woman's hair back for her."

"Yeah, if what you say is true, we cannot let more shame come to the family. We'll be lucky to get through the night without one of our brides trying to kill us," Ualan said.

Olek chuckled despairingly.

"And you, brother?" Ualan asked, turning to study Olek carefully. All knew that Nadja was aware that she was a Princess and wasn't too thrilled with it. "What ails your bride that she won't have you?"

Olek frowned, moving to stand. He held his hand down and

pulled Ualan up to join him. How could he answer when he didn't know himself? Nadja was a mystery that he no longer knew how to solve. He couldn't get her secrets out of her by asking or torturing or yelling. They were well guarded within her.

"I truly don't know," Olek admitted after a time. "But I think I am the most accursed of us all. My little solarflower wants nothing to do with me. At least your women fight you. Mine won't even speak to me, let alone yell. How can I fight a battle that won't be fought?"

"A battle can always be fought, brother," Ualan said wisely. "It's finding the weapon that proves most difficult."

The brothers walked through the forest, silently agreeing to go around the long way, away from Zoran and the exercise field.

"Ah, curse the married life anyway," Olek grumbled. "At least with warriors you can always draw your sword and lop off their heads when they get too aggravating. With a woman, what can you do? They should have sent directions along with these vixens."

Ualan agreed with hearty laughter. "That they should have, little brother, that they certainly should have."

Chapter Ten

Nadja doubled over in intense pain, pushing deeply at her stomach as she begged any god who would listen to end her agony. She rocked for a moment on the floor, trying to catch her breath. She had sensed its coming. She felt like such a wimp, as she again held her breath in an effort to stop the unbearable agony.

Nadja hated her period. Ever since she was a young girl, the cramps had been unbearable. Groaning, she looked around the bathroom. There were no pain pills, no hand held medic unit, no bottle of scotch. Hearing the outside door open, she tried not to whimper.

"Nadja?" she heard Olek call.

Nadja flushed in embarrassment, too hurt to stand. Swallowing, she called back in irritation, "What?"

"Where are you?"

Nadja flinched. She finally managed to push herself up. Wiping her teary eyes, she ground out, "Leave me alone."

"Nadja?"

Olek's voice was closer. She glared at him as he came through the bathroom door. He took her in.

"Don't you ever knock?" she asked.

"Nadja, what's wrong? What happened?" Olek asked in concern. He started for her and she flinched.

"It's nothing, go away," Nadja said, trying to turn from him. The pain steadily got worse and her face paled. She wanted to scream but she bit her tongue.

"Nadja, has something happened? Are you hurt?"

She felt his hand on her shoulders and stiffened. He massaged her and, oh, but it felt really good. Her eyes rolled in her head. Her body swayed.

Suddenly, Olek's body stirred with a curious feeling. Closing his eyes, he lightly leaned in to smell her. The pheromone his body detected lit a fire in him. She was breeding.

For the Draig, the woman's breeding time was almost regarded as sacred. The pheromones the woman's body sent off drove husbands mad with lust and the need to procreate. It turned them into true beasts. And, from what he'd been told, although women were not made to conceive at such a time it didn't stop the effect. Draig seed could stay within the woman, waiting inside her until her new cycle, causing a belated pregnancy. Olek didn't have such things as pregnancy in mind, as a light, passionate moan left his lips and he began kissing the back of her slender neck.

Nadja tensed. When she turned around, his eyes were glassy and he moved as if he would kiss her mouth next. She frowned. It didn't deter him. He cupped her face in his hands and pressed his lips to hers.

Nadja jolted in surprise at his instant passion. Not that she minded terribly when his mouth moved with such unrelenting skill. But, her breasts were swollen to the point of painful exploding and her hips throbbed in horrific pain. Lightly, she moaned and hit his shoulder.

Olek growled in primal response. He continued to mindlessly assault her, deepening the onslaught of his gently probing mouth. Nadja gasped as his hands found her backside, hurriedly lifting her up with his grasping palms only to set her on the side of the counter. He wouldn't stop. His lips tore more aggressively.

Nadja ripped her mouth from his. His lips instantly buried into her neck, sucking deeply. Weak with pleasure, she gasped, "Olek, stop."

He didn't hear her. His hands were on his pants, undoing the laces.

"Olek," Nadja said louder, wondering what had gotten into him. He was senseless. His eyes opened slightly, completely hazed over.

Olek leaned as if to again kiss her parted lips. Nadja pulled back. She hit him hard on the shoulder. He blinked in confusion. His eyes cleared and he looked at her, puzzled.

"What...?" Olek began, starting to pull away.

"What is wrong with you?" Nadja gasped with a look akin to dismay. "Didn't you hear me?"

Olek frowned. He looked down at his pants around his ankles. His manhood was bared and Nadja was glaring at him. He couldn't for the life of him remember how he had gotten like that. He quickly picked up his pants and tied them at his waist, clearing his throat in discomfiture.

Nadja hopped down from the counter, pressing into her hip as she did so. Glaring at him, the hormones making her surlier, she demanded, "What came over you? You were all … weird."

Olek cleared his throat. "Sorry. It's … you're breeding aren't you?"

"Breeding?" Nadja asked. Her cheeks flamed in a combination of apprehension and mortification. "No, I'm not!"

Olek let loose a deep breath, smiling sheepishly. "I can tell."

Her frown only deepened.

The scent of her filled his head and Olek took another steadying breath. It was hard to concentrate.

"I'm not pregnant!" Nadja denied hotly. "How dare you!"

Olek chuckled. "Not carrying, bleeding."

Nadja tried to skirt past him, mortified. "I'm not discussing this with you!"

He stopped her. Unconsciously, his fingers began rubbing a persistent trail against her arm. Olek's gaze threatened to turn cloudy again.

"Argh," he groaned, fighting his innate desire to procreate. Like an animal in heat he wanted nothing more than to bend her over the counter and take her wildly from behind.

"I need a medical unit," Nadja stated, seeing his growing reaction.

Olek blinked again, doing his best to concentrate on her words. "A what…?"

"A medical unit," she said, trying to meet his hazed eyes with her calm ones. Seeing that he was about to pounce mindlessly on her again, she added, "Fast."

"Are you hurt?" he questioned, his mind clearing in worry.

"Just cramps." Seeing his nostrils sniffing at her, she pulled back. "If I can use a medical unit it will take care of them. Please tell me you have one."

Olek smiled awkwardly and tossed his head. "All right, come on."

He led her from the bathroom. Nadja followed him out the door into the hallways. She kept a steady eye on him as he led her forward. Her cramps got slightly worse and she frowned, glancing down at her waist.

Before she could look back up, Olek had her pinned against a wall. His hand was on her breast and his mouth was seeking her throat. Nadja moaned in surprise. He found her thigh and was lifting it over his waist to come between her legs. His hard length pressed into her, already at full erection. Strange jolts of fire erupted all over her skin.

Nadja gasped, looking around the passageway. She hit his arm, hissing insistently, "Olek! Stop it!"

"Nadja," he breathed hotly to her throat and she thought she might swoon from the rush of pleasure that overcame her. "Just … a little longer, please. I just want to kiss you."

Olek wanted more than that. His mouth moved, nipping at her shirt, as he kissed a hot trail the breast cupped in his palm. His hips ground wildly up into her, thrusting against her clothing.

"Ah, Nadja," Olek rumbled to her nipple as it peaked beneath the cotton material of her shirt, right into his lips. His hand was at her back, twisting insistently into her waistband, ready to strip her of her clothes.

"Olek!" Nadja hit his arm harder, trying to get his attention. His wild passion was overwhelming, but she couldn't help noticing they were in danger of being caught. "Oleeek!"

Olek abruptly stopped at the panicked sound of her voice. Nadja heaved for breath. Olek breathed heavily, his eyes bore steadily into her, unashamed of his actions.

"Tell me to take you back to our bedroom." He dipped to kiss and lick playfully at her parted lips. "You won't regret it, I promise. I'll make you scream my name for hours."

Nadja shook her head in denial, although the proposal made her shiver with all it implied. "Take me to the medic unit."

Olek grinned, despite the raging fire in his body. He let her go. "Perhaps that would be best."

The medical wing was deserted when they arrived. There was a row of large, empty beds against one wall, a reception desk by the other along with rows of glass cases. In the back were two private exam rooms and an operating room.

Olek glanced at one of the empty beds, his eyes lit with suggestion. Nadja glared back at him, instantly shaking her head in denial.

"Don't even think it," she said under her breath, moving towards the back room to put distance between them.

"But," he began, looking very wounded by her heated denial.

She lifted her hand to stop his advance. "Where is the unit?"

He tilted his jaw indicating behind her.

Nadja backed away from him before turning to check the backrooms. The last room had a standard medical unit. Turning it on, she looked around. Seeing a long, thin instrument on a nearby table, she grabbed it and jammed it lightly into the unit's side panel. The controls slipped open and she grinned.

Olek came to the door and frowned. "What are you doing? We only have one of those."

"I'm not breaking it," she said under her breath, biting her lip as she reprogrammed the machine. She tried to concentrate over her pain.

"Are you sure you don't want to...." Olek began, his head tilting to the side to eye her firm backside as she leaned over. He licked his lips.

Nadja glanced at him only long enough to direct him a frown. "Stay back, barbarian."

Her words lacked heat. Olek shrugged, extremely disappointed.

Nadja finished. Pushing the panel back in, she said, "There."

Standing, she climbed between the two plates of the machine and reached around the corner to press a button before drawing her hand to her side. The plates came forward, trapping her within.

The cloud of desire lifted from Olek's one-tracked brain and he could again function rationally. The pheromone scent was gone. The machine beeped once and opened. Nadja climbed out, sighing in relief.

"Are you better?" Nadja asked wryly. She knew she was.

Olek frowned. Indeed he was recovered. The desire was still there, but no longer the desperate urge to procreate. "What did you do?"

"I took my period away," she smiled brightly. "No blood, no pain, no mess. I should market that little trick to women all over the stars. I would be a trillionare!"

Nadja felt so good that she was indeed very proud of herself for the moment.

"You mean you made yourself sterile?" Olek asked in alarm. He wasn't so pleased.

"Well, yes, I suppose you could look at it like that."

Olek marched forward and pointed into the machine. "Get back in there and fix it immediately."

"What? The unit? It's not broken," Nadja said, confused. "I just had to reprogram it so it would--"

"Fix your body," Olek demanded angrily. His face contorted

and he took her arm, urging inside the medical unit. She jerked away.

"Wha --?" Nadja gasped suddenly. She understood what he was referring to. He wanted her to get her hormones back so she would have the ability to get pregnant. "I can't change it back. It doesn't work like that."

Olek felt as if she kicked him. She didn't want his children.

"It's only for this month. It won't last," she rushed. "It's never permanent."

That eased him some, but he was still hurt.

"I thought we said we wouldn't have children right away," she defended against his silence. "I had no idea you wanted to knock me up so quickly."

"Knock you?" he questioned in disgust. Snarling, he said, "I have never hit you!"

"What? No. Knock me up, get me pregnant," she explained.

Olek scowled at her. Grumbling, he ordered, "Don't call it that."

"Okay," she sighed, shaking her head. "It's just a saying. I didn't mean anything by it. What's gotten into you?"

"Nothing." His look was dark and he walked away.

"Olek?" Nadja asked, going after him in concern.

"Let's just go! It's late and I have a lot to get done before tomorrow."

He was silent as he led her the rest of the way home. Nadja glanced at the spot in the hall where only moments before he had been pawing her like a mindless animal. Part of her told her she should have lived with the pain. Once home, Olek said nothing, only went to his office

Nadja shook in confusion, not able to forget his heated display of passion followed by his sudden angry dismissal. Well, what had gotten into him? If she didn't know better, she'd have thought he started a period of his own.

* * * *

Olek was still grumpy the next morning and Nadja stayed out of his way. He left with a case full of documents around mid-morning without saying more than two words to her. Nadja shrugged. She was content to work in her lab.

That was before the patients started coming. Apparently, word had spread in the village that Princess Nadja could cure naturally, just as well as a medical unit. The villagers brought her everything from skin disorders, to a burn, to cuts and scrapes. When she asked why they didn't just go to the doctor, one of the women told her that the man with the limp had proclaimed her touch to be a miracle and now everyone wanted to see for themselves what she could do.

The superstitious villagers, for some reason or another, seemed reluctant to try a medic unit, which was a new contraption to the planet. They kept her busy until the late hours of evening. Sending the last one out the door, Nadja sighed, shaking her head in wonderment.

Olek was still gone and she was too tired to wait up for him. Taking a quick shower, she crawled into bed.

* * * *

"What exactly are you doing?" Nadja demanded, her eyes narrowing in displeasure.

She stood in the doorway of the bathroom. She'd just woken up and was going to brush her teeth when she discovered Olek on the floor of the bathroom. He was surrounded by the contents of her beauty bag.

"Please tell me you are not putting on makeup," she demanded dryly, shaking her head.

Olek gave her a sardonic frown, pressing his lips together at her statement. "Zoran's wife needs to grow her hair. Do you have something for that?"

"That is an eyelash curler," Nadja said, reaching over to snatch if from his hands. He was eyeing all her things with an avid curiosity, trying to snap them open and make them work. "I don't think that's going to help you."

Olek picked up a pair of electric tweezers and began playing with them. Taking them in his hand, he pushed at it to make its jaws snap open and shut in loud clicks. Nadja grabbed it from him. He gave her a small grimace, before smiling slightly.

"Your brother, Zoran?" Nadja asked. She sighed, leaning over as she began putting her things back into the beauty bag the way she liked them.

"Yes." Olek stood. He held a blush tinter in his hand and began clicking through the color selector. Absently, he said, "It seems she did something and he had to cut off her hair as a punishment."

"That would be Pia, wouldn't it?" Nadja said, remember what the Queen had told her. She frowned. Pia was perhaps one of the most beautiful women on the ship. She had the prettiest blonde hair Nadja had ever seen. She frowned. "Why would he do that to his wife?"

Olek shrugged. "I hear she shamed him at the Breeding Festival."

"What kind of monster is your brother?" Nadja huffed, unable to imagine what she'd do if Olek tried to chop off her hair without her permission. Getting everything in the bag, she stood. Rolling her eyes, she held the beauty bag open for Olek to drop her brush tinter in it.

Olek frowned but gave the contraption back. "Do you really need all this stuff?"

"Yes," she defended as if it were the stupidest question in the world.

"But, you're pretty," he offered, confused.

"Thanks," came her wry answer.

"Well, do you have anything for Pia or not?"

"Yes," Nadja answered absently. She put her things back where they belonged and went underneath one of the counters. "Here. It's a hair extender. It will grow her hair back in about an hour or so."

Olek took the hair-growing apparatus and frowned. It had a giant suction cup on one end, a funnel on the other and more buttons than a computer. He looked it over. Then, glancing curiously over his wife's body, he motioned meaningfully at her lower stomach and asked in manly curiosity, "Can you use it anywhere?"

Nadja again rolled her eyes at him. He grinned, despite himself.

"How do does it work?" he asked when she refused to dignify his last question with a response.

Nadja smiled. Suddenly, she had an idea. She really would like to see some of the other woman--someone who understood her when she spoke and whose voices weren't marred with a handsome burring accent. "Why don't I take it to her and help her?"

"Would you?" Olek asked, almost relieved. He hadn't relished playing the role of hairdresser.

"Sure," Nadja said, in girlish excitement. She didn't have a chance to make many friends before leaving the medic ship and, though they never really spoke, Pia had seemed very nice. "I have to charge it today, but I can go tomorrow. I wouldn't mind visiting with her a little bit. I haven't seen any of the other women since we got here."

"Perfect." Olek nodded. He looked her over, before turning away from her. Clearing his throat, he said, "Now, I've got to go. I have to meet with the King and finish going over some trade agreements."

"So, you're not still mad at me?" Nadja inquired, biting at her lips. She wished she could take the words back because his face became a blank mask.

"No," Olek replied softly, sighing. He wasn't mad. He was hurt. She didn't seem at all interested in having his children and it tore at his heart. The words were unconvincing, but he added, "I'm not mad."

* * * *

Olek was gone with his father the rest of the day and Nadja didn't make the mistake of opening the door to the persistent knocking of villagers again. She didn't want to be the new village doctor. It was late evening before the knocks finally stopped and she wearily climbed into bed alone.

Olek was awake when she got up the next day. He reminded her to go to Pia's, giving her directions to Zoran's home. He was quiet as he again gathered up his case and left, telling her he wouldn't be home until late.

Nadja hated his inattention to her. However, the idea of visiting Pia lifted her spirits some and that afternoon she went to go see her. Moreover, she didn't relish another day of avoiding answering the door.

"Nadja?" Pia hazel eyes blinked in surprise when she opened the door to Nadja's knock. She glanced around the hall in confusion.

"Hello, Pia," Nadja said. She patted her light brown hair into the bun and smiled pleasantly, a little nervous. It wasn't as if they were great friends. Instantly, her eyes went to the woman's hair. Olek was right. Zoran must have cut it. Gripping a small bag in her hands that held the hair extender, she asked in hesitation, "Do you mind if I come in?"

"Oh, yeah," Pia said, with a forming smile of apology. "I'm sorry. It's just I've been cooped up in here for so long, I feel as if I forgot my manners."

Nadja smiled. Her nerves relaxed as she stepped inside. For a moment, she thought Pia was going to kick her out and she desperately wanted to stay and talk. As she stepped into the beautiful house, Pia ordered the door shut behind her.

"Can I get you anything?" Pia asked, beginning to move towards the kitchen. "I think we have juice."

"No, I'm fine." Nadja looked around the Japanese style home and smiled to herself. The walls were wooden planks of straight lines. A floor of matching wood was placed together in an intricate pattern of long cut strips, in the center of which was fashioned the impression a giant dragon on the front hall's floor. A chandelier hung beneath a giant center dome. The crystal shards reflected the light, brightening the room.

The interior doors separating the one level of rooms were paper thin and had no locks on them. From the front hall, a single step down led to an open living room with a marble fireplace, which had straight lines carved into the plain surface and a dragon head in the center top. A step back up, led to a dining room, complete with low table and cushioned floor seats.

A tapestry hung on the far wall, just behind the table. It was red with the depiction of a black forest. In the middle was a noble phoenix.

"I see you got the Princess suite, too," Nadja mused by way of starting conversation.

"You, too?" Pia laughed, almost seeming relieved that she spoke first.

Nadja nodded and an instant camaraderie was struck up between the women.

"It's just so nice to see one of the other women from the ship," Nadja admitted shyly. "This planet has entirely too many men, which wouldn't be so bad except they are all so mannish."

Pia chuckled, instantly seeming to understand.

"So which Prince did you get?" Pia politely inquired.

"Olek."

"Ah, the ambassador." Pia nodded wisely.

"What about you?" Nadja asked, though she already knew.

"Zoran," Pia answered. The women's eyes clouded softly as if she were in pain. Nadja politely looked away. Pia pointed at the bag Nadja was clutching before her. "What do you have there?"

"Oh!" Nadja lifted it up. She hesitated, feeling a little presumptuous in offering. "Before I show you, I have to apologize in advance."

Pia frowned, looking worried.

"It was my husband's request," Nadja rushed, not wanting to be rude. She reached into the bag and weakly pulled out the hair extender. "He said your husband cut off your hair and asked if I could…."

Nadja's voice trailed off weakly and she shrugged.

Pia gave her a wry grin to put her at ease. Easily, she finished, "Grow it back for me."

Nadja nodded.

"Zoran didn't cut my hair," Pia confessed impishly. "I did."

"Oh," Nadja said, horrified. "I didn't mean to insult you. I like your hair short."

"It's all right," Pia laughed, trying to put the nervous woman at ease. Nadja had been quiet on the ship but Pia found she liked her agreeable, unpresuming nature. "I guess it's called disfigurement. It means I shamed myself or something. You should see the looks the people gave me when I went outside. It was like an evil spirit came into their midst. I was waiting for mothers to rush their children away screaming."

Nadja giggled, relaxing once more. How could she not relax in Pia's laid-back presence? Sheepishly, she said, "Well, it's a planet of men. Go figure they'd come up with a tradition to keep their woman soft."

"The Queen stopped by just to look at it," Pia continued with a look of vast amusement. "I thought she was going to throw up on me."

"Mede was probably mad at her son. She says they are a handful," Nadja admitted. "The Queen isn't so bad."

Pia eyed her in disbelief. Nadja could tell the woman didn't know what to think of the Queen, so she thought it would be best to change the subject.

"So, do you want me to grow it for you?" Nadja asked, lifting the extender. "If anything, it should give us something to do today."

"Why not," Pia answered with little consideration and an easy shrug. Then, she turned her hazel eyes to Nadja and began looking her over.

"What?" Nadja blushed at the bold look and seemed shaken. She glanced down over her clothes.

"Do you think you could help me with the other stuff too?" Pia asked, her voice dipping timidly.

"Other stuff?" Nadja blinked in surprise to hear the woman

speaking so modestly. From what she gathered, Pia was one tough lady. She envied the strength in her. "What other stuff?"

Pia waved her hand at Nadja. "You know, beauty stuff-- dresses, hairstyles, makeup.

Nadja softly chuckled, a smile coming to her face. "Sure, I'd love to. But, honestly, I don't think you need all that."

Pia looked down.

"I mean," Nadja said, detecting something amiss in the woman's response to the compliment. "You have a strong, natural way about you that the men around here seem to respond to. I wish I could be more like that."

"What?" Pia asked. Her brow furrowed in question. "You want me to teach you how to defend yourself?"

"Oh, could you?" Nadja practically gushed in excitement. Her face lit up with a force of excitement. She hadn't been asking that, but the idea fascinated her. Her father never let her learn such things as self defense. Quickly, she said, "I mean, you'll probably hate teaching me. I don't even know ... I don't know anything."

"I'd love to," Pia insisted. Nadja could see she really meant it.

Nadja bounced in giddy anticipation. Grinning like a fool, she said, "All right, let's get started."

* * * *

By the time Nadja left, she felt as if she and Pia were long time friends. The woman was modest and didn't seem to know her own beauty. They finished her hair and Nadja invited the woman for dinner. Pia refused and Nadja had the feeling she was anxious about her husband coming home. She frowned, feeling Pia's apprehension when she mentioned the man. She'd also see the slight bruise in her chin and wondered if maybe Zoran hit his wife. She was too polite to ask.

Pia showed her a couple of self defense moves that Nadja could practice on her own. They tentatively scheduled to meet with each other in a day or two, thinking it would be best to hold off the real training until a later date when they were both up for it. Saying their goodbyes, the women smiled and Nadja bounced all the way home. She couldn't wait.

Chapter Eleven

"Where did you learn to do this stuff?"

Olek had been watching his wife in silence, liking the way she twirled her hair when she was in deep thought. He'd been standing in his office door for some time, just watching her. She didn't notice he was there, but he was always aware of her.

Nadja blinked in surprise, looking up from her notes. She sat at the table, figuring different formula combinations. It was a like a giant riddle that begged to be solved, and she loved every agonizing, headache-making moment of it.

"What?" Nadja was surprised that Olek was talking to her. When he hadn't been working with his father, he'd been in his office getting ready to work with his father. She hardly saw him and when he was there, she hardly felt like he was. He was always so preoccupied.

"Like what you did with the medic unit," he said. Lightly, he set a glass of wine before her and took a seat across from her.

"My father taught me," she answered, lost in his eyes for a moment. They seemed so kind and gentle, not like the hard eyes that had stared back at her for the last couple of days. Just one soft look from him and her heart would flutter.

"Your father?" he questioned, mildly surprised by the admission. Olek was all too aware of how little he knew the woman before him. Now that his trade negations were well in place, he could concentrate more on his home life.

"He's a doctor," she said, swallowing nervously. She trembled and the pen fell to her paper. She closed her notebook and took up the wine.

"Where?" Olek didn't miss the way she all of a sudden avoided meeting his gaze.

"He travels all over," Nadja answered the best she could. She swallowed, unable to meet his expression. It was too kind, too inquisitive. "I couldn't tell you where he is at the moment."

Well, it's the truth, thought Nadja in dejection.

"Will he travel here? He'd be welcome to visit. We have a wing specifically for guests."

Nadja wasn't so sure how welcome her father would be in a place like this. She gulped her wine nervously. Olek gave a quizzical smile as she set the empty glass down.

"More?" he asked.

Nadja shook her head. "No. I have work to do. Too much wine and I won't be able to concentrate."

She tried to stand. Olek reached a hand out to stop her. His fingers wrapped her wrist and he felt her pulse racing beneath his fingers. Instinctively, he smelled her fear.

"I don't want to talk about this," she said. "My father won't visit us here. He doesn't know where I am and I prefer to keep it that way."

"Nadja," Olek began, only to sigh. To his people family was very important. "But, he's your father."

He's a madman! her head screamed. She took a calming breath. "He's not in my life anymore. So can we drop it?"

"Sure."

Nadja relaxed greatly at the admission, though her eyes darted around the room as if searching the darkened corners for something that wasn't there.

Olek wasn't finished talking quite yet, and asked, "What about Pia? Did you get her hair fixed?"

Nadja smiled. "She actually cut it herself, but she did let me grow it for her. I don't think she knew that everyone would consider it a disfigurement. She's really nice and offered to teach me how to throw knives."

At that Olek grinned.

"She's very good," Nadja defended.

Olek's smile widened. He was glad she had a woman to talk to. "I'm sure she's wonderful. Just be careful. I would hate to see you hurt yourself."

Nadja blushed in pleasure at his concern. She nodded dutifully.

"So, how's your work coming along?" Nadja asked shyly. She hated to admit it, but his secretive nature when it came to what he did had her very curious. Several times she almost dug through his office for a clue. Only her self-respect kept her from going through with it.

Okay that and the fear of him catching her in the act.

"It's coming along," he said, sipping his wine. "I'm almost finished with what I was doing and will start a new project soon."

The vague answer caused her to frown. "Can't you tell me any more than that? What is it you're doing? What will you start on next?"

"It wouldn't interest you. It's just intergalactic politics--very boring stuff."

"A very diplomatic answer," she answered hesitantly in the Qurilixen language.

Olek laughed, "Not bad. I see you've been practicing."

"Thanks." A little blush fanned Nadja's features as he studied her.

"Ah, Nadja?" Olek began, looking down at his glass. He swirled the wine. "There is something I need to ask you."

Nadja frowned, worried. "What?"

"I know you don't like being a Princess," he began in apprehension. He'd been avoiding this conversation, but with the coronation in a couple days he had no choice but to bring it up. His father had been relentless in asking him about it. Olek couldn't blame the King. After all, he was practically hiding out in his father's office.

"Yes," Nadja said carefully. Her heart beat in panic. Was he going to get rid of her? The idea terrified her more than she thought it would have.

Olek sighed. Hesitantly, he reached forward, taking her hand in his. "There is a big celebration in two nights and I want you to go with me ... as my Princess."

Nadja blinked. Her heart let loose in her chest. He studied her expectantly, as if wary of her answer.

"It's very important to the kingdom for you to be there," Olek said, "or else I wouldn't ask it of you."

Her heart stopped.

"It's to be your and the other Princesses' coronation into the family." Olek traced the long line of her unmoving fingers beneath his hand. "There will be some diplomats there from a neighboring kingdom to bear witness. It's very important that they think you're happy, that all the brides are happy here with us."

Olek studied her face, wanting desperately to ask her if she was happy with him. She never said anything one way or the other, except to state she hated being a Princess and wished for a simple life. Thinking of the politics involved with this celebration, he knew that simple was the farthest thing from it.

"I know it's a lot to ask, being as you are ... that you didn't want this," he said carefully. He drew his hands from hers.

Nadja nodded. He wasn't asking her because he wanted her there with him. He was asking her because duty required him to bring her.

Olek saw the look in her eyes and mistook her disappointment for displeasure. He was sorry for it. An ache started in the pit of his stomach. He really wanted to take her with him. He really wanted her to want to be there as his wife, proudly proclaiming herself as his bride.

"It's fine, Olek," Nadja answered softly. Her eyes dipped, trying to hide her worry. "It's just a planetary event? There won't be intergalactic nations attending will there?"

"No, we don't really hold intergalactic events. Occasionally, we will entertain a foreign ambassador, but it's rare and often it's only one or two people, never a large group."

Nadja was glad for that. An intergalactic event would mean cameras and reporters and, worst of all, her name being printed all over the galaxy like a walking advertisement for trouble.

"What will happen?" she asked, softly. "What do I need to do?"

"Just show up and smile."

Nadja chuckled, liking the way he was looking at her. She looked at his mouth, longing to kiss him.

"The coronation is simple," Olek added. "The Preosts will crown you as you are seated in your chair. You aren't required to make a speech or to do anything special. We'll have dinner, dance if you wish, and that's all."

"I think I can do that," Nadja murmured. Her eyes again dipped to his mouth, wondering if he tasted of wine. A party didn't sound all that bad.

"I appreciate it, Nadja." Olek was unaware of her thoughts as she stared at his face. "I didn't mean to interrupt your work."

Nadja wanted to stop him as he stood to go. His boyishly handsome grin as he paused to look at her made her heart contract. She twitched to reach for him, but he turned away before she could get up the nerve to touch him.

* * * *

Nadja took a deep breath, looking pointedly at Pia. They were in the long exercise room in Pia's home. The wood floors were perfectly smoothed and polished. There were weapons everywhere--some of which Nadja had no clue about. The paper thin door leading between rooms was opened and Nadja could see Pia's dining room table from where she stood.

"Okay, Nadja," Pia said, trying to draw her friend's attention back to her. Nadja was drifting off again. "I want you to kick my hand."

Nadja was in comfortable black pants and a cotton shirt Pia had lent her for the lesson. Her own clothes hadn't been suitable for what they were about, according to Pia. Taking a deep breath, she looked at the woman's hand high in the air.

"Just like I showed you," Pia urged.

Nadja kicked, giving a light jump as she did so.

"Again," Pia said. Nadja kicked a second time and then a third and fourth on command. Pia smiled. "You're getting a lot better."

Nadja blushed. "I'm sorry. I'm just so distracted today."

Pia lowered her hand, sensing a talk. "What's going on?"

Nadja shrugged. "Have you been told about our coronation?"

"We have a coronation?" Pia asked, before laughing.

"I guess not," Nadja said. "Olek told me about it last night. He says it's important to the kingdom that we go and act happy."

"Ah," Pia said, perceptively. "He didn't say that it was important to him that you go."

Nadja blushed, but nodded in agreement. "He's just so frustrating! One minute I want to … kiss him and the next I want to…."

"Kiss him some more?" Pia said with a laugh.

"Exactly," Nadja said with a bashful grin. Pia lifted her opposite hand and Nadja kicked it repeatedly, as she continued, "And I shouldn't want to. He's not what I wanted at all when I came here. I wanted a sweet country doctor who was old and didn't make me want to kiss him all the time."

"Instead you got a Prince."

"Exactly," Nadja said, kicking harder and faster. Losing her breath, she paused. "I got the perfect Prince. Sometimes, it's like I married a title, not a man. I have no clue what he does all day. I know he's an ambassador and working on trade agreements, but every time I ask he changes the subject like I'm some kind of alien spy."

"Now a low kick," Pia instructed, holding her hand down low near waist level.

Nadja turned to use her other leg.

"Nadja," Pia began. "Why did you come here?"

Nadja froze. Her leg dropped down without striking. Pia dropped her hand. Taking a deep breath, Pia began reaching for a glass of water. Nadja, mistaking her as wanting her to kick, did.

Pia bent over just as Nadja's foot struck out. It hit her in the stomach, sending her off balance in surprise. Nadja gasped. Pia stumbled back, right into a standing display of swords. Her mouth opened in astonishment.

"Oh, Pia," Nadja gasped, running forward. She reached to grab her. "I didn't mean to. I thought--"

"No," Pia gulped. Her somber expression kept her back. Pia looked down at her side. Blood was spilling onto the floor. "Get a medic."

Nadja paled. She ran for the front door.

"Open," Pia yelled weakly. She heard the door slide. Her breath became shallow as she pulled forward, urging a blade from her back. She fell to the floor, whispering, "Please hurry."

* * * *

Tal, the royal household's personal medic, said Pia was going to be all right. She lost a fair amount of blood and her wound needed to be seared shut with a laser. He did the back first, before moving to the front. Nadja felt awful, standing pale and worried in the background. Pia told her to quit fussing, that it was just an accident and she'd been through much worse.

Nadja didn't feel better. She had never hurt anyone like that before. To think that her only female friend ever might have died because of her stupidity made her want to retch. Every time she closed her eyes, she saw her father's laughing face. He would think it a great irony.

Pia flinched, barely making a sound as the medic worked. She lay on her couch, arm raised above her head. Her clothes were drenched with sweat and blood. Lifting up to watch the medic work, the injured woman sighed.

"Are you sure you wouldn't like me to deaden the pain, my lady?" the medic asked when she jerked at a particularly deep section of the wound.

"No," Pia answered between her tightened lips. "It's fine. Just keep going."

Nadja stood behind him, worrying her hands. "I'm so sorry, Pia. I didn't mean to kick you that hard."

Pia chuckled, sucking in a breath as she was again seared with the laser. Through gritted teeth, she said, "It's nothing, Nadja, quit fretting. I should have been ready for it. You've got some power in those legs of yours. Next time, we'll just make sure we're no where near the sword display."

Nadja relaxed some, watching the medic closely for any errors. He was very competent and she sighed as his task was almost finished.

Pia closed her eyes waiting for the man to get done. Hearing the door slide up, her eyes popped back open. She moved to stand. The laser bumped and seared off course onto her undamaged skin. Pia grunted lightly. The medic huffed and turned the laser off.

"You have to sit still," Tal ordered.

"Zoran," Pia breathed, ignoring the man as her eyes went to the door.

Nadja glanced to the door in dismay to see the Captain of the Guards. She shivered in awe and fear of him.

Zoran was everything rumor made him out to be. He was a large man, with an overbearingly commanding face, broad shoulders, and a hard set to his passionless jaw. He was terrifying.

Nadja shivered anew as the extremely large man looked at her and frowned in what Nadja could only take as displeasure. Then, stepping forward, he eyed Pia's side. His voice was harsh, as he commanded, "What happened?"

Nadja took a step back. Zoran looked angry.

"It … it was an accident," Nadja said to the big warrior, hoping to direct some of his ire from her injured friend. She trembled before the giant Prince as he looked menacingly at her like she was one of his soldiers. She got the impression she shouldn't have spoken out of turn. Slowly, she glanced at Pia, feeling sorry for the woman.

Pia was staring at Zoran and Nadja suddenly felt like an intruder. Olek might be a large man, but Pia's husband was monstrous. At least Olek smiled and had the most brilliant laughing eyes that danced in gaiety and mischief. Zoran looked as if he didn't know how to smile, let alone laugh. It was no wonder Pia didn't talk about her husband too much. He was absolutely fearsome. Weakly, Nadja started for the door, "Pia, I'll see you later."

"Thanks, Nadja," she heard the woman answer. "Remember to practice!"

Nadja didn't look back, skirting around the warrior Prince as quickly as she could without touching him. To her immense relief, Zoran ignored her. Reaching the hallway, she had the strangest urge to run away. Pia's husband scared her. Now that man truly looked like a beast.

* * * *

"What's wrong?" Olek asked, as he wife came inside their home. He stood up from the table, closing the folder of drawings he had been doodling on. He'd been thinking about her, almost tempted to send a guard to search her out--only he was having a hard time coming up with a good enough excuse.

"I met your brother," Nadja said. Her round blue eyes shone wide from her porcelain skin. She was still shaken from the evening's events. Zoran had looked fit to kill. Pia was injured, and even though she claimed she was fine, Nadja felt horrible about it. Pia was her first and only female friend and she had almost ruined it. She didn't see how she could forgive her.

"Oh?" Olek asked, wondering why she was so pale. She trembled as she walked forward and stopped by the fountain. She swayed slightly on her feet, prompting him to question seriously, "Which one?"

"Zoran," she answered, weakly. The word was a shaken whisper and her lips quivered delicately.

"What happened?" Olek came for her, unable to stop from gathering her into his arms. He devoured her with his eyes, searching her mindlessly for injury or a clue as to why she was upset. She trembled beneath his hands and to his amazement the reserved Nadja cried. He pulled her to his chest, his hand cupping the back of her head to his shoulder. "Nadja, what happened? What's wrong?"

If Zoran had done anything to her, he'd kill him!

"Pia and I were practicing. She was trying to show me how to defend myself and I accidentally kicked her in the ribs," Nadja cried. Her breath gasped in between words as she tried to get her story out. "I thought she was ready for me, but she wasn't. She fell on a thing with swords and got hurt. I didn't mean to hurt her."

"Is she going to be all right?" Olek asked in a rush, patting down her hair.

"Yes, the medic said that she'd be fine." Nadja sniffed. Pulling back, her wet blue eyes studied him miserably. "But I think your brother wants to…. He looked really mad at me."

Olek frowned as she burrowed deeper into his chest. He wasn't sure what to say to her. He'd never seen her this vulnerable, this willing to stay in the comfort of his arms. His body stirred with hot desire. But, beyond the desire there was more. He wanted to keep her in his embrace, protect her. It was a strange feeling, a connection that stirred between them, pulling them together. He felt every nerve in his body drawing her closer, as if he could fold her inside his chest and keep her next to his heart.

Feeling her tremble, Olek soothed, "Zoran has a temper but he's a reasonable man. He won't hurt you, Nadja. I'm sure he's just worried. I would be if it happened to you."

Nadja pulled back to study him, her eyes wet. She didn't look so sure. "You didn't see his face, Olek."

"I'll tell you a secret. He always looks like that."

Nadja laughed through her anguish and hit him lightly on the chest. "You're not funny."

"Ah," Olek murmured softly, brushing a tear back with his thumb. "It'll be fine. You'll see. I'll even talk to Zoran first thing tomorrow for you."

Nadja looked into the deep, liquid pools of his green eyes. They were so soft and giving. How could she resist them? She could tell he wanted to protect her. He stroked her gently and for the first time in her life, she felt as if nothing could reach her--not even her father's wrath.

"You'll tell him I didn't mean it?" she hesitated. Olek nodded.

Olek's eyes dipped to her trembling lips. To his amazement, Nadja lifted on her toes and kissed him first. He groaned in surprise. She wound her hands up into his hair, pulling him closer. She pressed her body along his. Her lips were tentative, but she didn't stop.

Nadja couldn't help herself. She felt his protective arms, smelled the passionately tempting scent of him. His lips moved beneath hers and it was all she could not to devour him with her body. With a moan, she forced him back towards the couch.

Olek's knees hit the side and he was instantly pushed down. Before he knew what was happening, Nadja had straddled his hips with her thighs and was working her heated core onto his full arousal. She pulled back from her kiss, holding his face as she gasped for air. Her eyes bore into him, pleading. He read her passion for him, but also saw her confusion. She didn't know what to do next. It was a plea he couldn't resist answering.

Olek took control. He ran his hands up into her hair to free the silky brown locks before moving down to her hips. Fervently, he pulled her forward onto his clothed erection, grinding her hips to his. Nadja moaned, helping to rub herself along his extraordinarily thick length. Olek groaned into her as he thrust up to meet her. He felt her getting wet for him. Her heated center dampened her clothes. He kissed her throat as her head tilted back and her hair fell over her shoulders. His fingers gripped into her, forcing her hips to crush harder against his.

"My sweet solarflower," he said against her flesh. He artfully swept her onto the couch so she lay beneath him, his hand cradling her head. His body worked into hers. His hands were everywhere at once, on her stomach, curving to her hip, digging beneath her shirt to free her swelling breasts to the onslaught of his searching lips.

Nadja didn't try to fight him. She was tried of fighting her body. She only wanted to feel him and the safety he provided her. When he touched her it was as if nothing could ever harm her again. She was safe.

"Tell me you want me," Olek moaned hoarsely, desperately.

"Yes," Nadja moaned and was rewarded with the press of him between her legs. Her body arched. "I want you, Olek."

Her hands were on his shirt, pulling it frantically over his head. He let her strip him of it. Her finger boldly found his muscular chest, gliding effortlessly over the solid bulges of his muscles. Olek reached for the drawstring tie on his pants, intent on freeing his throbbing member. Suddenly, he stopped. A groan left his parted lips and he nearly collapsed with his frustration. Someone was knocking on the door.

Taking a deep breath, he saw Nadja blink. As her mind cleared, she covered her chest from view and drew her legs off him. A blush crept on her features. Olek grabbed her back and kissed her.

"Just leave it," he said, ready to continue. "They'll go away."

"But," Nadja began, having regained a bit of her sanity. "What if it's about Pia? What if she's hurt worse than I thought?"

Olek saw she was about to panic. He climbed off her tempting body and, with a frustrated sigh, he yelled, "One moment!"

He grabbed his shirt, tugging it over his head. Nadja followed suit. Leaning over, his kissed her cheek and whispered the heated promise, "We're not finished with this, solarflower."

Nadja hesitated at the heated admission. She trembled, now that she had time to stop and think about what she was doing. The old insecurities hit upon her hard. Olek had been so passionate, so bold, and she became frightened she wouldn't measure up to his expectations.

Olek strode determinedly to the door, walking around the fountain, eager to send whoever it was away. Nadja righted her clothes. Still on the couch, she used the fountain as a blockade between her and the door until she felt she could properly receive their guest.

"Draea Anwealda," a servant acknowledged. Olek frowned, recognizing him instantly as his father's man. He glanced over his shoulder to where Nadja still sat. Her cheeks and neck were flushed. "The King bids you to join him immediately in his office. Prince Zoran is back from his mission and has reported. The King wishes to discuss his findings with you. Furthermore, he said to tell you there is a problem with the trade agreement and he wishes to go over the final preparations for tomorrow's event."

Olek swallowed. Stiffly, he nodded. "Inform my father I'll be right there."

"Very good, my lord," said the servant, doing as he was told.

Olek turned. Nadja was already standing. Her clothes were smooth and her eyes were again guarded. Never had he cursed his position as much as he did in that moment.

"Nadja," he began hoarsely, feeling the need to explain.

"Go," she told him calmly. "I was just a little emotional. I'm fine now. Your kingdom needs you."

"But...." His eyes roamed desperately over her. His body strained horribly. He didn't want to leave her.

"I know, you have to go to work," she answered. Olek flinched. She was calm--too calm. What happened to the fiery passion of just moments ago? He wanted it back. Her voice was mild, as she urged, "Duty is duty. Now, go. The King is waiting."

He detected a sour note to her words. He hesitated, torn between staying and leaving. Knowing she was right, he growled and stalked out of the house. What else could he do?

Nadja watched him go. As soon as the door slid shut behind him, she let loose a ragged breath of tortured air and fell back onto the couch. She couldn't move to save her life. Her body sung with the tumultuous fire of his touch. But, as she had time to cool her thoughts, she grew frightened by the passion in him. His eyes had been so determined, so possessive. After what she did to Pia, she had been so vulnerable, his arms so comforting.

Nadja never acted rashly, never just leapt before thinking. This time, she just leapt into his arms, no debate, no considering the consequences. She shivered, her thoughts were thoroughly confused.

Chapter Twelve

To Olek's misfortune and bodily frustration, his father's need of him lasted well into the night. Zoran had nothing of relevance to report. He had followed a suspected Var spy into the swamps, but had to turn back without completely tracking the man down if he was to make it to the coronation on time.

The Lithor Republic returned a communication much more quickly than they had expected. It was nearly one hundred pages long and with it came a ten page request that basically asked to set up an official meeting between two of their dignitaries. By the time they were finished drafting a response to the smaller document, the King decided to put the ceremony's final preparations off until the morning.

Olek was in an unpleasant mood by the time he got back home. His head throbbed terribly from having to decipher the Lithorian mess. He deposited the hundred page communication on his desk, none to eager to sift through it.

Nadja was asleep. He looked at her for a long time, lying on his couch with a blanket and pillow. He wondered why she chose to sleep there instead of the bed where she had been staying. There wasn't room for two of them and he had no wish to wake her so late. His body aching, his head throbbing, he left her as he went to bed.

The next morning he awoke late. Nadja was already gone. He assumed she was checking in on Zoran's wife.

His dreams had been haunted by her kiss, overshadowed by the duties he faced and the attendance of the Var at the festivities. The Prince would not have admitted it, but the Var threat to the royal Princesses was in the back of his mind, though he had no proof of their conspiring.

Dressing quickly, he had no choice but to go back to the royal office to prepare for the night's ceremony. The sooner he could get it done, the sooner he could be back home with his Nadja. A smiled found his lips. Hopefully, she wouldn't be too averse to picking up where they had left off.

* * * *

Nadja's fingers trembled in nervous excitement, despite herself. She'd been to celebrations, balls, parties, and numerous other royal events before. She'd even been the guest of honor along with her father at many of those functions, giving joint speeches with him, shaking hands, and smiling pretty for the crowds. So tonight should have been no different--but it was.

Nadja smiled in nervous anticipation, taking twice as long with her hair to make sure it was perfectly upswept. She put on makeup and perfume. Looking at her bare throat and ears, she wished she hadn't been so rash getting rid of all her jewelry. A diamond necklace would have gone perfectly with the gown.

She'd spent most of the day with Pia, helping the woman get ready. Pia was fine, moving around as if nothing had happened. The woman really didn't hold a grudge and Nadja was glad, though she still felt guilty. To her relief, Zoran had been gone while she was there.

Finishing her makeup, Nadja practiced smiling into the mirror before going to get her gown. She pulled the light robe around her as she walked. Olek was still gone. She knew he was more than likely with his father.

Her gown was divided into two layers. The first was a softened, cream-colored, faille silk that overlaid a tight corset bodice on the top with non-existent sleeves. It pushed her breasts up, but not too much. The cream skirt then flared out from the hips in a light sweeping affect that glided beautifully when she walked.

The top layer was more of a high-collared jacket of dark green. She'd been told that green was Prince Olek's royal color and she would be wearing it in some form at most royal functions, whether it was a gown or a simple sash. The jacket met at her waist with silver miniature dragon clips. The overskirt flowed, though it was heavier than the cream.

Slipping into green dress slippers, she sighed, feeling every inch a Princess.

"You look ... lovely," Olek said in awe from the bedroom door. His gaze roamed hungrily over her.

Nadja turned, not having heard Olek walk in. She smiled, brushing down her skirt. "You don't think it's too much?"

"It's perfect," he murmured, unable to stop himself from going to her. He reached for her waist. Nadja darted out of his embrace. Olek jumped in surprise, confused.

"I spent three hours on this hair. You are not going to ruin it," she said, seriously. She lifted her hands to make sure he stayed back.

Olek couldn't help his easy smile. He took a step for her again, teasing her as he pretended to reach for her.

"Oh, stay back," Nadja cried. Her face fell in worry. "I mean it!"

Olek laughed. "Agreed, but only if you give me one kiss."

Nadja eyed him suspiciously.

"Just one," he urged, taking a step forward. He lifted his hands to the side. "I won't even touch you. See, I'll keep my hands right here."

Nadja, still watching him carefully, eased forward. His mouth stuck out expectantly and she pecked him on the cheek.

Olek instantly found her waist, pulling her to him. "You call that a kiss?"

Nadja struggled against his hold, though the power in his arms did excite her. She swatted at his hands, trying to get free. "Olek, come on, let go."

"Fine, but I want a rain check. Promise to kiss me later and I'll let you go for now," Olek said. His eyes dipped down to her cleavage with untold promises. Nadja knew that he would be expecting more this night than just a kiss.

Weakly she nodded. "Now let me go. I've got to go check on my hair and make sure you didn't shake it loose."

Olek grinned. Her hair hadn't moved. Murmuring into her creamy white throat, he asked, "What if I promised not to touch your hair? Would you at least let me see the rest of this dress?"

Nadja was confused. She looked down, trying to see what he meant. "This is the whole dress."

Olek shifted to undo one of the dragon clasps and his hand dipped beneath the jacket at her waist. Leaning forward, he nuzzled her neck playfully. "I want to see under here."

Nadja swallowed.

"And under here," Olek huskily continued, his hand trailing down the underskirt to her buttocks and thigh. She was naked beneath the gown. "Let me see what you're wearing underneath this skirt. Will you take it off for me?"

Nadja nearly swooned to feel his lips assaulting her neck. Passion readily flooded into her limb. She moaned.

"You smell so good," he murmured. "You feel so good."

Olek's fingers moved back to undo the second and third clasps, completely freeing the top layer. He groaned to see the tight bodice clinging to her flesh. He saw her nipples tightening under the gown, responding to his assault.

Suddenly, she swatted as his searching hands. Olek chuckled, surprised he'd gotten as far as he had.

"We're going to be late," Nadja said, though in truth she had no idea when the event was to start.

"Ah, solarflower," Olek moaned. Teasing, he added, "I won't take too long."

Her face scrunched up, not completely understanding, but not liking the idea of a fast whatever-it-was he was planning.

"Is that a no?" Olek asked, stroking her buttocks one last time and giving it a hard squeeze before letting go.

"Get dressed," Nadja ordered. Then, looking at the bed, she said, "Your clothes are right there."

Olek followed her nod. He smiled. She'd picked and laid out one of his formal tunics for him. Leaning forward, he smacked her loudly on the lips and let her go. Nadja was almost sorry to feel his protective arms leave her.

"Do you want to help me get dressed?" he asked mischievously.

"I have to go fix this mess you made of me," she scolded, walking from the room.

Olek smiled after her like a fool. Then, sighing, he went about making himself presentable.

* * * *

Nadja looked around the main common hall. The red stone floor was swept clean. It had steep, arched ceilings with the center dome for light. It was larger than the one in her home. Banners of the family crest lined the walls, one for each color of the family lines--green for Olek, red for Zoran, purple for the King and Queen, black and blue-gray for each of the other Princes. Each banner had the embroidered silver symbol of the dragon.

Lines of tables reached across the floor for dining, filled with villagers and attended to by servants who carted out endless pitchers of various drinks and set them out on the tables. Their murmuring voices could be heard all around the hall.

Frowning, Nadja realized no one had thought of decorations. There were table cloths and a vase of flowers on the royal table, but the walls were bare and only goblets and pitchers graced the lower tables.

Trust men to throw such a party, she thought wearily. She'd just have to offer in a hand next time. At least there were musicians setting up in the corner. That was something.

Glancing at Olek, her heart fluttered. He was seated next to her, on the left. On her right was the King. He had smiled at her politely and welcomed her. But, beyond that, he didn't speak to her and kept turned to his wife.

Pia was next to the Queen, looking uncomfortable. Zoran was by her side, looking as forbidding as ever in his red oriental style tunic. Next to him was Prince Yusef. Nadja had never seen him before. He was much darker than the rest of the family and looked as unhappy as Zoran. The seat next to him was empty.

The Princes, the King, and the Queen all wore silver crowns atop their heads as a symbol of their sovereignty. Queen Mede's was smaller in size, thought of the same plain design. Nadja glanced at Olek's.

"Where's your other brother at?" Nadja asked curiously, leaning into Olek.

"He'll be here in a moment. His wife has to come in and end her slavery first," he answered. For a moment, he was lost in the blue depths of her eyes. Those eyes hardened in dismay.

"Your brother made his wife a slave?" she asked in disbelief.

"She did it to herself," Olek defended, wondering why she was getting so heated up.

Nadja's mouth pressed into a thin line. It was just like these men to blame the woman! Suddenly, the hall grew very quiet and her attention turned forward.

Morrigan Blake drew to the center of the room, her head down-turned in a way that made Nadja want to scream. The woman looked absolutely subdued. Where was the spunky, sarcastic Rigan she'd known on the ship? Where was the woman, who always looked proudly to the distance, as if she were overrun with thoughts and ideas?

"Queen Mede, King Llyr," Morrigan said giving the royal couple a curtsey. Her voice wavered and she swallowed. Nadja's frowned deepened, urgently wanting to go to the woman's rescue. What sort of a man would make his wife humiliate herself like this in public? She shot a glare at Olek, wishing he would help the poor woman. Morrigan continued, "I come to you as a humble slave, begging for your royal pardon. I have restored my honor and wish to seek your blessing."

Nadja lifted her jaw. Her lips pressed harshly, turning white.

"Prince Olek?" the Queen asked.

Nadja glanced at her husband. He had something to do with this? He allowed this to happen? Maybe he wasn't the man she thought he was. Maybe she didn't know him at all. He never told her about his work. What if his work included enslaving women or selling children? She really had no clue. Just as soon as she could, she was going to raid his office and find out what he was up to once and for all.

"Yea," Olek answered boldly. She turned her eyes forward, waiting quietly as the Queen named her sons and husband, getting the same answers.

"And I say 'yea'. She has spoken well," Queen Mede allowed when she had finished. "We have agreed. It is up to you, my son. Will this slave receive her pardon, Prince Ualan?"

Nadja couldn't listen to anymore as Prince Ualan made his way down to his wife. Turning her head to Olek, she asked, "How could you have allowed this to happen?"

Olek frowned, not understanding. "I didn't allow anything."

"But, you're taking part in it!"

Olek blinked, not understanding what he had done. Ualan's wife enslaved herself by her own will. Not even Ualan had any say in it.

"Yea," Ualan announced. "I shall pardon my wife. She has proven herself very worthy of her title and of my family's honor.

"Arrogant wretch," Nadja mumbled under her breath, watching as Ualan led his wife to the table.

"What?" Olek asked, leaning in to hear her better.

"Nothing," Nadja grumbled. When Morrigan looked up at her, she could tell the woman was upset. She looked ready to kill. Nadja smiled at that, glad to see the woman's spirits hadn't been completely broken.

"It is glad I am that all my sons have found brides. We are a house blessed," the King announced when Ualan and Morrigan were seated. "Preosts, crown the Princesses."

Nadja felt a crown being placed over her hair and automatically reached up to help the Preost ease it on her head without messing up her upsweep. She didn't turn around to look at the man as he spoke Qurilixian words she didn't understand. She glanced around, happy and very much relieved to see there weren't any cameras in the hall taking her picture.

Olek affectionately took her hand and stiffened. He glanced at her, smiling kindly. For a moment, his gaze almost drew her in, but she looked away before she let it.

"Nadja?" he asked, thinking she might be upset about the coronation. He knew she didn't want this.

Instead of answering his silent entreaty, she inquired, "So who are the ambassadors we are trying to impress?"

Olek's face fell, but he nodded slightly towards a distant table. A group of silent, blond men sat solemnly, ignored by most of the hall. Only one servant approached them, seeming to hesitate as he filled their goblets. The men held still, not looking at the servant as he made his way around them.

"Who are they?" Nadja asked. The ambassadors were the only ones not enjoying themselves in the hall. Nadja shivered as one of the largest warriors subtly returned her stare. He almost appeared to snarl at her as if he would like nothing more than to snap her neck between his flexing fingers. She hastily looked away.

"The House of Var," Olek answered evenly, keeping his attention carefully trained on them without appearing to do so. "They are the kingdom to the south. We rule this half of Qurilixen, they rule the other."

"Your family rules half a planet?"

"Our planet isn't so big," he said modestly, taking a drink.

Servants came around with plates of food, serving royalty first and the Var guests second. The Vars lifted their hands, silently refusing the meal. The servants moved on, giving their plates over to the next table. The hall became more subdued as the people began to dine. Musicians played soft music in the corner.

Nadja tried to keep from staring at the blond warriors, but it was hard. They drank in silence, rudely taking in everything with obvious displeasure. To her surprise, no one paid them any attention, pretending as if they didn't exist. Nadja would have thought her husband and his brothers completely unconcerned by the visitors until she heard Price Ualan lean over to speak to Olek.

"What are the Var doing here?" Ualan questioned in English. His tone was hard and she could tell he wasn't happy to receive the Var guests in his home.

"They are our guests," Olek answered. Nadja looked up at him. She saw Olek's jaw tighten to match Ualan's look. Maybe he was more worried about it than he let on.

"See that they are watched," Ualan said. "I won't have their deceits in the House of Draig. There will be a big price to pay if we must punish them."

"Yusef is taking care of it." Olek paused. Then, easing purposefully into their native tongue, he said, "I wanted them to see the royal marriages for themselves."

Nadja frowned. She wanted to hear more of what they said, but Ualan only answered his brother in kind. It was annoying, like parents spelling out the bad words so the kids couldn't understand. She'd really have to step up her practice of their language if she were to learn anything.

Nadja realized Morrigan was looking at her, a serious smile on her strained face. Nadja tried to smile to get the woman's attention, but Morrigan just nodded stiffly and turned away.

For the most part she ate in silence. A servant came to take her plate and she let him. Olek occasionally spoke to his brother in their language. Nadja glanced at him, seeing his head was turned from her. She thought of how Olek and Ualan really did look alike, though Ualan's eyes were blue and Olek's were the much sexier green.

Pia smiled at her and Nadja smiled back. She wished she could switch places with Zoran so she'd have someone to talk to. Seeing her head turned, the King glanced at her and grinned. He turned back to his wife, murmuring softly to her.

As she watched, Nadja saw Pia's face fall in horror. A shout of laughter had resounded over the hall in front of her. To Nadja's amazement, Pia jumped up from the table and rushed down to the floor. Leaning forward, she saw a young boy limping to his feet. One foot turned in slightly and started to drag.

Several large Draig warriors chuckled harder as they watched the slender, sickly boy from the nearby table. The boy blinked as Pia sidled next to him. He tried to bow, but his position was precarious and he stumbled before righting himself.

Unconsciously, Nadja's hand found Olek's leg beneath the table and kneaded it with her agitated fingers. He tensed as a rush of pleasure shot through his system. He turned to study her.

"Leave him be!" Pia ordered the table of warriors. Nadja noticed one of the Var stood up amidst the distraction. The scolded table quieted and looked at Pia in question.

"What do you want with Hienrich, my lady?" a burly man with a beard asked. "Does he offend you? I'll have him removed."

Pia turned red, her blonde hair flying as she spun to glare him down. "He does not offend me! You, however...."

"My lady," the warrior defended. "He knows we mean no harm. Don't you lad?"

Hienrich dutifully nodded his head at the man's hard look.

"See," the man said.

"Yeah," another added, shorter warrior with a pock marked face. "He thinks to become a warrior, don't you boy?"

The table's occupants laughed louder.

"Well I am a Princess," Pia announced, "and he will be my personal warrior."

The men looked shock, but no more so than Heinrich whose mouth nearly fell to the floor.

"If my lady wishes for a warrior, let us battle for the position. Don't insult us by naming a boy," the burly man insisted in return.

Prince Zoran came around to gather his wife as the soldiers shouted in agreement.

"Let us have a tournament," one of them called. He was met with excited shouts

"Do you dare to question a Princess?" began Zoran, his voice booming with an authority they automatically respected. The hall fell deadly still.

Nadja shook. She saw Pia's hard eyes searching over the crowd. Pushing up from Olek's leg, she yelled to his surprise, "He is my warrior too!"

Olek choked on his wine to hear the reserved Nadja shout out in command. All eyes turned to his wife, including his.

"And mine as well," Morrigan piped in, rising to her feet.

Nadja looked at Morrigan and smiled. They both turned to watch Pia who nodded gratefully in return.

"There you have it," Zoran said, trying not to laugh. "You cannot deny the wish of three Princesses. Heinrich is now under royal protection and will be treated according to his new station."

The stunned hall broke into a murmur of talk. At Zoran's nod, the musicians picked up their tune once more. Nadja watched as he led the boy to the head table to sit by Pia in Yusef's wife's empty seat. Pia waved at a servant to bring the boy a plate.

The dark Yusef nodded at the boy before standing. He went to the musicians who welcomed him good-naturedly and handed him a guitar looking instrument. He began strumming a few tunes with them and proved himself quite up to the task. Someone joined in, singing in the Qurilixian language. It was a beautiful sounding ballad.

"That was very kind," Olek said as Nadja once more settled beside him. He skimmed his hand across her lower back and she shivered. "The boy has no family. It is good that you all claimed responsibility for him. It shows you as compassionate in your rule."

Nadja blushed, seeing his pleasure in her. All too aware of being on public display, she eased slightly back from his face, which was dipping closer as if he would kiss her.

"Do you play?" Nadja asked, nodding her head toward where Yusef sat with the musicians.

"I never really took to it," Olek answered. He moved his hand to her waist, pulling her closer to him, as he took in her exquisite mouth and the brilliance of her shining eyes. Her hair was piled perfectly on her head. She was the loveliest woman in the room and she belonged to him.

Nadja saw his eyes again dip to her mouth and blushed. She gently pushed his hand from her hip and turned away to pick up her goblet. Olek sighed in loud, groaning disappointment.

The King glanced at him. Nadja nearly chocked on her drink. The Queen chuckled at the purposefully wounded look her son was affecting.

Nadja turned to Olek. Under her breath, she scolded, "Stop it!"

"What?" he asked innocently, his green eyes shining with liquid gaiety.

"You know what," she said, doing her best not to blush profusely as he licked his lips and looked at hers. His brow rose slightly as if considering her taste. "Stop looking at me like that."

"Why?" he feigned a frown, though his eyes still shone.

"Because we are in public! It isn't appropriate!"

Olek glanced around to the lower tables. Some wives sat lovingly on husbands' laps. Couples kissed as freely and naturally as breathing.

"But--" he began.

"No," she commanded him regally, already knowing what he was going to say. "I am well aware of what everyone else is doing. However, you're a Prince and you should act with a little more decorum."

Olek leaned to look over her shoulder and winked. To her mortification, the King began laughing behind her. She turned, her stunned cheeks paling.

"Ah," the King said to her. "Well spoken, my dear. I see you have him well in hand."

The Queen punched his arm lovingly and King Llyr instantly leaned over to plant a big kiss on her lips for all to see.

Nadja turned her face away. Olek laughed at his parents and no one seemed to notice from the lower tables.

"So solarfl--" Olek began hopefully.

"Don't even try it," she warned, cutting him off.

Olek chuckled loudly. Leaning into her ear, he couldn't help himself as he said, "Until later, then."

Olek nipped playfully at her earlobe before drawing away. Nadja just shivered. She was unable to look back up from the table for a long moment. But, hearing a dark voice calling up from directly below her, she forgot her embarrassment.

"King Llyr," the large blond Var who had snarled at her acknowledged. He bowed and she saw the emblem of a tiger embroidered on his chest where the Draig usually had a dragon. She unconsciously inched closer to Olek, leaning into him for support. She rested her hand on his leg beneath the table. His arm was stiff as it came around her side and pulled her closer into a protective embrace. The Var warrior didn't look directly at her.

Nadja couldn't understand what was being said. She held quiet, studying the man's face intently. She hoped Olek would fill her in later.

"Many blessings on your unions," the stranger said. "May your reign be long."

"As may yours, King Attor," the Draig ruler returned, standing to show a respect that didn't reflect wholeheartedly in his eyes.

Olek gripped on her waist. She shivered in fear. King Attor's eyes shifted to the side, glancing over the table before he moved away.

"What just happened?" Nadja asked, turning to see Olek's eyes were focused on the Var's back.

Without answering her, Olek tilted his head to Yusef. Yusef ended his part in the song early and passed his instrument back to its owner. Nadja watched as he got up and moved to follow the Var out of the common hall.

"Is everything all right?" she asked, moving closer to get Olek's attention. He blinked, breaking his concentration to study her curious face. Unable to stop himself, he kissed the tip of her nose. "Everything is fine, solarflower."

Nadja frowned, not liking his placating tone as his eyes turned once more to the door the Var had disappeared through.

Chapter Thirteen

The celebration livened up after the Var ambassadors left. The musicians played louder and couples gathered together to dance. Nadja watched Olek from the corner of her eye. She hoped he would ask her to join him on the dance floor, but he seemed preoccupied.

Some time after Yusef followed the Var out, a beefy giant of a man came to the head table, speaking first to the King in a soft murmur. He drew the attention of the Princes, who leaned in to hear his words. Nadja watched their faces stiffen and their eyes narrow, but other than that, they nodded and turned back to their wives.

"What's going on?" Nadja asked, turning to Olek. His eyes were hard and his breath controlled. "What's happening?"

"There's been a little trouble with the ambassadors," Olek answered, trying to smile for her. "Nothing for you to be concerned about, but I've got to go."

"Olek, wait," Nadja began, wanting him to confide in her. She felt his unease and it scared her.

"I'll have one of the men escort you home," he said, waving down to a nearby table. Nadja blinked, looking down at the guard. He bowed at her as Olek gave him his orders.

Leaning over, Olek lightly kissed her cheek, "I'll be back as soon as I can."

"But," Nadja gasped. Her mouth opened to try and stop him. It was too late. He was already down the raised platform to join his brother Ualan. They walked leisurely out the side door, trying not to draw attention to themselves.

The King stood and bowed to his wife. "My Queen."

She took up his arms and, smiling, she made her way down the platform on the arm of the King. She lightly took up Zoran's arm as she passed by him, urging him to join in escorting her out. They acted as if nothing was amiss.

Nadja blinked, looking down to where the soldier was waiting for her. He bowed again, offering up his hand to lead her around the table. Morrigan was already being led away by a servant. She looked uncommonly pale.

Nadja, at a loss, stood and moved to follow the guard. He was quiet as he took her through the passageways to her home. Once Nadja said the command to open the door, he moved to the side and put his back to the wall, standing guard.

"Do you want to come in?" she asked politely. "You don't have to wait out here."

The guard nodded his thanks to her but didn't speak.

"Goodnight, then," she murmured. His face turned straight and stiff to the opposite wall. Nadja shook her head and went inside.

* * * *

Olek and Ualan rushed through the castle passageways to the medical wing where Yusef was being delivered. Agro hadn't been able to tell them much, but that Yusef had been attacked from behind while seeing King Attor out of the keep and off Draig land. Agro seemed fairly confident that it wasn't the King and his ambassador's who dealt the blows, but the Var were not dismissed as suspects in the tragedy.

Hearing Yusef's howl of pain, the Princes ran. Llyr, Zoran, and Mede were quick behind them. It had been hard not to run out of the hall, but it would do no good to alarm the castle until they knew what was happening.

Seeing Agro pinning his brother to a bed as the doctor's worked, Ualan and Olek stepped in to relieve the man of his position. Agro backed away, his face strained. Yusef fought like a bear, but he had lost so much blood that he was weakening quickly.

"They stabbed him in the back. He didn't have time to shift," Agro said to Yusef's family.

The King nodded his thanks to the loyal man. Agro was a good friend, having grown up with the four Princes. Speaking low, he commanded, "Agro, gather the trackers and see if they can't pick up a scent."

"I'll lead them myself," Agro stated purposefully. Shifting into his fearsome Draig form, he took off down the hall in lightening speed.

"My wife," Yusef moaned, nearly incoherent.

Ualan turned to his father as Yusef finally passed out. He let the man go. Olek followed suit. "We should send someone to the Outpost to gather his wife."

"She's in chastisement," Olek said. "Send someone discreet,

someone who won't scare her with Draig. We don't know how much he's told her. She might not even know she's royalty."

Zoran nodded in agreement, looking over from where he spoke with a guard. He waved the man away.

"I've taken care of it," Zoran said. "They go to get her right now."

The family turned to where the doctors worked in silence. The faces held tight as they waited for Yusef to pull through. A half of an hour later, Yusef was bandaged up but still unconscious. The doctor told them that, since he hadn't been given time to shift into Draig and the knife wounds had penetrated deeply beneath the surface of his skin, he was still in danger. But, they were hopeful for a complete recovery.

* * * *

Olek silently made his way down the red halls to his home. Seeing the soldier he'd sent to guard Nadja still at attention outside his door, he waved the man from his post. The guard bowed dutifully and said nothing as he left.

Nadja was still wearing her formal gown when he walked in. She looked as if she had been frantically pacing the floor, waiting for his return. As the door slid open, she spun to him, rushing forward.

"Are you all right?" she hastened, her face drawn with worry as she looked him over. "What happened?"

Olek didn't wish to alarm her. She hadn't asked for the burden of their royal life and he didn't want to trouble her with it. "Everything's fine, solarflower."

"Then? What was that all about?" Nadja demanded, breathless with relief to see him safe. "Why was there a guard left at the door? I thought we were being attacked."

"Yusef had a small accident. The doctor's say he'll be fine."

Nadja took him at his word. She let loose a heavy sigh. "You had me so worried, I was sure something bad had happened with the ambassadors."

Olek's eyes turned to liquid fire as they dipped over her gown. Nadja saw the look and instantly backed away.

"Oh, no," she declared, pleasure and awareness coming over her at once. "I'm not through talking."

"Who said we had to stop talking," Olek dismissed, beginning to stalk forward. Nadja backed away, around the water fountain. "I just want to collect on that kiss you owe me."

"What kiss?" Nadja asked, feigning innocence. She batted her eyelashes at him.

"Before we left tonight, you promised me a kiss," Olek murmured. "Here, let me remind you."

Bursting forward, his hands wrapped her waist. Nadja gasped, awed by his speed. His fingers hit a clasp and pushed the overdress' material aside so his fingers could slide over the cream colored gown to her backside.

"I believe we were right around here," he said, giving her a playful squeeze. "And you promised to kiss me if I didn't mess up your hair."

Nadja shivered as his body edged closer. He firmly pressed his hand to her back, forcing her cleavage to push up against him. He looked down, devouring the creamy globes of her breasts with his hot gaze.

"I'm waiting," he murmured, his breath falling over her bare neck and the top of her chest. "Where is my kiss?"

Nadja leaned forward to quickly peck his lips. When she pulled back, he wasn't smiling.

"Naughty solarflower," Olek said, shaking his head in denial. His eyes pierced her with fire and need. "That is no kiss."

"You didn't specify," Nadja declared. "Now let me go so I can talk to you."

"You talk," he said, a mischievous grin coming to his features, "and I'll show you what a real kiss is."

Nadja gasped as his head dipped down to the top of her breast and he instantly began devouring it with his passionate lips. She gasped, weakening into his arms. Her heart pounded beneath his tongue, thundering wildly.

When he thoroughly melted her will to his, he lifted his head and grinned. "You don't speak, solarflower? I thought you wanted to talk."

"I," she began feebly, trying for the life of her to remember what she wanted to ask him. Nothing came readily to mind.

"How about I speak, then?" Olek mused. "Shall I tell you what I have been thinking about all night?"

Nadja froze. The hands on her back grew bolder, working her skirt up her back to expose the backs of her legs.

"Should I tell you what I am always thinking about?" he continued passionately, claiming her with his deep gaze.

He found a firm cheek of her backside and caressed the naked globe roughly in his hand.

"Yes," Nadja said, not turning her eyes away. Her body was getting moist just listening to his seductive voice. All of a sudden, she was hot--almost too hot--and she was having trouble catching her breath.

"I think about you, solarflower, all the time. I think about having you in a hundred different ways."

Nadja panted at the bold admission.

"Shall I tell you how I think about taking you?" Olek asked, leaning forward to lick at her neck.

"Yes," she breathed, her eyes fluttering closed. "Yes, Olek."

"I want to make love to you here on the floor, on that couch, in the bath, on the fur rug in our bedroom before the fireplace. Every time I see you, I want to strip you naked and have my wicked way with you. I want to tie you up and conquer you. I want to bend you over my office desk and take you from behind. I can barely think straight anymore." Olek grew bolder, licking, nipping, kissing his way along to her collarbone. "I'm always hard. Feel it, feel how hard I am for you. I'm going crazy, solarflower. I need to be inside you. I want to feel your wet, soft…."

Olek didn't wait. He grabbed her hand and brought it to his erection. Nadja gasped at the deep power of him.

"This is what you do to me, Nadja." Olek lifted the back of her skirt. He edged his fingers around from behind, digging to test her response to him. He wasn't disappointed as he slid into her moist lips. "Tell me you're hot for me. Tell me to take you right now, right here. Don't make me wait any longer."

"Ah," Nadja's mouth fell open about to scream her agreement.

"Draea Anwealda!" came an ungodly high-pitched screech.

The shout was followed by a frantic knock on the door. Nadja jolted in alarm, blinking heavily.

"Draea Anwealda!" a woman's panicked voice called louder. "Come quickly, you and the Princess!"

Nadja blinked again as Olek's eyes cleared. He let her go. Her body jerked in protest. He wasn't going to leave her in this condition again, was he?

"What is it?" Nadja asked. "What is she saying?"

It was hard, but Olek managed to tear himself away from her. His body couldn't take much more of this painful denial.

"She's saying we need to go," he answered hoarsely. Oh, but

his manhood throbbed and pulsed in a hard erection. His gut clenched painfully. Under his breath, he swore, "Come on."

Nadja righted her gown as Olek yelled for the door to open. He took her hand, leading her forward.

"What is it?" he asked the woman.

"You are needed in the medical wing," the woman said, her Qurilixian words coming out fast. "It's the Princesses, they've been poisoned!"

The woman ran off to warn the others. Olek turned to his wife. She was pale, trembling as he looked at her.

"What happened?" Nadja asked, as Olek grabbed her hand.

"Come on, we've got to go," he answered, terrified. Without waiting for her to answer, he ran, pulling his panicked wife behind him.

Nadja saw that Olek was leading her to the medical wing. Her chest heaving from the run, she pulled her hand from his as he slowed.

"What's going on? Is someone hurt?" she asked, following him inside. His family was there. Ualan looked tortured, as he stared blindly at the operating room door. She saw Yusef on the bed in bad shape. His skin was pale and he was bandaged over his entire upper body. Turning to Olek, her brows furrowed in confusion, "You said it was just a little accident."

Olek didn't have time to answer or explain. Nadja blinked. There was a rush of talk around her that she couldn't understand. The Queen was there along with the King. Mede was shaking her head, speaking frantically to Olek and motioning at Nadja and Pia.

"Olek?" Nadja insisted loudly, confused.

Olek turned back to his wife, his face drawn. There was no time to explain what was happening. He took her hand, ushering her forward to an awaiting doctor. Zoran was doing the same with a confused Pia. Nadja trembled. The doctor was covered completely with protective gear, down to his goggles. It didn't look good.

"Go with the doctor, Nadja," he urged. "We'll talk as soon as you're done."

"I'll go with them," the Queen said following the Princesses to the back room. But, the doctor turned and motioned that she should stay out. The Queen blinked in confusion but obeyed the man.

"But," Pia began, protesting Zoran's insistent shove. "I feel fine. I haven't been poisoned."

Nadja's eyes widened in horror at the statement and she spun around to stare at Olek. His lips tightened as he nodded for her to go on. Mede's hand was on her arm, pushing her forward.

"Go, dear," Mede said. "Hurry."

Nadja was led into the room with Pia. The doctor turned to the women, taking out two handheld medic units. Without comment, he grabbed their arms and took a sample of their blood. Neither woman spoke as they watched the man go to a counter to test it.

Outside the room, Olek felt as if he was dying. Morrigan had fallen to poison and possibly lay dying in the other room. Yusef was still unconscious. Suddenly, Ualan spoke, stating what they were all thinking.

"If any in our family die," Ualan swore to his father. His voice deepened into a growl as his face hardened with a shift. His eyes glowed with a deadly yellow as fangs extended into his mouth. Resembling the beast he could become, he roared, "There will be blood."

"There will be blood either way," Zoran said, his eyes dark.

Olek nodded in firm agreement, staring at the door that kept Nadja from him, unable to speak until he knew his wife would live.

* * * *

Pia and Nadja's blood tested fine. They were unharmed. Olek almost swooned with relief when the doctor told him. Nadja was stiff as Olek pulled her into his arms, but she said nothing and didn't pull away. Afterwards, they all quietly sat together in the medical wing by the motionless Yusef, as they awaited news of Ualan's wife.

Morrigan was very ill and didn't stop throwing up, even in her sleep. She had been poisoned. Her body fought with a bravery and in the end she won the battle for her life--albeit barely. Ualan sighed heavily with the news and was instantly ushered to his wife's side, where he stayed.

The King ordered all the food and wine tested, starting with Morrigan's. The poison was instantly found in a goblet. The servant responsible for serving her the drink had been dealt with. It was soon learned he wasn't at fault. One of King Attor's men had distracted him as he was preparing to serve the royal drink.

The drink had been meant for the King and Queen. But, when King Attor went up to speak, the servant had placed the goblet before Morrigan instead as not to get in their way. He never realized Princess Morrigan wouldn't recognize the King's seal and would indeed take the drink for herself. If Mede or Llyr had taken a sip, they would have died instantly. The poison worked slower on humans.

The family relaxed some, until the soldier Zoran sent to gather Yusef's wife came back alone. He looked worried, standing in the doorway, eyeing the royal family.

"Where is she?" Zoran barked, as soon as he saw the man. Pia jumped slightly by his side at the noise.

"My lady is gone," the soldier announced. "There looks to have been a struggle. We smelled Var blood, but no human. She should still be alive."

The King growled.

"We picked up their scent in the forest. I ordered the others to follow it," the soldier said to Zoran.

"You should call the soldiers back and get one of your best trackers on it," stated Olek quietly. Nadja, who was standing by his side, turned to look at him, surprised by the darkness in his voice and glad that they all spoke so she could understand what was going on. "Let them think they have escaped into the shadowed marshes. Once we find their location, we'll go after them alone and reclaim her for Yusef."

"Olek's right," Zoran stated to his father, switching his language in deference to the listening women. "If they wanted her dead, they would have killed her right then. They take her for a reason. If they hear the men coming after them, they could be forced to get rid of her to escape."

Nadja held quiet, though she didn't like the idea of Olek going out to do battle.

The men looked at each other, nodding in agreement and knowing that the revenge was going to be theirs.

* * * *

When it was determined that nothing else could be done, the royal family departed for their homes. Only Ualan stayed to sit vigil over his wife and brother, promising to send news if there were any changes.

Nadja yawned as Olek called open the door. She stepped wearily in front of him, her feet dragging. As the door slid shut locking them in, he tugged her into his arms, resting his chest along her back. He tenderly leaned his chin on her hair.

"I'm so glad you're not hurt," Olek said, leaning into her neck to give her a light kiss.

Nadja stiffened.

"Nadja?"

"Get away from me, Olek," Nadja said, ripping away. She turned to stare at him. Anger seeped from her skin, but her voice was deadly quiet. "You lied to me about your brother. I can't talk to you right now."

She left him standing in the hall, going to the bedroom. Sighing, she unbuttoned her overdress. She threw the formal gown over a chair, sliding into more comfortable clothes before crawling into bed.

Olek's body stung with the rejection. Slowly, he walked over to his office. Running his hand over the wall, a hidden liquor cabinet opened. He poured himself a stiff drink and sat down, sipping at it wearily.

He knew Nadja never wanted to be a Princess. She'd told him that from the beginning, but he had foolishly hoped she'd come around.

Finishing his drink, he went to the bedroom and changed his clothes. He debated whether or not he should sleep on the couch, but then decided that his bed, by his wife, was where he belonged. He slipped next to her beneath the coverlet.

Nadja sighed, but didn't wake. Olek was glad that she didn't resist him when he pulled her into his protective arms. His body curled intimately around hers and the thickness of their cotton clothing wasn't enough to keep the softness of her body from stirring him to full attention. Cursing his one-tracked erection, he refused to let her go. No matter how much holding her made him ache, the alternative was that much worse.

Chapter Fourteen

Nadja awoke with a start. Olek's arm was draped around her body, hugging her back close to his chest. There was a hardness pressed intimately into her backside. In a sleepy daze, she turned to him. She reached up the side of his body, unable to see his face in the dark room. She ran her fingers lightly against his naked waist, tripping on his shirt as she moved up to feel him. She rocked her hips naturally closer to where he lay, moaning to feel him. She searched blindly to kiss him.

He had been in her dreams again. Maybe she was still dreaming. She didn't stop to think as she opened her mouth to lay claim to his.

Olek gasped with a start, instantly waking, only to groan as Nadja's soft body worked into his. Her mouth was parting against his lips in a tender, sleepy kiss. Her hands were on his chest, rubbing up to his neck as she urged him to her. Her thigh was over his hip, restlessly digging to feel him, pulling him closer.

He glided his hands over her body, unable to resist the hot passion she awoke in him. He held quiet, wrapped in the dark spell of her lovemaking. Her hands were on his waist, lazily urging the shirt from his chest. She inched over his muscles, grazing his nipples. He threw the shirt off his shoulders and came back to her. Nadja moaned lightly as the tight folds of his warm arms embraced her.

Olek rolled her to her back. He placed kisses on her mouth, moving to her cheeks and throat. He pulled the shirt off her and tossed it away, loving the feel of her skin beneath him--so soft, so fragile, so warm. The only sound was the panting of their intermingling breaths as they explored in aimless directions.

Nadja discovered the delight of his lower back, sloping to his butt beneath his loose pants. She dipped her hands beneath the cotton material causing him to groan against her breast. The sound sent chills over her body, shooting like fireworks throughout her skin. His hips jerked and flexed as she worked her way around to the front. He pulled his stomach up to allow her access. Soon, her hands were on his arousal, stroking him, feeling him, discovering him.

Nadja wasn't scared--she'd never be scared of such a sweet dream. Her eyes were closed, so she must be dreaming. Her body felt as if it were in heaven. Olek was so hot against her.

"Olek," she moaned, wanting him to touch her as she touched him.

Olek heard her plea and pulled back. With supernatural speed, he rid them of their remaining clothing so there were no boundaries. Her smooth legs rubbed against his hair-roughened thighs and it was more than he could bear.

Wanting to make sure she was ready, he kissed a fevered trail down her stomach. Nadja gasped in surprise. Olek's tongue flicked her navel before he dipped lower to taste her sweetness. His mouth pressed a light kiss onto each hip. Nadja tried to close her legs, but his hands strayed to her thighs, parting her for him.

With a moan, he tested her wetness with his tongue. Her hips bucked in astonishment, a ragged moan falling from her mouth. Olek's kiss only deepened, pleased to discover her body was more than ready to accept him. He couldn't deny himself the sweet taste of her in his mouth. The whole kingdom might come to his door, but he wasn't stopping this time. He drank deeply from her, causing her legs to tense and her hips to arch against him. He felt a soft tremor start. Oh, but she was close. He couldn't help but smile.

Swiftly, he crawled up over her, rising on his hands as his hips sought to burrow naturally into her. Nadja felt a momentary wave of apprehension. She'd felt how big he was to her hand, had seen the size of him. The heat of his arousal was searing her thigh, edging ever closer to stake claim.

"Olek," Nadja breathed, wanting to trust him but frightened.

"Oh, Nadja," Olek moaned, seeing that she was about to hesitate. His words came out in a hoarse whisper, "You feel so good. I have to have you."

Olek guided himself to her. Her body tightened around him as he eased his way inside her silken depths. Nadja's eyes got wide. Her fingers gripped his arms. Olek groaned in ecstasy, fitting himself deeper.

Nadja's body burned and stretched. Tears came to her eyes. Olek pushed on and she panicked, hitting at his arm.

"Stop," she breathed, frightened that she could feel so full and hot and so wickedly wet at the same time. Her mind tried to adjust.

Olek blinked in surprise, feeling her tight muscles spasm around him. He wanted to go deeper, but he held still, allowing her body to get used to him.

"It's all right, solarflower," he eased, his voice trembling. "Try to relax."

"I don't think this is working," she said earnestly.

Olek's laugh was painful. He eased a little deeper. Oh, but it was bittersweet agony. Leaning down, he said, "You were made to take me like this."

Nadja tensed, not so sure. Olek pulled back, taking shallow thrusts as he tried to stretch her to accept him. He'd waited too long to have her, had been pushed so far without release. Now he finally had her where he wanted, he could barely stop to think. It was hard, but he kept from delving fully into her silken depths.

"That's it," he urged, moving his hips a little faster. Nadja felt a fire beginning to build inside her as his movements hastened, replacing the white heat of his initial testing. "Oh, that's it, solarflower. I just want to go a little deeper, just a little … oh, ye-ah."

Nadja trembled, feeling a sensation coming over her flesh. Before she could discover the true depths of what her body was trying to show her, Olek tensed. His sweaty skin slid beneath her hands, shuddering violently. His yell resounded over her, loud and conquering.

Nadja's hand fell away at the sound. Her lungs gasped for breath. It was like nothing she had ever experienced. A curious warmth spread over her limbs, making them weak. Her body hurt, but it wasn't all bad.

Olek groaned as he slid himself from her, completely sated. Reaching for her, he pulled her into his arms, tiredly kissing her temple. He brushed her hair with his nose, snuggling into her, curving his body to fit hers.

"I'm told the first time is always a little rough," he said into her hair. Nadja shivered. "As your body gets used to me, it will be better. I promise you, my sweet solarflower."

Nadja shivered, not sure she could take anymore of what he had to show her. Olek held her there, in the dark, as they both fell asleep.

* * * *

When Nadja awoke her body stung. Her first thought was that it was too early to be having another period cramp.

Her second thought was, *What happened to my clothes?*

The third thought, coming to her as her eyes popped wide awake, was, *Why is someone kissing my neck?*

"Fire," she croaked with a hoarse pant. Nadja pulled up in the dim light as the fireplace lit. Grabbing the blanket to her chest, she looked over at Olek. He was lying next to her on the bed, grinning like a fool.

Nadja stared at him, her mind trying to focus on what was happening.

"Lay down," he urged her, his hands coming for her naked back. Her skin instantly lit with memories as he ran his palms over the flesh of her back. Bumps rose over her skin, though she wasn't anywhere near cold.

Nadja jumped, scooting away from him. Her eyes wide, she pulled the blanket with her as she nearly jumped out of the bed to get away from him. When she turned, Olek was on the bed naked, wearing nothing but a confused frown and a very disturbingly ready arousal.

"What are you doing?" she breathed hotly. Her body twinged as she tried to move. Her eyes traveled over his form, trying not to stare at the most predominate part of him vying for her attention.

"Nadja?" Olek asked in confusion, sitting up.

The full force of what they had done hit like a ton of brick to the head. She gulped. Her eyes went to a telltale red stain on the bed where she had been sleeping. She shook her head. Staring at the stain, she said in disbelief, "I was dreaming. That wasn't real."

Olek smiled, he moved to sit, completely unembarrassed to have her look at him. Nadja didn't look. She turned her eyes away as she began rushing into the closet looking for clothes.

"Nadja," he laughed. He was in too good of a mood. His body sung with released tension and he felt like he actually slept instead of tossing and turning all night. If she wasn't too sore, his body was more than willing to try it again. "It's all right, come back to bed."

Nadja rushed out of the closet, shaking her head at him. Her arms were laden with clothes as she hurried past him to the bedroom door, still sporting the bedcovers around her naked body.

"Nadja," he said sternly, his good mood quickly leaving him in light of her outrage. To his surprise, her voice actually rose and she when she answered she was yelling at him.

Angrily, Nadja cried, "We couldn't have done this! I'm still mad at you! Oh, how could you do this to me?"

"Nadja," he tried to reason. "You woke me up. You were kissing me."

She stopped, turning to glare at him. "I told you I was dreaming. If I had been awake I would never have kissed you. I don't even like you right now! Why would I kiss you when I don't like you?"

Olek stood to follow her, moving behind her without bothering to dress. Nadja quickened her pace, slipping on the covers as she tried to get away from him.

"What are you so mad about?" he asked in exasperation, at a complete loss. His arms tossed into the air.

"You lied to me about Yusef! You said it was no big deal," she shouted. She turned, kicking the bedspread as she moved back to glare at him. He was gloriously naked and she tried her best not to look at his handsome body. "You're always so secretive about what you do. Oh, your so important Princely duties. Let's not tell Nadja about them, she obviously can't be trusted!"

Nadja stormed into the bathroom, slamming the door behind her. She dropped her clothes on the floor, whirling to lock the door. She was too late, Olek barged through.

"I didn't want to burden you with it."

"You didn't have to lie about it. You said he was in an accident. I saw his wounds, Olek. What happened? He fell onto a knife about fifteen times?" she demanded back, her eyes wide in disbelief.

"I was trying to protect you! I know you hate being a Princess and I didn't want you to be frightened by this."

"That isn't your decision to make! I have every right to know if my life may possibly be in danger."

"I am your husband," he announced, his face red with anger. All he wanted to do that morning was make love to her again and again and now he found himself in a full blown fight. "It is my job to decide what is best for you!"

"What's best for me?!" she howled with bitter laughter. "You just want to control me. You may talk sweet, Olek, but you're just like my father. You just want to tell me what to do and where to go and who to be. Soon you'll be telling what I can and can't eat! Well, I've had it with being controlled and I don't need you or anyone trying to protect me."

Olek swallowed, seeing the strange light that came to her eyes when she spoke. The dam he had feared for so long broke within her until she was raging mad. He couldn't fight that kind of passion, not until she cooled, not until she came to reason.

"Now get out!" she screamed. "I'm going to take a bath and go check on Morrigan to see if she's up."

"Fine," he growled.

"Fine!"

Olek slammed the door behind him. Nadja locked it for good measure. Then, turning around, she dropped the covers and climbed angrily into the bath.

* * * *

Olek was gone when Nadja finally came out of the bathroom. She didn't care, storming her way through the halls to the medical wing. The place was deserted, except for a kind lady at the reception desk. Nadja discovered she was married to one of the doctors and just helped out when the men took breaks or when there was a patient to watch over like now.

Morrigan had awakened and had been allowed to go home to finish recovering. The woman told her that the pain medicine they gave her would keep her knocked out most of the time. Prince Ualan had been with her, but now he was meeting with his brothers.

Yusef was still unconscious. The woman at the desk asked if Nadja was going to stay for awhile and if she would mind sitting with the patient until she got back from a short errand. Nadja agreed, pulling up a seat by Yusef.

As soon as the woman was gone and she was alone, she studied her brother-by-marriage. Finding a pin light, she lifted one of his eyelids and then the other. She took a reading of his levels with a handheld unit. Next, she examined his wounds, rotating him over to the side to see his back. She lifted back the bandages. Grabbing some gloves, she probed them gently. Hitting a particularly long gash, she frowned.

Going to the glass cases behind the desk, she was surprised to see they weren't locked. Within seconds she had several bottles lined up and was mixing ingredients together. She had helped her father with post operative care enough to know what she was doing.

Going to Yusef, she rolled him onto his back and brushed a piece of dark hair from his forehead. Taking a deep breath, she asked, "Yusef?"

No answer.

"I'm just going to give you a shot," she continued. "It will make you feel better. It's much better than those pain killers. It will help you heal faster."

Still no answer.

Finding an old fashioned syringe, she filled it with her mixture and injected it into a vein in his arm.

Almost instantly, Yusef opened his eyes. His body shuddered with pain. He looked quizzically at her and then down at the needle in his arm. His eyes narrowed.

"Sh," she hushed, drawing the needle away. "This will help you."

Yusef's eyes fluttered closed, seeming to relax.

Nadja dumped her supplies into a trash compactor and pressed the button. Then, she put the bottles back where she found them. By the time the receptionist got back she was sitting innocently by Yusef's side.

The receptionist took one look at the patient and shook her head. "I've been staring at him almost the whole night and I haven't seen a change. But I actually think his color is coming back to him. Whatever you have been saying to him must have worked a miracle."

Nadja smiled kindly and said nothing. She walked out of the medical wing, feeling like she might have actually done something right for once with the knowledge her father had given her.

* * * *

Olek gripped the center horn of his mount. The ceffyl's wide back shifted with each stride, used to the weight of the warrior rider. His fanged mouth darted open with a hiss of its long tongue. It had the eyes of a reptile, the face and hooves of a beast of burden, and the body shape of a small elephant. It was wickedly fast for an animal of its girth and equally as deadly.

Olek's hand strayed to the sword at his waist as he slowed, lining up behind his warrior brothers as they neared the shadowed marshes. The trackers said it had been difficult, but they found Yusef's wife and her Var captors camping in the area. It was an awful place. The rotting smell of molding plant life and animal carcasses masked even the barest traces of scent from most of their kind, from all but the trackers, an elite bunch of Draig who were chosen for their highly developed sense of smell.

He rode with Ualan, Zoran and his father. The trackers had said the Princess was still alive. She appeared unharmed, though she was tied to a tree and half naked. The Princes all silently wondered if she had been ill-used. It wouldn't matter to Yusef. He would take her back, so long as she hadn't been willing.

Fuming, he thought of Nadja. He didn't know what he'd do if the frustrating woman was ever taken away from him. Even when he wanted to strangle his lovely wife, he wanted to kiss her. She was his other, very aggravating, half.

Olek growled, drawing the glances of his brothers, who shared his dark mood. The King frowned, knowing all his sons were in torment.

Last night had been so achingly sweet. It was the best he'd ever felt. His arms had hurt for it for so long to hold her, to claim her body with his. Even now, he wanted to turn his mount around and go to her. But, this morning she had ripped the feeling away from him. How dare she yell at him for trying to shield her from a harsh world? He only sought to protect her.

"Save your anger for the Var," Zoran commanded. His eyes glowed with deadly intent. "If spilling their blood does not placate our wrath, then nothing ever will."

* * * *

They were all spattered with blood from the battle with the Var. None of Olena's four captors were left alive. Olena herself had killed one of them by breaking his neck with her legs as he hung from a tree.

"Hold, woman!" Olek yelled, fighting to keep his seat as Princess Olena tried to wiggle out of his arms. He had half a mind to take the fiery red-head back to the Var and drop her off. He was sure he would be doing Yusef a favor.

Grabbing at the center horn of his mount, Olek pulled himself back up the beast's bare shoulders. Only, this time, he was careful not to touch the fiery woman in front of him. Fine thanks that was for trying to keep her astride the ceffyl when she was passed out.

Zoran and Ualan broke into snickering laughter. King Llyr watched with a vastly amused smile on his face. His brothers had refused to carry the aggravating woman before them.

Princess Olena flinched, her emerald eyes hot as she turned around to glare at the moody Olek. She wore Zoran's overtunic. It flowed over her slender body. When he didn't make the mistake of touching her again, she relaxed her tense arm.

"Where are we going?" Olena asked, as if she hadn't just tried to throw him from his seat.

"Good morning to you too, Princess," Olek grumbled, rubbing his stomach. How he missed his gentle Nadja at this moment. After seeing the menace Yusef's bride was, he wasn't so disappointed in his married life. She might frustrate him, but at least Nadja didn't try to kill him with her fists.

Olena grimaced at being called a Princess and Olek felt somewhat vindicated. She had just discovered her new title and ranking.

"Home," Ualan stated in answer to her question when he saw Olek had no intention of speaking to her.

Olek ignored the others, concentrating on keeping his body out of Olena's arm's way. The traveling party made it to the small village, riding through the center street. People came out of their houses and shops to watch the blood-covered soldiers. They were hardly shocked by the scene, though they were curious as to what caused it. Young boys waved at the passing Princes, some cheered and shouted. The Princes waved back solemnly, acknowledging them.

Olena jolted around in surprise as Olek reined in near the front gate. Her face grew pale. Olek swung down. He was glad to finally be rid of the woman. He lifted a hand to her to help her from the animal's back. Olena ignored him, jumping off the other side on her own.

Olek and Ualan grabbed the reins and began walking the animals to the stables. When they were out of earshot, Olek grumbled, "Fine thanks that was for saving her life. It makes me appreciate my wife's silent treatments."

Ualan chuckled in dark humor. Olek shook his head, feeling that his ribs were bruised from the ungrateful, accursed she-devil. But, she was Yusef's wife and a woman so he couldn't strike her back. Nadja's softness was getting better and better each passing moment.

Determining that he was going to have a long talk with his wife to clear up a few matters between them, he tossed the handful of reins to a boy at the stables and took off for the castle gate. He wanted to stop and see Yusef, but knowing the fiery wench his brother had married would be there, he decided against it. He had had enough of Princess Olena to last him five Qurilixian lifetimes.

Chapter Fifteen

The news arrived that the men had safely retrieved Princess Olena from capture and were heading back to the keep. Nadja refused to go to meet them. She was still too upset at Olek. He didn't even bother to tell her he was leaving and so the news that he was back had come as a particular surprise to her.

"Typical," she had said to the guard who delivered the message. She shut the door in his surprised face.

Nadja was staring at her notebooks of information, not really seeing them for her anger, when Olek came home. She glanced up from the couch, gasping to see his blood-covered clothing. Instantly, she shot to her feet. The notebook fell forgotten to the ground as her heart squeezed bitterly in her chest. Her lips worked frantically, but no sound came out as she rushed to him.

"Olek," Nadja breathed in horror. She reached to touch him, but held back. "What...? Are you hurt?"

Olek couldn't have been more pleased by her innocent horror or concern. He knew that she didn't mean to question his manhood as her wide eyes looked him over. She didn't know that it was an insult to assume a man had been hurt in battle. Her eyes shone out from her chalk-white skin. Her lips were trembling and he had the strongest urge to comfort them with his kisses. Pulling his arm from behind his back, he held out a bouquet of flowers.

Nadja blinked, swallowing and gasping in confusion to see the peace offering. The flowers were beautiful with white porcelain petals, a lovely light blue center ring, and a light brown stem that looked as soft as silk.

"They're called solarflowers," Olek murmured. "I though you might like them."

"I do." She blushed.

Nadja had never seen flowers so beautiful, and that he named her after something so lovely melted all the anger from her until she was left panting in pleasure. She shook as she reached to take them.

"Do I put them in water?" she asked.

"You can." Olek let the stems slide from his fingers. Her round eyes were shining with pleasure. "However, if you take the center bud out and plant it, you can grow them in your garden."

Nadja nodded. She would definitely have to do that. Leaning over to smell them, she found they were of the most exotic perfume she had ever sniffed.

"Thank you," she breathed, turning up to look at him. She again found his marred clothing. "So you're not hurt?"

"No. It's not my blood, but the blood of our enemy. I told you I would protect you, Nadja, and today I have."

She still studied him.

"Does it upset you?" he asked.

"What?" Nadja inquired, finally meeting his eyes. "Blood?"

He nodded.

Nadja wanted to laugh. Ever since she was a child, she had seen more blood and gore than she cared to remember.

"No," she answered instead. "Blood doesn't bother me."

"Because of your father's work?"

Nadja nodded. Feeling rather soft from the gift of flowers, she admitted, "I used to help him take care of patients after surgeries and when I was older I actually assisted him."

"What about your mother?" Olek kept his voice quiet, not wanting to scare her away.

"She's.…" Nadja paused, thinking of a delicate way to paraphrase her mother and not thinking of one. "She's an ornament. My father married her for her beauty, which he helps her maintain, and nothing else. She smiles prettily and throws parties and never raises her voice to him."

Olek listened, wondering at her hardening tone. He could tell she didn't approve of her mother's lifestyle, but he sensed that deep down she loved the woman.

"Though, to tell the truth, no one ever raises their voice to my father," Nadja chuckled darkly.

Yeah, she thought, if they did, he'd surgically remove their voice box while they were still awake.

"Why are you running away from them? Did they hurt you?"

Nadja blinked wearily at the question. Instead of answering, she said, "Why don't you go wash up? I'm going to put these in some water before they wilt."

"Nadja." Olek began to lift his hand to touch her smooth cheek. Seeing the dirt marring his fingers, he let it fall to the side. "I won't let anyone hurt you. You know you can tell me anything."

"I know," she said.

Olek watched as she walked away from him, holding her gift. Well, that admission was something at least.

Olek took his time in the shower, letting the cool water beat against his skin. Merely thinking of his night with Nadja, made his flesh heat. With a slight smile on his face, he tried to come up with ways of wooing her once more to his embrace.

Finally forcing himself out of the water, he dried and wrapped a towel around his waist. Kicking his dirty clothes into a pile, he went to get dressed. Almost immediately, his Draig senses detected her scent in the bedroom. His pace quickened.

Stopping in the doorway, his face fell in puzzlement. It wasn't his wife who stood in next to his bed, but a buxom blonde wearing his wife's clothing as she posed in front of the mirror. Sniffing, he smelled Nadja but couldn't see her.

Coldly, he demanded, "Who are you? Where is my wife?"

Nadja spun from her trashy reflection in horror. Her mouth fell open. Olek was glaring hotly at her in accusation. His eyes flashed and for a moment, she thought he was going to rip her heart from her chest.

Olek looked in repulsion over the busty woman, whose large backside and over abundant chest was stretching Nadja's clothing. Her platinum blonde locks were piled and fluffed high over her head. Her blue eyes were surrounded by an ungodly amount of green makeup, contrasting the awful pink blush on her cheeks. Big, gaudy jewels graced her neck and hands. Her fat red lips moved as if to speak.

Nadja lifted her hands to keep him from attacking. In a whiny voice that wasn't her own, she said, "Olek, wait."

"Who are you?" he demanded, storming forward.

The towel dropped from his waist and Nadja stared. Olek frowned to see the ugly woman staring at his member as if she wanted to touch it. Instantly, the half erection he was sporting in thought of his wife drained from him.

Nadja gasped to see his member become flaccid.

"Olek, don't, stop," she whined in her high pitched resonance, reaching for her finger. "It's me, Nadja."

"You are not the least like my wife," he spat. He reached out to grab her throat. "Tell me what you have done with her."

Nadja gasped for breath at the power of him. Finding the large gemstone on her ring finger, she managed to turn it clockwise.

Olek recoiled as the tasteless woman's features melted beneath his hands. The lips thinned, the makeup faded. Even the hair tamed and wound itself into a neat brown bun. Within seconds, Nadja was as he knew her.

"What trickery is this?" he croaked in horror. His eyes devoured her to make sure she was complete. His nostrils flared to take in her scent, proving to himself that she was really his wife.

"You weren't supposed to see that," she said, her voice low and pleasing once more. She tore the only jewel left on her finger and held it up to him. "It's a morphing gem."

Olek eyed the gaudy ring with the big diamond and frowned. Placing his hands on his naked hips, he asked, "Why would you have this?"

"I…" Nadja pulled back, seeing his scowl hadn't lessened. She didn't hear him get out of the shower. "It was a gift."

"Who would give you such a thing?" he asked, repulsed. She was so beautiful that it didn't make sense that someone would want her looking like a cheap, used whore.

"We … you asked earlier why I left my father's house," she began.

"Your father wanted you to look like that?" he inquired, disbelieving.

"No," she said. "My father wanted me to marry a man who wanted me to look like that. This horrid thing was my engagement ring."

Olek frowned. She had been promised to another?

"Don't take it like that. I never agreed to marry Hank," Nadja began. Suddenly, she babbled, nearly incoherent, as she rushed to tell Olek the truth of it. "My father took us to a district where arranged marriages were permitted and just made the announcement one night at a dinner party he was throwing for some business associates. I had no idea."

Olek didn't move, listening patiently, trying not to grin at the way her eyes widened and her lips moved. By all that was sacred, she was beautiful.

"Then, later, Hank found me and gave me this. I was horrified when he showed me what it did. The worst part is that in order for him to have the ring made, he must have stolen a piece of my hair or a nail clipping when he saw me last, which would have been when I was like fourteen." Nadja shivered in repulsion, taking a deep breath. "That only means that he knew for a long time that he was going to marry me, which means my father knew, which means that is why he kept such a tight rein on me. He was saving me for that fat, creepy slug of a pervert."

Olek's mouth twitched slightly at her confession. Oh, but she was lovely--even more so now that he had the blonde beast to compare her to.

"Are you laughing at me?" she demanded, her cheeks flaming. Playfully, she hit his arm.

"Never," he said, but his laugh rolled pleasantly out at the word. "I was just thinking of Hank's particular tastes."

"Well," Nadja said. "If you like it so much, why don't you wear it!"

Nadja threw the ring at him and he caught it in one hand. Taking it between his fingers, he called, "Fire."

The fireplace roared to life and, without looking, he threw the offensive ring into the flames.

"That is why you signed up to be a Galaxy Bride? To get out of marriage to a slug?" Olek asked.

"It's why I ran away," Nadja admitted. "I didn't have a clue where I was going when I snuck out of my engagement party. Galaxy Brides happened to be leaving from the same space port that night and I climbed aboard. They were short some passengers and were more than happy to take me."

"Ah," Olek said, his voice dipping seductively. He became aware of his naked state. His body stirred back to life and he moved to tower over her. "It was fate."

Almost desperately, she said, "That is why my father can never be told where I am, Olek. He would come after me."

"But you are my wife," he stated as if that solved every problem. "Your father cannot touch you now. This Hank will be forced to step aside."

"He won't see it that way," she said, her eyes fearful. Olek didn't like the trembling in her voice or the overwhelming wave of fear he felt coming from her. "He'll try to punish me."

"Surely he won't mind being related to a rich Prince," he concluded, logically.

"Yes, he will," she persisted. "When I left as I did, he would have been humiliated in front of his business associates. They are very powerful men. You don't know what they are capable of."

"Then it's a good thing you have a very powerful husband with a very powerful family," he murmured, dipping to capture her lips.

Nadja stiffened. She had been so wrapped up in her thoughts that she hadn't seen his mounting desire for her. How could she have missed it? It was blatantly obvious, shining out of his liquid eyes.

"Olek," she sighed, her knees weakening. "I don't want anyone hurt because of me."

"You are my wife," Olek growled possessively, deepening his kiss. "I'll kill any who dare to take you from me."

Nadja moaned. Her arms instantly wrapped around his neck. Olek jolted in surprise but didn't protest as she forced him back to the bed. Nadja's hands delved into his hair, as she returned his kiss with an overwhelming rush of passion that he didn't expect.

When his legs hit upon the bed, she shoved him back. Olek landed hard on the soft mattress in awe. Nadja tore the shirt off her back and came topless to straddle his naked hips. Leaning over him, her breasts grazing his heated flesh, she kissed him deeply.

Olek's hands found her slender hips. Pulling the drawstring tie at her waist, he loosened the material and plunged his fingers around to her naked backside and squeezed. With a moan, he pulled her down so her thighs spread and she was seated fully on his arousal.

"Mm," Nadja groaned in pleasure. Unable to take the barrier of her clothing, she pushed up from him.

Olek's grip tightened. He didn't want to let go. He thrust her forward to grind against him. His eyes lit as he watched her breasts bob with the motion. Nadja fitted her hands onto his chest. Panting, she pushed away from him. Reluctantly, he let his hands slide from her smooth hips.

Olek pushed up on his elbows. He watched as she stood before him and pushed her pants off her legs. Her body was bared to him. She stood, letting him look at her, thrilled by the desire in his eyes and the heavy rise and fall of his chest as he tried to gasp for air. His already full erection lurched, standing tall from his hips.

Olek reached forward and stroked himself as he looked at her. His molten gaze dipped to her sex. Nadja licked her lips, her eyes watching his expert hand.

"Ride me," he ordered boldly, heated and breathless.

Nadja obeyed his growling command, eagerly crawling forward on the bed. His hand fell to rest above his head and he dropped from his elbow to lie beneath her. The firelight glowed around her, framing her body with a golden halo of light. It glinted teasingly off her breasts as she moved astride his waist.

"Yes," Olek said, his hips searching for her, thrusting up to meet their aching bodies all the quicker.

When his hands reached to guide her, Nadja grabbed his wrists and put them back over his head. She pinned him down. Olek grunted in rough approval. His eyes lit to see her breasts so close to his face. He leaned up, nipping playfully at one tip and missing it completely.

Lifting up her hips, she let his arousal brush her. Her body shivered but she didn't give him what he sought.

"Do you want me?" Nadja asked him audaciously, never knowing where the words came from.

Olek closed his eyes at the obviousness of his answer, knowing she had every intention of torturing him.

"Yes," he groaned. His hips urged higher, searching.

She brushed her heat against him, letting his tip part her slightly. Again his hips pushed up and he was denied.

"You want me to ride you, don't you?"

"Oh, yes, Nadja," he said, sweat beading his brow. "Do it. Ride me."

"How do you want me to ride you?" Nadja persisted, giddy with her power over him. She was nervous about feeling the fullness of him inside her again, but she didn't think to stop as she kept his wrists pinned beneath her hands.

"Hard," he growled. His breath drew I ragged pants. "Ride me hard."

"Is this what you want?" she asked, sliding her legs down so that she impaled herself slightly on him. Olek spasmed and quivered. His strong stomach muscles jerked.

"Deeper," he ordered harshly. He knew he could throw her hands from his wrists, but he didn't dare to move. Her torturous movements were too sweet to resist. "Take me deeper."

"Like this?" Nadja asked, feeling herself stretch around him. It was agony, but she was having too much fun tormenting him. It didn't hurt nearly like before.

"Deeper, woman," he pleaded and commanded at the same

time. His eyes opened as he gasped for ragged breath. Already his hips were flexing as he took what shallow thrusts he could.

"Like this?" she asked. Her words were not as confident as before.

Olek jerked his hips hard, bouncing her knees on the mattress. The movement forced her down. Her voice rose to call out as he neared her center flame. Olek grinned, quite pleased with his own cunning.

"Yes, just like that," Olek urged, seeing her losing her composure and delighting in it. Her fingers gripped and worked around his wrists. He could have freed himself if he wanted, but he let her control their pace and depth. A bond strained between them, strengthening. She made him feel whole and he knew that he did the same for her. Their lives were joined, just as their bodies would soon be. Seeing how it excited her when he voiced his needs and passions, he said, "Now finish it, Nadja. Take me all in."

"Oh, Olek, you feel so big," she gasped, not sure she could get him any deeper. Already her body was pushed to the brink. "I don't think you'll fit."

"Just a little lower, solarflower." He took in her breasts. Their budding peaks called to his lips. Sweat beaded her flesh, matching a light sheen forming on his. "That's it, just spread your legs and let me in."

Nadja did as he commanded and was rewarded with a deep pleasure. Her thighs opened, dropping her completely onto his erection. Her fire-hot flesh drove him mad.

"Ah, yes," Olek called through gritted teeth. "Just like that. Oh, Nadja, now ride me."

Nadja was still getting used to the hard, conquering feel of him and didn't move, save to squirm slightly as she tested the feel of him.

"Is it always this size?" she asked in wide-eyed wonderment.

"Only for you," Olek said, passionately. "You make me so hot, solarflower."

"I feel like I'm on fire."

"Yes," he agreed. "And your body is moist for me, isn't it?"

"Yes!" Nadja cried.

"You're made to glide over me."

Nadja lifted up at the words. Indeed, she did slide against him and was rewarded with a pleasurable friction.

"Now, ride," he urged.

Nadja dropped her legs to impale herself once more.

"Argh," Olek shouted in approval. Oh, but her slow thrusts were the most horrendously exquisite torture he had ever felt.

By small degrees, she quickened her body's pace, watching the approval on his taut features. A delightful sensation took her over, making her mindless and driving her forward at a maddening pace. She couldn't stop. She lifted her hands from Olek's wrists to support her as she leaned back over him. Olek's fingers flew to her bouncing breasts only to tweak her nipples and slide down to take control of her thrusts. He urged her faster, showing her how deep he could bring himself into her, how fast and hard.

Olek's stomach tensed as he bent forward to better see Nadja's body. Strands of her long hair had worked themselves loose and wrapped in small waves over her shoulders. Her head thrust wildly back as she began to tense and explode above him.

"Olek!" she shouted, fearfully, beyond any point of reason.

The feel of her quivering body caused his member to erupt, draining him into her with hard gasps. His yell joined hers as their bodies met in a brilliant climax.

Nadja stayed frozen above him, too overwhelmed by feeling to move. As her breath slowly came back to her, she fell forward onto Olek's chest. Her face buried into his neck until Olek realized she was hiding from him.

"Agh," he sighed against her temple. "You can do that whenever you wish."

"So you liked it?" Nadja asked, almost shyly.

Olek growled at the soft question. Turning over, he swung his leg onto her thighs and pinned her beneath him. His soft kiss molded against her lips, showing her his pleasure in her.

"I don't think the word like could possibly begin to explain it," he said softly.

Chapter Sixteen

After discovering the depths of pleasure her body was capable of at Olek's hands, Nadja wasn't so quick to turn him from her bed. Sanity slowly returned to her sated body. She was mindful of her aching limbs, limbs Olek had gladly twisted and turned into multiple positions as he showed her extraordinary ways in which they could come together. His bed was a virtual playground she found herself longing never to leave it.

During the day, work kept him from her, taking him to the royal offices or to check on his brother. Truthfully, she didn't know what he did. He would never tell her. She knew he didn't want to worry her, but not knowing worried her even more.

She spent time with the other Princesses, excluding Olena, who spent every moment caring for Yusef. Nadja managed to sneak into the medical wing to check on Yusef. Her injection seemed to be working because the doctors were baffled by his quickened recovery.

She took her meals in the common hall along with the rest of the family. A high alert had been set on the kitchen and staff after Morrigan's poisoning, so it was a little more tense than usual when they gathered together. The men didn't join them often, taking their meals wherever they practiced and strategized.

When Nadja mentioned how Pia was training her to fight, Morrigan had been only too happy to join in the lessons. So, when they weren't roaming about the village with the Queen, they were self-defense training in Pia's home. It made the days go by quicker and Nadja would wait breathlessly for the evening when Olek would come home.

Olek didn't press her about her father again, and Nadja was glad for it. Let him think that Hank was her only reason for running away. He didn't need to know the details of who her father was. Hank had been the spurring effect that finally made her leave, but he was only a small reason in a sea of many.

Three days passed in such a way. Nadja, who had overheard the Queen talking to her husband in their Qurilixian tongue, had taught herself enough to make out the words danger, spy, and family.

Knowing Olek wasn't going to tell her anything, Nadja decided it was time to do a little investigation of her own. She felt only mildly guilty as she snuck into her husband's office to pry, armed with her translator.

Scanning a few pages left on his desk, she made out that they were import and export agreements between other planets. Sitting in his chair, she looked around, pulling out drawers. There were old communications in files, nothing of real interest. There was an electronic word translator, which looked as if it hadn't been used for some time.

Sighing, she leaned back against his chair. She rolled her neck over the back, about to give up, when she saw an edge of a notebook peaking out from a thin, hidden space beneath the desktop. Smiling, thinking she hit the jackpot, she leaned forward and pulled it out.

Setting it atop his messy pile, she pulled forward to study the book. It looked old, the leather binding a little frayed at the edges. She remembered him carrying it around with his other documents. She opened the first page.

Nadja gasped. She never would have suspected. Her husband was an artist. There were pictures of young boys playing in the colossal trees of the surrounding forest. There were drawings of soldiers at practice, vicious imaginary beasts that looked like man-dragons, the mountain fortress, the village, villagers doing everyday things.

Then, as she continued to flip, she gasped again. From a pencil-smudged page, her face stared back at her. Shadows danced across her drawn features, until she recognized the veil she had worn at the Breeding Festival. It was how he saw her the first night they met.

Her hand shaking, she turned to see what else he had drawn. After the first portrait of her, she realized that she was all he had drawn since. She found a couple incomplete sketches of her at the festival--sitting at the table, wrapped in fur inside the tent. She chuckled. He drew her in her laboratory, looking out in irritation, her hair frizzed unattractively around her head. There were drawings of her in the library reaching for a book, at the dining room table poring over her notebooks, asleep on his bed.

Nadja was speechless. Olek was really very good. She had seen a lot of professional artists over the years in her travels and

Olek could hold up to many of them.

Flipping again, she saw herself in the gown she wore to her coronation. There was a small, unfinished drawing of her with her crown. Her lips were parted and she would have sworn the dreamy look on her face was a figment of his imagination. Touching her mouth, she was positive her lips never pursed like that in invitation.

She shook her head, moving on. Nadja pulled her hand back from the next page in surprise. Now that was something she had never done. Her cheeks instantly flamed. Olek had her posed atop his desk, her legs spread indecently, and her hand looked as if it crawled up her thigh. She was wearing a most revealing piece of see-through material that didn't hide a bit of her flesh.

Swallowing over her constricting throat, she continued to turn the pages, mesmerized. He had her restrained in the water fountain, water pouring over her naked form. He drew her in the bath, steam making her hair cling to her face and nipples, as she knelt over what looked like the back of his head.

He drew her from behind, bending over in thigh-high boots and nothing else as she peeked over her shoulder at him in invitation. He even had her small black tattoo down to perfection. Nadja blushed, but she couldn't look away. There were an array of differently erotic poses and naughty outfits. In some she touched herself. In some she touched parts of him. In one particularly interesting portrayal, she was looking up at him from his lower stomach and her tongue was licking the tip of a very large erection. It would appear the things Olek had done to her in bed were tame compared to what his imagination did to her.

"What are you doing?"

Nadja jumped, automatically slamming the book shut as her cheek flamed. Olek had caught her and he didn't sound pleased. His eyes darted to the book, narrowing before turning back to her.

Olek's body tensed. He never thought she would find his drawings. His face was harsh as he waited for her to say something, anything. He'd seen the portrait she'd been staring at in what looked like horror. His gut was rigid.

"I was," Nadja began weakly. "I was looking to see if you had the jewelry I gave you in here and I ... I found your book."

Olek didn't move. He didn't quite believe her but he was too tense to think perfectly clear.

"I didn't know you were an artist," she said softly. Olek didn't say a word. "I didn't mean to pry."

Even as his pictures embarrassed her, they aroused her too. Licking her lips, she glanced down over his body. She took a hesitant step around to face him.

"Is that how you see me?" she questioned delicately.

Olek's jaw tightened. Nadja realized that he was waiting to see her reaction. He waited to see if she would be angry.

"Is that how you want to see me?" Nadja asked, her tone growing husky. She touched the edge of her shirt and lifted it up. His eyes lit with fire. He didn't move.

Nadja slowly undressed. Standing naked before him, she turned her back to him and leaned over to mimic the pose exposing her back side to him. She flipped her hair over her shoulder to study him.

Olek still hadn't moved and he hadn't looked away. His eyes roamed over her exposed flesh.

"Or do you want me on your desk?" she inquired, breathless. She turned around to push up on his desk top. Scattering papers to the floor, she lifted her legs to fall open. Her fingers moved to her thigh, tracing in slight circles.

Olek's nostrils flared and his body lurched.

"Or like this?" Nadja licked her finger and touched her nipple, budding it for him.

Aware that she had him as her captive audience, she slowly brought her legs back down to the floor. Sliding off the hard wood, she took a step for him. With a shove, she pushed him into the door frame. Olek's face was stiff with control. Only his deepened breaths gave him away.

She ran her hands over his tunic to his waistband, deftly freeing him of his pants. Licking her lips, she slowly bent down on her knees before him and looked up at him from the ground. Pushing his tunic up and over his arousal, she asked softly, "Or was it like this?"

Nadja flicked her tongue to taste his hard heat. His body jerked and he groaned. He brought his hands forward to touch her face. He breathed heavily.

She stayed back, not touching him. "You must show me what you want before I'll give it to you."

Olek tensed, not believing his ears.

"Where do you want my kisses?" Nadja asked, looking

meaningfully at his arousal.

He twisted his lips as his hand moved from her cheek to the back of her head. He pulled her forward. Nadja licked him again, more fully. Her mouth parted and Olek took advantage. To her surprise, he thrust himself between her lips and groaned in approval. He pulled back out, only to run the tip over her lips as she kissed him. Pulling her forward, he delved again into her soft lips.

"Suck," Olek urged her.

Both hands found her hair as she did what he asked. He leaned against the door frame, working his erection back and forth into her wet, hot mouth. His head fell back, his eyes closing as his face lifted to the ceiling in ecstasy. Her teeth grazed him and he nearly choked her trying to feel more of her.

"Argh," he cried, pulling her off before he lost himself between her lips. He yanked her to standing. "Lean over the desk."

Nadja gasped at the rough command, but couldn't deny him. She turned from him and offered her backside. Olek pushed her down so she was pressed flat against the wood. He reached to grab her hips, his erection sliding forward to target her moist heat.

Nadja's breasts rubbed against the leather book of his sketches. She felt his power as he brought himself to her from behind. Her fingers gripped the opposite side for support as he brutally thrust without testing her wetness. She gasped, surprised at how well he fit, how deep.

Olek didn't need to feel if she was ready to receive him. He smelled the intoxicating perfume of her desire. His hips pumped behind her. His buttocks tensed as he forcefully prodded her depths. He took and gave as he sought to go faster.

Nadja thrashed helplessly beneath him. She built and exploded under the guidance of his force. Olek grunted in manly release, his hips thrusting in shallow spasms as he rode out the wave of her climax. Nadja whimpered, breathless, panting, weak.

As his heart slowed and his eyes to clear, he pulled back from her. Nadja weakly pushed up. That's when he saw her translator laying on the corner of his desk.

Still wearing his tunic shirt, he reached over to pick the translator up. Nadja turned, puzzled at his swift movement away from her.

Angrily, he asked, "What is this?"

Nadja paled. She grabbed for her shirt. Tugging it on backwards and inside out, she said, "It's not what you think."

"I think you were trying to spy on me."

"All right," Nadja squeaked, pulling on her pants. "But it's not for the reason you think."

"Quit telling me what I think!" he yelled. "What were you doing in here? If you wanted something all you had to do was ask!"

"Oh, really," she shot back, just as infuriated. "I have asked you a thousand times in a thousand ways. What do you do all day Olek? What's going on with the Var? Why does Mede think there are spies in the palace? Why do you have to be so damned secretive all the time?"

"Nadja--"

"No," she shouted, turning his tirade back on him. Suddenly, she took a deep breath and affected the deadly calm that had frightened him in its coolness when they first met. "I don't know what it is you're hiding from me. But, mark my words Olek, I'll find out."

Nadja turned. She stormed away from him, intent on locking herself in the bedroom for the rest of the night.

Olek looked down at his desk. Picking up his papers from the floor, he sighed. He shouldn't have jumped to conclusions. He knew Nadja wasn't a spy for the Var. She didn't even know the Var. He'd just seen the translator and couldn't help it. Day and night, they searched their walls for whoever sold their palace blueprints to the Var with no luck.

Grabbing his pants, he pulled them over his hips. He knew he would be spending the night on his couch. A shiver worked its way up his frustrated body. Damned if his wife wasn't an enjoyable vixen, even if she did frustrate the hell out of him.

* * * *

"None of the men will fight us," Zoran said darkly to his brothers. He glanced from Ualan to Olek and then back again.

Olek frowned, glaring over at the cowering soldiers. Here the bravest of their whole race was refusing to let the Princes take out their frustrations on them. He should have Zoran stick them in the swamp for a full year.

Snarling to his brother, Zoran growled in irritation. "They say our mood is too black. They are frightened we will kill them."

Olek couldn't say he blamed them. With the only outlet for

their rage quickly retreating, they were stuck. But it didn't mean he had to like it.

The soldiers' frowns deepened at the dark royal looks.

"What the hell are we supposed to do now?" Olek asked, voicing his brothers' sentiments as he stormed away to the palace.

After Olek left early in the morning with no more than a grunt directed at her as he passed, Nadja took it upon herself to invite misery to share her company. She wasn't disappointed as the Princesses arrived.

Pia came first, her face glowering. She was soon followed by Morrigan, who looked sickly and pale and reeked of stale liquor. She had bathed, but the smell of a night of binging still softly came from her pores. Olena came last. Her red hair was pulled back into a bun and her eyes flashed with continuous mischief, even when she wasn't up to something. She looked none the worse for wear for her ordeal with the kidnappers, but she also wasn't speaking of it.

Looking around at the other high-backed chairs, Nadja sighed. The relaxing sound of the natural water fountain didn't do a thing to soothe the sour temperaments of the four women.

"Hienrich is now training as a soldier. I released him from his duty to us," Pia said in answer to a question about the boy.

Olena didn't understand, but the others nodded in agreement.

Stretching her arms over her head, Morrigan yawned. It was the most movement she had made in awhile.

"So, have any of your husbands lied to you about whom they were?" the dejected Princess Olena asked.

"I thought mine was a prison guard," Pia chuckled darkly to herself.

"I used to call mine a gardener," Morrigan admitted, tucking her hand beneath her head on the high-backed chair. Mumbling softly, she said so as not to disturb her delicate head, "And a caveman."

The women laughed.

"I call mine a dragon," Nadja shyly admitted. Bringing to mind his latest bout of anger in the office, she did indeed think he had a dragon-like temper.

"They're all dragons, if you ask me," Morrigan winked at Nadja.

Nadja halfheartedly laughed as she rose to answer a summons

from the door. Blinking in surprise to see the Queen, she allowed her in.

Mede stepped into the intimate circle of women and nodded. "I heard you all were hiding out here."

Nadja smiled weakly at the Queen. Seeing Mede's good mood didn't match theirs, she sighed, but invited her in anyway. More than likely the woman would run for the hills once she felt the melancholy they were nurturing.

"How's Yusef?" Olena asked, suddenly blushing at the outburst. She refused to glance around at her comrades.

"Still awake," the Queen answered. "And still with his brothers. They speak of fighting, and fighting always makes warriors happy, for it is something they know how to do."

Olena nodded, leaning back in her chair and trying to pretend she didn't care either way. No one was fooled.

Mede glanced at the hung-over Morrigan and slightly raised her delicate brow. Morrigan had to turn away. To her credit, the Queen said nothing.

Nadja suddenly asked if anyone wanted something to drink. Morrigan balked and instantly declined, turning a shade paler. They all laughed, despite their moods.

"No, dear, we're fine," the Queen answered. Silence followed. Mede was disappointed that the women weren't going to continue to talk freely. She had heard their soft laughter and had been anxious to be a part of it. But, she also knew the women were troubled in their own ways. She couldn't blame them. Her sons were great men, but were sometimes too stubborn for their own good. Announcing, she said, "Daughters."

The Princesses looked at her expectantly. Nadja blinked, surprised that the woman deigned to stay in their depressed ranks. Mede came forward and took a seat amongst them, looking them over in turn. She not only intended to stay. She intended to cure them of their woes.

"Enough of this. This planet is in desperate need of more women and I intend to see that each one of you explores the power you possess," the Queen said. Nadja couldn't help her smile at the motherly tone.

"Your husbands are warriors," Mede stated. "I expect each of you has a clear idea now of what that means. But just because they made the rules, doesn't mean you can't use them. You have more power than you think. So, tell me your problems with my sons and I'll give you the Qurilixian solution. I think it's time that the royal women had the upper hand for once."

Slowly, one by one, the women smiled, growing more and more trusting of the earnest Queen. The Queen nodded, happy. Yes, this was how it was supposed to be with daughters. She had waited too many years to let her sons ruin her plans for a giant family.

"Pia," the Queen began, looking pointedly at the woman. "Why don't you go first?"

Nadja grinned, nestling into the chair as she listened to Pia's problem and awaited her turn for council.

Chapter Seventeen

"Olek," Nadja announced to her husband when he came through the door that night. He looked tired, his eyes red from little sleep. "I am your wife, your other half. When you don't speak to me, it makes me very upset and when I am upset, you will be upset. Our lives will be stressful and unpleasant. I don't expect you to trust me right away, but you will have to trust me sometime. Life is too long to spend in misery."

Nadja kept a straight face, repeating the words exactly like Mede told her to. She didn't think it possible, but after speaking to the Queen, Nadja felt three-hundred percent better. She had a plan of action, a clear way of handling her stubborn husband. The Queen was a great source of information and had been only too glad to inform her daughters in how to receive the upper hand in their marriages. The chat had made the women closer too--like family. Nadja never knew family could feel so good and safe.

According to Mede, the best way to handle Olek was directly and honestly. He had a lot on his mind and at any given time and a concise, blunt attack was the best way to get him exactly where you wanted him.

Besides, he was suspicious by nature, always trying to read into half-words and looks. He had to be that way with the sort of double-tongued people he dealt with all the time. He was an expert at avoidance, never answering or giving more than what was needed at the time. So, given the nature of his work it was only natural he would try to read into everything Nadja said with suspicion.

Olek blinked at her strange greeting, but stopped to listen with an open mind.

Nadja smiled. It was working. She would have to remember to give Mede a big thank you gift next time she saw her.

"I'm listening," Olek answered seriously. His eyes were intent as he came forward to sit across from her on one of the high backed chairs.

Let the negotiations begin, thought Nadja.

"According to Draig law, because you are an ambassador your wife has the right to be an ambassador," Nadja stated. "Now, I had every intention of finding a job. Ambassador duties might not be what I had in mind when I came here, but is the most logical option. According to Mede, you have quite a heavy work load. I know it will take some training before I am ready to be a real help to you, but the sooner started, the sooner ready."

Olek was quiet, listening to her calm words. Nadja knew that he was reading into her, judging her. She opened herself up and let him. There was no mischief or malice in her face as she spoke. He didn't detect any falsehoods or deceit. He nodded for her to go on.

"I don't expect to take over your job, but to help you with it," she continued. "I am educated. I can learn if you will but teach me. Having done some research, I find I could be of immediate use in local disputes. I already have earned the trust of the villagers...."

Olek frowned, not following.

"Do try to keep up," Nadja scolded. "See what I mean, you are way too overworked. You don't even know what goes on in your own house everyday. The villagers have been here quite often seeking medical attention. I am the new ... oh, what is it they've been calling me? Gullveig?"

"It means witch," Olek said, knowing that it was a term applied fondly to natural medics.

"Good, then were agreed on that point," she stated, not giving him a chance to deny her claim. "I can help out in local disputes, minor things for now. If I have questions about law I'll come to you."

Olek didn't move.

"Also, I have a few ideas I would like to approach Zoran about for the men. I've finished testing on the cream I made and would like to have him try it out on the soldiers during practice to see what they think. Feel free to run it by your doctors for tests." Reaching beside her, she handed him a bound report. "Here is everything they will need about the chemical makeup as well as the active and inactive properties. I also took the liberty of drafting a small antidote in case of an allergic reaction."

Olek took the report and set it aside without opening it. He eyes traveled her face, thoughtful and probing.

"I have also talked to Mede about changing the decorating

arrangements in the hall for traveling dignitaries," Nadja continued, not losing her grace for a moment as she hopped from one topic to another. "Really, Olek, some flowers and silk banners wouldn't hurt one bit and can be put up with minimal effort. First impressions are a key to any negotiation and our hall just screams, uh, 'barbaric planet full of warrior men who would rather fight than talk'."

Olek let the side of his mouth curl up. He couldn't help it. She was ravishing. Leaning back, he crossed his arms over his chest and rested his foot over his knee.

"Now, my first act as the newest Draig ambassador is to call an official meeting with you," she stated boldly. "Right now I think would work perfectly for both our schedules. Update me on the Var situation."

His finger lifted to press against his chin in thought.

"All right," Nadja stated. Her face remaining professional and business like. "I know that spies are suspected within our walls. What have we done so far to locate them?"

"It is being handled," Olek said. Nadja frowned slightly and he added, "There is nothing to report. Servants and soldiers are being questioned, but it is a long process and so far we have nothing."

"Fine," Nadja said. "And the attack on Morrigan and Yusef?"

"Morrigan took a drink from a goblet meant for the Queen and King," stated Olek. "We don't believe it was meant to kill her but them. Yusef was attacked from behind. Whoever did it knew the back passages of the palace well enough to escape. It's why we suspect a spy. That and the royal offices were broke into. Only the palace blueprints were disturbed."

Nadja nodded. "Anything else?"

"The war council convenes tomorrow," he answered. "I'll be gone all day presiding over it. We are giving King Attor the right of defense, though it's likely he will deny everything and nothing will be accomplished."

"Fine," Nadja said before announcing, "I will go with you."

"I am afraid that's not possible. You are not on the war council," Olek said, liking how she took on the initiative with her new course of action. He would gladly accept her help. When he traveled to other planets, it would be nice to have her lovely presence by his side charming the foreign ambassadors. Not to talk about how much more interesting the journey would be with her lovely presence in his bed.

"But I am an ambassador," she stated.

"An ambassador in training," Olek corrected.

Nadja grinned at his words. He accepted her idea.

"You have to stay here tomorrow in the house. Attor's men are here and everyone is ordered to stay within their homes. We won't have bloodshed. We aren't going to risk losing anyone," Olek stated. He stood. "But, since you are an ambassador now, I have plenty to get you started."

Olek strode over to his office, a mischievous grin coming to his features. Reaching in his desk, he pulled out the hundred page communication from the Lithor Republic. He also took her translator from the desk. Coming back to where she sat on the couch, he handed both to her and said, "Look over this document and write a summary of what it says so you may report its conditions to the King."

Nadja, only slightly daunted by the thick document, didn't complain. She set it aside on the couch for later. "Not a problem."

"Glad to hear it," he murmured. Looking down at her, he asked, "Meeting adjourned?"

Nadja nodded, a small smile of happiness coming to her face as she looked up at him. Oh, but he was so handsome, strong. He reached for her hand and pulled her up.

Wrapping his arms around her waist, he asked, "Anything else?"

Nadja shook her head. "I can't think of anything."

"Then may I schedule our second meeting?" Olek murmured, leaning to kiss her earlobe. He bit it gently, sending sparks of delight all over her neck.

"When did you have in mind?" she asked, giggling as his breath tickled her skin.

"About three seconds from now," Olek growled with promise.

"Where?" Nadja breathed, her hands journeyed to his shoulders, loving the feel of him.

"Bathtub." He bit her earlobe only to soothe it with a kiss. "I want to negotiate some marital relations."

Nadja giggled. Olek swept her up into his arms, carrying her across the living room to the bathroom. Depositing her directly into the water, clothes and all, he stepped inside with her. Kissing her deeply, he proceeded to negotiate--for most of the night.

* * * *

King Attor denied all charges with a misleading grin. He knew so long as he was under the protection of the convened council, he wouldn't be touched. Nothing was accomplished during the seven hours of talks. But, then again, nothing had been accomplished in the centuries of fighting that had occurred between the two kingdoms. Death attempts on both sides were nothing new, though none had occurred for over a hundred years.

Zoran was in charge of military matters, representing the Draig with a Var warrior of equal ranking opposite him. Olek presided over the whole affair, doing his best as ambassador to keep the peace, though all brothers knew he would like nothing more than to spill King Attor's blood for his insults to the royal Draig family. He was tired from his night of love play with Nadja. It seemed his wife wanted to try out every one of his fantasy sketches, not that he cared to complain. In fact, he had a few more ideas to draw for her.

After the meeting, it took another four and a half hours to insure that Attor and his men were gone. A thorough search of the castle revealed nothing and the high alert was taken off the village so that the villagers could again leave their homes using caution.

Olek knew that soon they might be facing another war with the House of Var. Wars were terrible affairs for their kind. They could last for fifty to a hundred years with much death and seldom any clear progress or victory. At the end they would have an uneasy truce while each side replenished their warriors and concentrated on rebuilding the population.

Olek came home late that night, exhausted to the bone. Nadja was just finishing up her translation of the Lithorian document. She looked as if she had been at it all day. But, yawning, she didn't complain.

Glancing at Olek, she said, "The Lithorian are requesting the exportation of ore and wilddeor meat. This is an outline of how they wish for us to deliver it, down to the formal greeting they wish our representative to give their representative. I have outlined all the important facts for everyone."

"Tedious lot, aren't they?" he laughed. "You still want the job?"

"How often do they write?"

"Once about every five years to renegotiate."

"Then yes, I want the job." She smiled. "But I am putting in for a vacation in about five years and will need it approved of in advance."

"We'll see." He leaned over and kissed her nose. "Come on, let's get some sleep. We both look like we could use it."

"What I didn't get from this is what we get in return for the trouble," she said, shaking the frustrating documents at him.

"The best chocolate the galaxy has to offer," Olek admitted with a playful smirk, "and some other things."

"Chocolate, you say?" Nadja grinned. She hadn't forgotten her last experience with it, but thought that maybe it was time to give it another try--on a lesser scale. "As the new Lithorian ambassador, I am afraid I need to test this chocolate before I can endorse this proposal."

"Coming right up." Olek disappeared into the kitchen only to return with the red foil bag from the refrigerator with her name on it. Falling on the couch, he laid his head on her lap and handed up a piece.

Nadja took it between her lips and sighed, "You're right. This is well worth their tediousness."

Olek grinned. Sticking a second piece between his lips, he offered it up to her. Nadja smiled, leaning over to bite. As she did, he kissed her and she was again lost.

"Maybe we don't need to go to sleep quite yet," Olek murmured to her chocolate flavored mouth. Nadja just laughed, continuing to kiss him.

* * * *

The warriors cheered good-naturedly as the four Princesses, wearing dark breeches and tunic shirts, aimed knives at the practice post. Olena was the first to throw. She did fairly well as each knife made it into the center. The gathered soldiers clapped and stomped. She glanced at Yusef, trying to act like she didn't seek his approval. A white bandage slashed across his arm but he looked well.

Nadja gulped nervously. She didn't think there was going to be such an audience. Looking at Olek, she watched him nodding at her. She had already confessed to him numerous times that she had never thrown a blade. Pia came up to her, urging her to aim at her target.

Nadja threw. The first and second were too short, the third too long, the fourth hit the post with the hilt and the fifth hit it with the blade, but it wasn't forceful enough to stick. Embarrassed, she glanced at Olek. He merely grinned at her, not caring if she could throw a blade or not. To her surprise, the watching soldiers cheered her effort, charmed by her reserved smiles and shy looks.

Morrigan threw next and managed to hit the post on her turn, though they weren't centered. She curtsied impishly as she received her cheers.

"Maybe you ladies should let a man show you how it's done," a voice from the crowd called.

Morrigan rolled her eyes at the others, retrieving the silver blades for Pia's turn. Nadja laughed as she went to stand beside Olek.

"Ach," Agro shouted. "You're hardly a man, Hume!"

"Have you given my cream to Zoran yet?" Nadja asked her husband, looking at Pia's formidable husband. He looked massive, with his crossed arms. Suddenly, Nadja wasn't so sure she wanted to approach him.

"I am having the doctors look at it," Olek admitted. When she frowned, he said, "Not because I don't trust you, but because a second opinion never hurt anyone. Besides, if you go around them, they could get their feelings hurt and the last thing we need is a testy medical staff on top of everything else."

Nadja nodded, conceding to his logic. She turned to watch Pia, anxious to see how well the woman did. She had no doubt Pia would outshine them all.

Pia took the knives, weighing them carefully in her hand as she tested them. Getting to the third one, she lifted it and studied the blade. Frowning, she went to her husband and handed it to him. She took the knife from his waist to replace it, testing his blade as she did the others.

At Zoran's curious frown, Pia announced loudly, "You need to check the balance on that one. It will pull a fraction to the right."

With hardly moving a muscle, Zoran threw the blade over her shoulder. It stuck just to the right of the target. The men laughed heartily.

Not turning around, Pia said smartly, "Told you."

Zoran's smiled at his wife and Nadja almost fainted. She was sure it was the first time she'd seen him show any emotion aside from displeasure. Olek chuckled.

Going before the target, Pia took a deep breath. Flinging one of the blades, she rapidly dropped to the ground to throw two more in roll. Then, coming to kneel, she threw the last two. The fourth blade struck against Zoran's to knock it free, before sticking in its place. The fifth, she turned her arm and it missed the post completely. The warriors watched in stunned silence, their eyes following the path of her last throw. It was a foot before Hume.

"You missed," Hume said, to break the silence. The men went wild cheering. Pia took a graceful bow. The women jumped in excitement, basking in Pia's victory.

"Did you see that?" Nadja asked her husband with a bright smile. "Do you think you can teach me to do that sometime?"

Olek grinned, "First things first and first you have to learn speak my language."

"I have a few words you can teach me," she murmured naughtily, looking him over with hungry eyes.

Olek growled low in his throat in response.

Nadja turned back to the show. Olena had the blades and a very irate looking Prince Ualan had just joined his wife. Nadja couldn't hear what was said, but soon Morrigan was being led away by her husband to the nearby forest path.

Nadja frowned, "I'm glad you didn't get your brothers' temperaments. I would have drowned you long before now."

Olek grinned. With a wink, he said, "You did try to drown me last night."

Nadja blushed. He was referring to when she'd wrapped her legs around his diving head as he showed her the meaning of the phrase, 'returning the favor'. Weakly, she hit him, unable to think of a comeback. Olek chuckled.

"We're waiting!" came a cry from the crowd.

Nadja watched as Pia turned to glare good-humoredly at Hume. Wryly, she called, "Don't make me aim higher, Sir Hume."

Pia meant his chest, but the rowdy warriors were only too ready to guess something much bawdier.

Zoran gulped. Pia looked in confusion at the men's snickering. Olena laughed, understanding the soldiers all too well.

Olena threw her turn, hitting the post four of the five times. The last blade was close, but teetered off without sticking. The men cheered as she went to retrieve the blades. Olek looked down as

Nadja waved away her turn. She had no desire to try it again in front of the crowd. Carefully, Nadja placed her hand onto Olek's arm. She watched Olena turn expectantly to Pia.

Olek's heart gripped at the simple public display. His people were openly affectionate, but his wife wasn't naturally so. It was good to see she wasn't as embarrassed by her feelings for him as before. At this rate, he'd have her on his lap, feeding him by hand, in a month's time. His body tensed at the thought, but he forced it to calm.

"We need a blindfold," Zoran called. Miraculously, the call was quickly answered as one was passed over the front to Zoran. Zoran crossed over to Pia and tied it around her head. Zoran then smacked his wife hard on her backside. The men laughed. Quietly he backed up.

"I bet she makes it," Nadja said in fascination.

Olek patted her hand and she looked at him.

"Make your throw!" Zoran called.

Pia lifted her arm, taking aim. Holding her breath, she threw, hearing the blade land on wood. Pia threw the second and third time. Each blade landed in the post. Suddenly, a loud cheering came up over the crowd.

Zoran grinned as she stiffened. He'd motioned the men to make noise. Nadja watched the large warrior Prince in awe. That was the second smile she'd seen from him today.

Pia lifted the blade, trying to concentrate over the shouts. She threw. The fourth hit, though it wasn't as deep as the others.

"Oooo," the men shouted in unison.

"Zoran!" came a sudden panicked shout. "Olek! Yusef!"

Nadja jolted, looking around at the call to see who it was. Olek stiffened under her hand, moving out of her hold. Nadja blinked in confusion. Zoran ran towards his brother's voice, drawing the sword from his waist. Yusef nodded to one of the men, who instantly tossed his good hand a blade. Olek was right behind them, drawing his own sword.

Nadja stepped forward. Pia tore the blindfold from her head. Gripping her knife, the woman chased after her husbands. The warriors murmured, but following Agro's command, they didn't move. Nadja glanced at Olena and they were both soon behind the others.

Olek saw Ualan pursued by twelve light blond Var warriors from the trees, over the forest path. Their bodies grew with fur as they shifted to the vicious, snarling features of wild cats. Ualan dragged Morrigan with one arm. She was unconscious, a dart sticking out from her throat.

Ualan was forced to shift to Draig, using his arm to deflect the enemy's blows as he fought them off with his free arm. He tried to protect Morrigan, her feet trailing in the dirt. Soon all the Princes were by his side, shifting into the Draig as they fought against the Var. The one-armed Yusef bravely hacked forward with his sword, giving Ualan time to get Morrigan to safety.

Ualan dropped Morrigan behind them on the ground as gently as he could. He turned back to join the fight against the attackers. Pia didn't hesitate, but ran swiftly to the men, throwing her blade into one of the creature's throat. When Zoran swung his arm, she ducked beneath him, grabbing the knife from his belt.

Nadja's feet ground to a halt. Her lips trembled as she watched Olek shift to do battle. For a moment, she blinked, thinking the suns were surely playing tricks on her. It was very real. She stiffened in fear to see the fighting creatures--human dragons against human tiger-like beasts. Her husband was a dragon. Those drawings he had done were not of mythical creatures.

Her mouth went dry. Olek's skin had hardened, turning a dark brown beneath his clothes. His hair remained the same, but a line grew out from his forehead, pushed forward to make a hard ridge of impermeable tissue over his nose and brow. His eye flashed with golden danger. Talons grew from his nail beds and deadly fangs grew from his mouth. The low, beastie sounds they made caused her blood to run cold.

"Nadja," Olena yelled. She was by the unconscious Morrigan. "Help me!"

Shaking herself, Nadja darted forward to the fallen Princess. She trembled to see a dart sticking from Morrigan's throat. Nadja shivered anew, her eyes dashing around to look into the trees.

"Help me," Olena demanded, trying to drag Morrigan away from the fray.

Nadja and Olena pulled, dragging Morrigan down the path to safety. The sound of battle still rang out. When they were far enough away, Nadja stopped. She dropped down to her knees.

"Should we pull it out?" Olena asked.

"No," Nadja answered. Again she trembled as she looked at the trees. She searched them for movement but saw nothing.

"Don't touch it."

Olek didn't stop to consider his wife as he fought bravely at his brother's side. Soon the Vars were retreating in the forest. Ualan turned, smelling Morrigan's trail as he took off down the path, Yusef and Olek were behind him. Zoran hung back with Pia to make sure the men weren't followed.

Olek froze, instantly detecting Nadja's pale face. She was by Morrigan's side, her narrow eyes examining the wound. The dart was still embedded in Morrigan's neck and the woman wasn't moving.

Nadja jolted to see Ualan's Draig face as he came beside her. He immediately shifted back to the way she knew him. Looking around, she warily eyed Olek's human features. Olek watched her mouth tremble before she turned away from him. He didn't know what to say.

Ualan reached forward.

"Don't," Nadja commanded, her voice raw with fear. Olek saw her jump away from Ualan's hand. Ualan drew back in surprise, but Nadja only nodded at his arm where red blisters were forming on his skin. "She is poison to you."

Ualan's jaw tensed, but he held back.

"You can't move her yet," Nadja said, trying to remain calm. She wanted nothing more than to run away, but she couldn't. She knew the alien dart all too well. She was the only one who understood its poison.

"But, the poison…" Ualan tried, desperate to help his wife.

"Quiet," Nadja said. Zoran and Pia approached from the battle. They hung back in silence. Nadja refused to look any of them in the eye. She shook as she pretended to concentrate. Inside her heart pumped furiously. Her stomach knotted in fear until she wasn't sure if she was going to puke or pass out. "Let me think. I need to concentrate."

Ualan looked at Olek. Olek shrugged. He was worried about his own wife. He detected her quivering hand. He saw her shoulders shake ever so slightly. And, with the connection that was built between them, he felt the full blown blast of her terror.

"Give me your knife," Nadja said suddenly to Pia, holding out her hand in determination. The woman instantly handed it over. Taking a deep breath, Nadja cut into Morrigan's throat where the dart embedded into the skin. Instantly, a dark green began to drip and ooze from the wound. Soon, she had dug out the star tipped points of the dart.

Nadja dropped the blade and continued to bleed the poison out. When she had finished, she quietly commanded Ualan, "Try touching her."

Ualan did. He was left unharmed.

"It's as I thought," Nadja breathed. The knowledge brought her little pleasure as she again looked frantically to the trees. It was like she could feel eyes on her but couldn't find them. Weakly, she admitted, "I've seen this kind if poison before. Usually jealous, old lovers do it for revenge. If you had torn the dart out of the skin, it would have released a poison into the blood stream. She would have lived but you never would have been able to touch her again. It's ironic really. That way it's the current lover that poisons the woman, sealing their fate."

Olek saw her looking at the forest, searching. He wondered if she considered running or if she was scared the Var warriors remained hidden within them.

"You should get her to a doctor," Nadja said, her tone lowering to a mere whisper.

Nadja stood, wearily trying to edge away from the Draig shifters to go down the path they'd come.

"I would say that whoever poisoned her didn't want you to be with her," Nadja said. Feeling she had done all she could, she turned and ran away from them, desperate to get away from the hidden eyes that she looked out at her from the forest.

Olek was right behind her.

Chapter Eighteen

"Nadja, stop!" Olek ordered softly, not wanting to scream at her in front of his family. He knew she heard him just fine. When she only ran faster at the words, he darted forward, using the unfair advantage of his Draig speed to stop her.

Nadja inhaled noisily as he touched her. Her shoulder trembled violently beneath his hand. Olek was sorry for it, but didn't let her go.

"Nadja," he began. Trying to caress her through the dark cotton of her shirt, he said, "Please. Don't do this. Can't --?"

"Let go of me Olek," she said fearfully, not turning around to look at him. She desperately tried to tug her shoulder from his grasp. Her ears turned to the trees to see if they were followed. She couldn't hear anything, not the call of insects or birds. But with the recent battle, that wasn't unheard of. Knowing she couldn't risk being seen with a shifter touching her, she jerked away from him.

Olek let her go. His eyes narrowed. He detected her deep fear and was sorry for it. He wanted to hold her, to comfort her. But, believing he was the cause of her fear, he held back and waited for her to speak.

Nadja knew her father was in the forest. She couldn't see him, but she wouldn't would she? No, she wouldn't see him until he wanted her to. He was going to play with her first, punish her with her own fear. She looked around the colossal forest anyway, seeing the red earthen path before her surrounded by yellow ferns that looked almost green in the shadows.

She knew what that dart was. It was very alien to this planet and only traded on the highest of black markets. She had transported them in her hair through customs before. Usually only spurned Kings could afford to buy the poison and they did so to punish the local village beauty for not returning their 'attentions'. It was a valuable commodity. For the Var soldiers to have it meant someone very high up in the Medical Mafia had sold it to him. Her father was about as high up as any could get.

If Olek had only been a human Prince, Nadja could have clung to the barest of hope that her father would understand and forgive. It wasn't likely, but there was always the chance.

However, Olek wasn't human. He was a shifter and that made all the difference in the world. Doc Aleksander, as her father was know by his 'Medical Alliance' associates, was a human purist. He put up with alien races out of necessity, but he didn't think they were good enough to lick the bottom of a human's boots.

Oh, if he discovered she'd fallen in love with and actually slept with a shifter! It would mean horrible death for the entire royal family. Nadja's heart squeezed with unbearable pain that she couldn't let Olek detect. Her father might only disfigure her, but he would skin alive each and every person she'd come in contact with. And, if they were lucky, the other human Princesses would only be sold as slaves to the lowest form of humanoids possible.

But no fate would be worse than Olek's. Looking at his handsome face, she knew it didn't matter how strong he was or how brave. He couldn't fight Doc Aleksander or his genetically altered goons. When Olek was caught, as he surely would be if his connection to her was found out, his death would be the most slow and painful. And she would be forced to watch the whole thing.

Nerves jumped all over her skin. She'd heard what her father did to people who merely looked at him the wrong way. He'd surgically remove their eyes without putting them under general anesthesia. If they fainted, he would revive them so they didn't miss an agonizing second of his torture.

Olek watched as Nadja's face shifted from fear to a calm, unmoving mask. The link between them was severed until he was left feeling hollow and dead inside. He could no longer detect her fear. She cut herself from him, refusing to let him feel her.

Olek took a desperate step forward, his arm reaching to pull her back to him by force if necessary. Nadja's eyes darted away, looking again at the trees. He glanced, trying to see what she looked at.

"Stay back, Olek." Nadja had no doubt that her father knew she'd recognize the dart, just as she knew he'd sent it to her as a calling card. If her father was close, then he already knew these men were shifters. She could only pray that she could convince him that she didn't know until today--which was true--and that she didn't have anything to do with any one of them.

She would tell him that she just got scared, hitched a ride, and ended up here after she realized her foolishness. The Princes were nice enough to put her in a room of her own until her father could come and find her. It had to work. Seeing Olek's tortured face, she was sorry for it. His feelings for her were the only kink in her plan. She had to sever them immediately.

"Just stay back. Don't come near me," she warned in a low voice.

"Nadja, please," he begged. He reached for her again, silently imploring her to him with his eyes and she wanted nothing more than to go. "Have I ever hurt you?"

Nadja held back. If she loved him, then she would be forced to hurt him to save him. Letting a distasteful snarl hit her lips for the sake of her father's watching eyes, she asked, "What are you?"

"I am Draig," he said, not caring for the look on her beautiful features. "Nadja...?"

"I don't even know you," she answered before he could give her away. She let her voice rise, praying they were overheard.

"You know me, Nadja," Olek pleaded, his tone soft, tortured, caring. "I'm the same man. Here, take my hand. See. I won't hurt you, solarflower."

"Just stay back," she ordered, refusing his offered hand. She glanced around for the sake of her spying father. Her head chanted that she dare not show any affection.

Growling, so her voice only carried a short distance between them, she said, "I only asked two things, honesty and loyalty. And so far you haven't been very honest. You never told me you were a shifter--"

"You never asked," Olek defended.

"Well I'm asking now. Is there anything else I should know, your highness? Any other surprises, like do you have five other wives and twenty kids hidden somewhere?" Nadja let an expression of utter loathing settle permanently on her features.

Olek flinched to see it. He felt as if his soul was being ripped from him and leaving him an empty shell.

"I told you never to lie to me, Olek," Nadja continued, quietly. "You lied about being a Prince--"

"I said I worked," he broke in. Why was she bringing this up now? It made no sense! They were past this!

"You knew what I was asking," she proclaimed. It was too hard. Every fiber in her being hated what she was doing to him.

"Why couldn't you have just been a small time farmer?"

Olek's heart thundered to a stop.

"It doesn't matter." She realized now that a small time farmer wouldn't have been able to protect her any more than a Prince. Doc Aleksander wanted his daughter back and he would get her.

"I never lied," he said in return.

"And yet, you never really told me the truth," she replied. "Go check on Morrigan, Olek. I need to be alone for awhile."

There. It's done, Nadja thought, her heart breaking into a thousand different pieces. Her body was cold and she suddenly wished the Var had poisoned her instead. She looked out over the distance, hoping her father enjoyed her little performance.

Olek nodded. He didn't try to touch her again, but moved past her, down the red trail leading to the palace. Hopelessness and despair surrounded him. Nadja was soon behind him, keeping her distance to make sure she didn't encounter him again.

Once she came to the front gate, she ignored the guard on duty, who merely glanced up at her entrance. She took quick steps through the passageways, running when no one could see or hear her. She knew everyone would be with Morrigan in the medical ward. She wanted to check on the woman, but couldn't risk being stopped.

Getting home, she ran inside. Looking around, her heart ached for the life she would never lead here, for the children she would never have, for the ambassadorship she would have worked at with her husband, for all the smiles and laughter she would never have married to a man like Hank.

She had been a fool to think she'd ever escape marrying Hank. She'd been a fool to think she deserved more. After the years of her life she spent standing aside, saying and doing nothing to stop her father, she didn't deserve Olek. She'd known what her father was doing to those poor victims, victims he forced her to help recuperate. Their endless faces flashed across her mind.

Now there was only one thing left to do. She had to go find her father first, before he came to claim her.

Olek did as his wife asked, and he went to check on Ualan's wife. He told himself that if he just gave her enough time, she would come around and accept his shifting. He had won her once, he would do so again. He had to. There was no other option to his troubled mind. He needed her like he needed air and food, even more so. She was his heart, his soul.

Morrigan was checked over by the doctors and released to go home with Ualan. Ualan was getting ready to take her when Olek got there. He caught him up on all that had happened.

To his surprise, Princess Pia had discovered the identity of their spy using a video feed Morrigan had taken of the coronation. It seemed Morrigan was a reporter and was doing a story on him and his brothers' royal marriages. Thinking of his marriage, he scowled--some story that would be.

It had also been determined with this last attack on Morrigan, that King Attor planned on striking the Princes' most vulnerable place--their marriages. By killing the Princesses, King Attor would assure that they never produced heirs and their line would end.

If Olek lost Nadja, there would never be another for him. It was the way of the crystal. When she broke it, she joined them forever. The Draig mated for life. If they lost their mate, they lived the rest of their days alone, never taking another to their bed. If Olek lost his wife, he wouldn't want any in his bed to replace her. No one ever could.

The news came soon after Olek checked on Morrigan in the medical ward that Pia's servant was apprehended almost immediately upon the Princes entering the palace kitchens. They found him hiding behind one of the big brick ovens, ducking from his work. Zoran's nose picked up the Var smell beneath a too potent scent of Draig.

The spy must have known that he was found out, because he tried to run. It was no use. Yusef was standing in the doorway and with a swing of his good arm he punched the man square in the jaw, laying him out on the floor.

The Draig servants blinked in surprise at the sudden attack, but as they witnessed the lazy man sprawled on the ground, they cheered even without knowing his deceit. As a fellow worker, the Var spy wasn't well liked in the kitchen.

The royal family was relieved as news was spread of the spy's capture. Olek arrived just in time to help escort the Var soldier to the lower prisons. A Draig guard was sent to retrieve Agro for the interrogation. It was believed that if any of the Princes questioned him, they would most likely kill the insolent man for the harm he intended to their wives. It was better to have someone with a cooler temper. Olek had no doubt that the beefy giant would discover much from the man. When Agro chose to shift, he could be most persuasive.

Nadja tried to pack, but she couldn't risk carrying too much and being discovered. She debated whether or not she should leave Olek a note trying to explain, but in the end decided against it. It wouldn't do to give him hope. If he tried to come after her, then everything she had just put them through would've been for nothing and she would have to watch him die.

Taking a deep breath, in the end she took nothing, leaving the house exactly as it was. It was getting late. Dusk had formed some time ago. There was no time for good byes. This was it.

Nadja took a deep and steadying breath. It did no good. She instinctively knew where her father would be waiting for her. He would be at the scene of Morrigan's attack or close to it. Walking down the earthen red trail, she clutched her fingers before her. The dusk made the forest darker that usual, but if she squinted, she could see fairly well where she was going. The deeper sections of the forest were a mystery.

Tears entered her eyes and only the thought of saving Olek kept her moving. Her body trembled with an uncontrollable fear, dread making it worse. Her steps faltered as she neared the place Morrigan fell.

Nadja stopped, as she looked around the colossal forest, seeing the red earth before her, surrounded by yellow ferns that looked green in the shadowy twilight. She didn't move until she detected movement at her side. It was the flick of a match and a light of an old fashioned cigar that first drew her attention. Her mouth opened to speak, but her voice only left in a squeak.

She saw the orange glow of her father's cigar brighten, illuminating his sinister face. He leaned against a tree as if he had been watching and waiting for some time. Aleksander stepped out from the sanctuary of the forest, brushing off the rough bark as if he were in the finest of gentleman's clubs. His movements were graceful and refined. He wore a dark suit, expensive and handsomely cut. His black hair was slicked back, matching the black of his thick mustache that twitched when he spoke, or when took a long draw as he was doing now. He smiled as the smoke curled out of his lips.

Instantly, she felt like a child, about to be punished for eating a scrap of her mother's chocolate, or being reprimanded because some handsome foreign dignitary held her eye a second too long.

"How did you find me?" she asked, looking piously to the

ground.

The comment caused a chuckle to rumble along his deep voice. When he waved his cigar around, it was with an air of elegance. "Nadja, darling, come give your father a hug."

Nadja couldn't disobey. Taking small steps, she didn't look him in the eyes. Her arms spread and she put them around his arms. He lifted his cigar up as she pressed her cheek to his chest in a brief embrace. As she pulled away, his cigar tip hit against her arm. She jolted back.

"Oh, sorry dear," he said, his eyes hard and unforgiving. "How clumsy of me."

Nadja didn't say anything, didn't reach to touch the little burn. She pressed her lips together to keep from screaming for Olek. This was her responsibility. No matter how bad she wished for him, she wouldn't call him to his death.

Aleksander reached to touch her shoulders, rubbing her arms gently. "Oh, Nadja, how you gave us a scare. Your mother has been frantic with worry over you."

Nadja lowered her head, stiffening as she awaited another burn. It never came. Meekly, she said, "I'm sorry, father. How did you find me?"

"You didn't honestly think an act of privacy would keep me from finding you, did you?" he mused. "You would be surprised what laws can be broken with enough money and persuasion."

Nadja has seen this man's form of persuasion.

"You," she began. Pausing, she took a deep breath and tried to look him in his dark eyes. "You didn't hurt anyone, did you? They didn't know who I was when they let me aboard."

"No, darling," he said, as if he was the most caring man in the world. "But you've hurt me. You embarrassed me and your mother. She was very upset. She hasn't left her room aboard the medic ship since your engagement party. You looked me in the eye and said you were going to marry Hank. You lied to me."

"No," she whimpered. Tears sprung to her eyes when she looked up at him. "I didn't lie."

"Oh," he soothed. "Don't cry, Nadja."

"I don't want to marry, Hank," she said. "He scares me. Please don't make me marry him. Let me stay with you and mother. Hank wanted to ... to...."

"Boys," Doc announced coldly, not giving her a response. His large, genetically altered henchmen came from the forest as if they grew from trees. "Take my daughter here to our camp and have her arm looked at. It seems she burned herself on my cigar."

"Miss Aleksander." One of the men bowed. Nadja recognized him, but didn't know his name. He was one of the many mindless clones her father grew in his lab. She saw by the look on his face that if she didn't follow willingly, he would take her by force.

Nadja nodded at him to walk. And, as he led her into the forest, she knew her fate was sealed.

* * * *

Olek frowned at the servant who stood before him and then the note he tried to pass him. The man had said it was from Princess Olena. Shaking his head, he said, "That letter is not for me. You seek my brother, Prince Yusef."

"No, Draea Anwealda," the man assured. "Princess Olena bid me to find only you. She was very specific. She told me to give it to you tonight."

"Very well," he answered, "I'll clear up this mistake myself."

Olek took the missive and nodded the man away. Why would that fiery tree witch be sending letters to him? The very impropriety of it made him sick. As far as he could tell, she didn't even like him. He clutched the letter in his fist, not wishing to read it when eyes could be on him. He could only imagine the rumors that would be started by this little stunt of Olena's. He hoped they didn't get back to Nadja before he had a chance to explain.

Thinking of his wife, he finally managed to get the courage to go home and face her. It was late and, if he was lucky, she would be fast asleep.

"Nadja," Olek called softly as he stepped into his home. He began tearing open Olena's missive, not eager to read what was inside. He looked in the bedroom. She wasn't there. He searched the whole house, his gut aching when he didn't find her. Taking a deep breath, he wearily sunk down into a chair. Where could she be? Would she even welcome him looking for her?

Chapter Nineteen

Nadja was led to a campsite buried deep in the forest. She felt like she walked forever on her trembling legs. No one spoke as they moved. Nadja felt her father's eyes behind her. She wished he'd have just killed her and gotten it over with. His silence could only bode ill.

"Have a seat, my dear," Aleksander said, motioning to a chair set up in the middle of the ground.

Nadja eyed it wearily. "No thanks, I'm fine."

"Sit," her father growled, his dark mustache twisting into a snarl.

Nadja nodded, not daring to naysay him again. She moved slowly to the chair, her body trembling in fright as she sat down. She knew this chair, saw the manacles that would bind a person's wrists to the arms and their ankles to the thick oak legs.

Nadja crossed her arms over her chest and pressed her ankles together, careful to stay away from the manacle's bite.

"Are you hungry?" Doc asked, eyeing her carefully. His eyes narrowed in disgust as he took in her waistline. "I see you have been eating more."

It was true she hadn't watched her diet since leaving the medic ship, but she had been working out too.

"What else has changed with you, daughter?" he asked, not bothering to send his men away so they could speak in private. The clones were loyal and probably didn't hear him anyway.

"N ... noth ... thing," she lied, her voice quivering.

"Sit back," he urged. "Relax. You look so tense."

Nadja looked at the chair arms as he meaningfully glanced at them. She shook her head furiously, moving to stand. Arms came around her from the back like vices, pulling her down hard as she screamed. Soon the men had her strapped to the chair, helpless. Nadja cried, but her tears had no affect on the emotionless henchmen.

"Father, please," she begged, meeting his eyes with hers. Whispering, she pleaded, "Don't do this."

"You did this," he answered with false sympathy, as if he was the victim and she forced his hand.

"What ... will you do?"

Doc lifted his hand and motioned his fingers. One of his men came forward holding his medic bag. Nadja tensed, gasping frantically for air, trying not to pass out as fear overwhelmed her.

"Father, no!" she cried out. Her mind called for Olek in terror.

"There, there Nadja." Doc's brow rose as he reached into his bag. "If you're telling me the truth, you have nothing to worry about."

Nadja gulped. She was so dead.

* * * *

Olek jolted to awareness, his skin prickling. He waited, listening. Nothing. All was quiet. Thinking he imagined the sound of his name, he sat forward to run his fingers through his hair.

Suddenly, Olena's missive caught his eye. He had dropped it on the floor in his preoccupation with Nadja. With a frown, he picked it up and finished tearing it open. His eyes narrowed as he read.

Your wife's father is coming for her. Ask her what that means. I go to put him off. You must keep her safe. He is an evil man.

Olek's hand trembled. The missive made no sense. Frowning, worry overcame him. Clutching the missive in his hand, he was going to find Olena and force her to tell him what she meant by the cryptic message. Then, he was going to find his wife.

* * * *

"Father?" Nadja gulped as he came near her. Pricking her arm, he took a reading of her blood. She watched his face in horror as he paled.

Suddenly, he waved his hand at the group of men. "Go. Make sure she wasn't followed."

They nodded and scurried off.

"Father?" she asked.

He ignored her, going back to his medic bag. When he withdrew his hand he held a laser scalpel. Nadja tensed.

"Who is he, daughter?" he asked quietly, eyeing the instrument as if he didn't trust himself to turn to her.

"Wha ... at do you mean?" she asked, trembling.

"You know what I mean," he said. "Tell me."

"There is no one, father, I swear," she put forth.

"Your blood screen says otherwise." Shooting forward, his

eyes flashed unnaturally in the blue glow of the camp lights. "Who have you whored for?"

"No one," she said, trying to block Olek from her mind. She couldn't let him find the love she had for him.

Taking the scalpel, he lightly pressed the end of it to her cheek. With one press of the button, it would light up and slice her eye in two.

"My patience grows thin, Nadja." Drawing the blade over her cheek to her neck, he laid it against her racing pulse, and said, "Give me his name."

Nadja pressed her lips together. Her father pulled the scalpel back and pressed the button. Taking his hand to her wrist, he clamped his fingers over her and moved the lighted blade to hover over her arm.

"Last chance," he said. "I will have a name."

Nadja tensed, closing her eyes as she braced herself for the cut. It came like a strike of lightening, snaking along her forearm in a deep gash. She whimpered in agony, knowing it was no used to cry out. No one would hear her. She didn't want to alert the Draig guards. If they came, Olek would follow.

Her breath ragged, she opened her eyes to look at him.

"I can do this all night," he said.

Nadja trembled. She knew he could.

"But, unfortunately, I don't have all night," he murmured. "You see, daughter, I have made some friends of my own on this accursed planet. It seems your precious Draig aren't liked by my friends. And if I help them, they'll help me. So tell me, which Prince is yours?"

Nadja shook her head, trails of tears streaming silently down her face.

"You are such a disappointment." He sniffed in disgust. "Well, if hurting you won't get us anywhere, what if I hurt one of your little friends?"

Nadja stiffened. Blood ran from the wound on her arm, but her father had been very precise in his cut and didn't hit an artery. Doc Aleksander went to one of the tents, and drew back the flap.

"Bring out the pirate," he ordered.

Nadja tensed as Olena was carted out. She lay flat on a long operating table, her arms strapped to her sides.

"She had nothing to do with this," Nadja rushed.

Doc Aleksander shrugged as if it were of no concern to him.

"Olena," he called down to the red haired woman. He tapped her face lightly. "Time to wake up."

Olena blinked, automatically stiffening against her bonds. Nadja saw her mouth was gagged. Her head thrashed back and forth on her shoulders.

"What shall I do to her, Nadja?" he asked. He took his scalpel to her face. Olena stopped moving. Her wide green eyes followed the laser blade as it moved down. "Carve out her eyes? Her nose? Take off her lips?"

"Don't," Nadja said, weakening.

"Then tell me what I want to know!" he ordered. "Who is the father of that bastard you carry?"

Nadja tensed, sure she had misunderstood him.

Olek stiffened, hearing Nadja's father's words ringing clearly over the forest. He dashed forward, already shifted into Draig. Yusef's hand on his arm stopped him. He nodded his head to go around the far side of the camp for a better view. Olek, reluctantly agreed. There was a fear inside him, so deep, as he heard Nadja whimper in pain.

"I'll never tell you," his wife answered, bravely. Olek swallowed in amazement and pride in her strength. She was protecting him.

Nadja shivered as her father reached into his bag once more. Leaving Olena alone, he turned back to Nadja.

"That bastard inside you will be dissolved," Doc Aleksander told his daughter. He lightly stroked her face.

To her surprise, the manacles were freed from her wrists and she was allowed to move. Her fingers shook as her father lifted her hand into his. He pulled her up. His fingers lifted to brush her face, Nadja tensed, closing her eyes to him as she swayed on her feet.

"The time for being a child is over, Nadja," he said. "It's time for you to take your place amongst your peers."

Nadja felt cold, hard metal being placed into her fingers. She jolted in surprise to see the large laser scalpel. It was much larger than the fine, precision tool, her father had used on her arm. Her fingers trembled as she looked to him in confusion.

"Do you love me, Nadja?" he asked her.

"Yes," Nadja answered. She cursed herself. It wasn't all a lie. She did love him. He was her father. But she didn't like him, couldn't respect him.

"Then dissect her," he ordered, pointing at Olena.

"What...?" Nadja breathed, her wide eyes turning wild as she looked at Olena strapped to the table.

"She is a common thief, a pirate," he said. Doc Aleksander gave his daughter a shove towards the bound woman. "She broke her word to me."

"No," Nadja gasped. The scalpel fell from her fingers to the ground. She turned to run. Her father caught her easily.

"Cut out her eyes," he ordered. "Or I'll burn your lying ones from your head."

To prove his point he motioned for a hot poker to be brought from the fire. Nadja watched the angry red metal smoke and curl with heat.

"Hold her down," ordered Doc. His voice was calm, unattached, weary.

"No!" Nadja screamed, flailing. Hands were all over her, gripping her shoulders and her arms, lifting her legs into the air when she would kick. Her father took off his jacket and rolled up his sleeves. The hot poker waved dangerously at the action.

"It's time you learn, Nadja," he told her. "You don't lie to your father."

Nadja kicked, trying to get free. The poker loomed closer to her face.

"Will you do as you're told?" he asked, his voice mocking her with its composed, almost soothing rendering.

Nadja nodded. How could she not?

"Let her go," Doc ordered. He handed the poker back to one of the men who tossed it back into the fire. Then, reaching to the ground, he retrieved the scalpel for his daughter. Nadja took it, her fingers shaking horribly as she pressed the button. A long laser shot out, nearly six inches long and sharper than the most deadly of blades.

Nadja sniffed, unable to breathe. Doc led her forward to Olena. Olena moaned, shaking her head as her eyes pleaded.

Nadja's fingers trembled as she lifted her hand to Olena's cheek. The woman's eyes pleaded with her to stop. Nadja's fingers slipped in Olena's tears, her own falling to splash in droplets on Olena's shoulder.

"I'm sorry," Nadja said lifting the scalpel close to Olena's eyes. Turning to look at her father, she said, "I love you."

Doc Aleksander smiled. Nadja, using a move Pia had shown

her, turned, thrusting the blade into her father's heart. The man blinked in surprise. Nadja held completely frozen, unable to move as a fine mist of blood sprayed over her from his chest. In slow motion, she watched him fall to his knees.

Chaos erupted all around her. Yusef and Olek burst from the trees, subduing Doc's men with slashes to the throat and rips through their gut.

Nadja stared down. Doc was looking at her, his lips hardly moving. His hand lifted as if to touch her. Nadja fell to her knees, pulling his palm into her own.

He pulled her ear down to his mouth and whispered. When Nadja sat back up, he was dead.

Yusef freed Olena, hugging her to his Draig chest as he assured himself she was unharmed. Olek stood above Nadja, motioning his brother to get his shaken wife home. When he looked down, he saw the scalpel protruded from a patch on the man's shirt that matched Nadja's tattoo. His wife grabbed the hilt of the scalpel, pulling it from the man's chest and turning it off. She tossed it over to his medical bag on the ground. Around the edge of the badge he read the words, Medical Alliance for Planetary Health.

"Nadja?" he asked. She blankly turned to look at him and he felt a hollowness forming inside of her.

"He said he forgave me," she said. Then, bursting to her feet, she buried herself into her husband's arms and didn't say another word.

* * * *

Draig soldiers came to the campsite at Yusef's command, shifted and ready for battle. Olek ordered them to remove the bodies. Nadja still hadn't spoken after the single sentence. No tears fell from her eyes.

She pulled back from Olek to watch the Draig soldiers taking the bodies.

"Nadja?" Olek asked quietly.

"Burn the henchmen," she ordered. "They're genetically altered clones, human drones. They had no feelings."

Olek nodded, calling out her order to the men. He saw the blood on her arm, but she ignored it. The wound didn't seem to trouble her. Her beautiful features were spotted with blood.

Nadja knelt beside her father. Unbuttoning the top button on his shirt, she pulled a small oval locket from around his neck. Jerking it, she broke the leather strap. Olek watched as she twisted it. Her picture was on the inside of it. She pressed in her miniature face. A beam of light came up and then a screen appeared, floating in the air.

"We are recording," came a voice.

"This is Nadja Aleksander," she said calmly to the burly man who answered the call. Her face gave nothing away. The man saw her face clearly, but didn't flinch to see the blood splattering it. Nadja's eyes hardened as she looked back at him.

"Medical identification?" the man asked.

"Morning Dove," she answered.

"Number?" The man's voice was emotionless.

"Ten ... twelve ... one," she stated. Olck was shaken by her unmoving features. He couldn't even feel a trace of emotion coming from her. It was like she was dead inside.

"Miss Aleksander," the man acknowledged.

"My father is dead."

"Yes, Lady Aleksander," the man said. Olek saw him rise to his feet and bow to her. "How may I serve you, Lady Aleksander?"

"Follow this signal," she ordered. "Transport his body and dismantle the camp. Take everything."

The man nodded. "It will be done, Lady."

"Tell my mother he died nobly and well," she continued. Olek frowned at the obvious lie. "Tell her it was an accident. Don't let her see the body until the mortician has finished his work."

"Yes, Lady," he answered. "And shall we be coming for you?"

Nadja glanced at Olek. Slowly, she shook her head.

"My father was the head of this family. Now, as his heir, I am breaking apart the family. Tell Doc Truman that I'll not be taking my father's place at his side. He died before he could name a second."

"Yes, Lady."

"My mother gets everything, every penny," Nadja said. "I want you personally to see to the funeral. Bring him to the Hazare Complex. Doc Truman will undoubtedly meet you there to give you a new assignment. I go to Datlis to start over. Wipe this planet from the records. There is nothing here for the Medical Alliance but a bunch of primitives who won't serve a purpose."

"Yes Lady," the man said. His fingers moved over to a computer to do as she commanded.

"Morning Dove, ten, twelve, one, out," Nadja stated. Flipping off the communicator, she dropped it on her father's chest. It blinked a signal for the ship to trace.

"Nadja?" Olek asked.

She shivered as if really looking at him for the first time. Weakly, she said, "Just let them come, don't get in their way. If you give them no trouble, they will take this all away and leave for good."

"Nadja," he breathed, worried about her. Suddenly, she paled. Olek darted forward, catching her as she blacked out into his arms.

* * * *

Nadja awoke in the medic unit. She saw her husband speaking to Yusef. Olena was no where to be seen. Yusef's face was tightly pulled.

Sitting up, she asked, "Olena?"

Olek glanced at her, rushing to her side. "She's fine. She was injected with something and they have her in the medic unit trying to discover what it was."

"I want to see her," Nadja said. She moved to stand.

"In a moment," Olek said.

His eyes darted over her with caring, but she was still too numb to see it. She had to make sure Olena was all right first. If her foolish actions in running from her home had caused any harm, she would never be able to forgive herself.

Olek looked at his pale wife. She hardly moved. Her eyes stared out of her head with an eerie, foreign light.

She blinked, looking at him. "There is a baby."

Olek grinned, nodding happily. "I know. He's fine."

Nadja nodded. To his disappointment, she didn't return his smile. Her gaze drifted back to the door where Olena was in the medic unit.

Suddenly, the medic, Tal, went to the door and opened it. Yusef was right behind him in the doorway.

Nadja stood, brushing past Olek to go forward. Lightly, she touched Yusef's arm and asked, "Can I have a moment?"

Yusef frowned, but nodded his head. He motioned for Tal to leave the women alone.

"I'm sorry," Nadja said when the door shut behind the two men. She was glad to see Olena was indeed live and well. A dam broke in her, as she rushed, "I didn't mean to scare you."

Olena chuckled lightly. "Don't apologize. You saved my life."

"I couldn't let him kill again. You have nothing to worry about," Nadja said. She swayed slightly on her feet and Olena could tell she was worn. "As Doc's heir, I dissolved the family. They won't be back."

Nadja moved over to the machine as it beeped. Absently, she moved to the panel and pushed a button for it to continue. She pulled up a chair, waiting as it cycled and then she again pressed a button.

"Nadja, I'm sorry. I know he was your father," Olena began.

Nadja trembled, holding back a well of grief. She held up a hand to stop her. "I am one of the few who could have done it without a backlash. No, it was time for his terror to end."

"Still," Olena began.

Tears came to Nadja and she sniffed. Shaking her head, she held up her hand for silence. No more words were needed on the subject. A part of her was saddened. He was her father and a part of her loved him. But she didn't regret her actions. "Thank you."

The unit beeped again and Nadja glanced down to the screen.

"Are you in pain?" Nadja asked at the panel's prompting.

"No," Olena said.

Nadja pressed a button.

"How's your baby?" Olena asked.

Nadja sniffed and wiped her eyes. She thought of Olek, desperately wanting to see him. It was as if she was coming out of a nightmare. Reading the panel, she grinned. Laughing lightly, she said, "Hopefully as healthy as yours."

* * * *

Nadja was quiet as Olek walked her home. There was so much she wanted to say to him, but she was scared. He didn't mention what he thought about her father or about what had happened. And she was too ashamed to face him.

As they went to bed, Olek didn't say a word. Nadja lay down beside him. He pulled her into his arms, hugging her back tightly into his chest. That night, he didn't let her go.

Chapter Twenty

A sweet, exotic scent curled around Nadja in her dreams, causing a smile to touch her lips. All around her was the small brushes of silken softness. Blinking awake, she realized Olek was gone, but petals of solarflowers were sprinkled all around her.

She sighed, running her fingers over his pillow. Her fingers met with a paper and she instantly sat up. It was a portrait of her sleeping, surrounded by the petals. In the corner, Olek had written, I have to go meet with my brothers. We have discovered King Attor's camp and will go to face him. I couldn't bear to wake you when you looked this beautiful asleep. I'll be home as soon as I can.

Nadja felt tears coming to her eyes. She rushed from the bedroom, out into the hall to see if she could catch him. The portrait was clutched in her fingers. He was long gone. Her fingers trailed to her flat stomach. He couldn't go to battle without her speaking to him first. She had so much she needed to say to him.

"Open," Nadja ordered the door, ducking under into the hall before it was even up. Calling, she yelled, "Olek!"

Nadja began running down the passageway barefoot.

"Olek, wait!" she yelled, not caring who heard. Coming around the corner, she nearly toppled over the King. "Oh!"

"Hey, easy," King Llyr said. "What's going on? Are you hurt?"

"No," she mumbled, trying to get past him. "Olek...."

"Sh, daughter, wait," Llyr said. "You can't go to him now. He's in the lower dungeons. Agro discovered from the spy that King Attor is camping along the southern border planning an attack."

"Then take me down to the prisons," she began in an order.

"No," he denied gruffly. "They are no place for a lady."

"But...." she tried to protest.

"Now, come on," the King said. He took her elbow and began leading her down the hall to her house. She still held the picture and he glanced at it briefly. "Let's just get you back inside. You shouldn't be straining yourself in your condition."

Nadja blushed, following her father-by-marriage's guiding hand. The King ordered the door to her home shut behind them. He led her to the couch and urged her to sit.

Staring up at him, she asked, "He told you about the baby?"

"Of course he told me!" the King snapped. "He's told everyone."

Nadja sighed. "Then he does know."

"He heard your father mention it," Llyr said. He turned serious as he took a seat. "How are you, daughter?"

"Fine," she mumbled absently. "And he wasn't upset about it? He was ... happy?"

"Of course he was happy," Llyr bellowed in his gruff voice, but Nadja could see the caring in his eyes. "We all are."

Llyr saw her relief and wondered at it.

"I don't know what that man did to you, girl," he grumped. "But he's not your family. We are."

Nadja blinked, tears forming in her eyes.

"Ah," the King frowned. "Don't go getting all emotional on me."

Nadja bit her lips, sniffing her tears back, and dutifully nodded.

"All right, then, good," Llyr said, when he saw she wasn't about to start bawling. "Now, why would you think he wouldn't be happy? Surely you sensed his feelings about it."

Nadja shook her head.

"Well, why didn't you read them for yourself if you were curious," said the King in awe. "That is why he gave you the gift of it."

"The gift of the baby?" she asked, confused.

"Did those Galaxy Bride people tell you nothing?" he asked, frowning in dismay. "The gift of himself."

Nadja just stared at him blankly.

"Ah," he sighed heavily. "You remember the whole crystal smashing, right?"

Nadja nodded.

"All right, then," he said. "Our crystals have magical powers. They glow and we find our wives. We choose to take them back to our tents for ... well," he paused, growing slightly distracted as he remembered his own wedding night clearly. It had been torture--glorious torture. "You stay and choose us, you crush the crystal, our life extends yours and there you have it. You're joined."

Nadja blinked at the rough, manly description.

"You understand?" he asked, his tone nearing a grunt.

Nadja shook her head. The King sighed.

"Qurilixian men are given a crystal when they are born," he stated. "They're magical."

Nadja nodded, trying not to laugh at his exasperated face.

"When you were paired by the crystal, your lives became joined in such a way that can never be taken back. You exchanged part of your souls, or so the women keep telling us. By crushing the crystal, you assured that the exchange would never be reversed. And in the process he gave you some of his years so you could live long together," the King paused, eyeing her. "You got it so far?"

Nadja again dutifully nodded. She didn't dare smile too brightly at the King, lest he stop his explanation.

"All right, good," he said, his chest heaving with breath. He clenched his hands into large fists, keeping them on his lap as he forced himself on. "Each of you are like half of a … a sword. Without the other side, you can't…"

"Lob someone's head off," Nadja offered.

"Exactly!" the King exclaimed with a smile. "It means he's yours and so on--"

"So on?" Nadja probed.

"Yeah, he's done sleeping with other women," the King answered with a throat clearing. Nadja balked in embarrassment. "Now, since you've bonded together, you can read each other's … you know--ah, hell! Ask your husband. It's his job to explain all this. I only came by to tell you Zoran approves of your cream. He's requesting a larger batch to issue to the men. Make a list of what you need and I'll get some worker right on it."

Nadja smiled and nodded, thinking more of Olek than her herbal creation.

The King stood, his hands on his hips, as he ordered lowly, "Now stay here. Olek should be back by tomorrow morning at the latest. I don't want you running about risking my grandson."

"Is that a royal decree?" Nadja asked with an impish grin. She couldn't help it.

"Yes," he grumbled, trying to frown at her but failing. He was too happy about her delicate state to care. Walking out the door, he yelled, "Yes, it most certainly is!"

The news came that night that the men were off to battle with King Attor and his Var warriors. The Draig trackers managed to confirm the spy's words as to the position of Attor's encampment of Var. Nadja was worried, lying in bed for most of the night, the dome curtains drawn, as she tried to sleep.

She'd found the box of jewels her father had given her and had spent most of the day crying over them as she tried to remember the good things about him, though they were few in number. Replacing the last piece in the box and closing it forever, she finally wiped away the last tear she would ever shed for him.

Doc Aleksander was the past. Olek and their baby was the future.

Olek didn't make his way home until late in the next afternoon. Nadja was waiting for him when he walked through the door. To his surprise, he was greeted with a sprinkling of kisses on his face and a long pair of legs wrapping around his waist.

He instantly cupped beneath her buttocks to hold her to him. He parted his lips in astonishment and she moved to kiss him deeply, her tongue dipping to explore his mouth as she tried to steal his breath.

"Mm," Olek moaned, pulling back. A quizzical grin on his face, he asked, "What's this?"

She roamed her hands over his shoulders and suddenly she flinched, realizing the hilt of his sword was poking her in the upper thigh.

"Ow, your sword," she replied, swinging her legs back around to the ground. Olek chuckled. When she was safely landed, he let her go and unstrapped the weapon from his waist.

"I am so sorry I didn't tell you about my father, Olek," Nadja rushed, trying to get everything out at once. "He was one of the leaders of the Medical Mafia. The Alliance is just a front. They could easily save lives, but they don't. They take them. I couldn't stay there and marry his associate, Hank. That's why I ran away and wanted a farmer. I was scared he would find me. And then I saw that dart in Morrigan and I knew that he," Nadja gulped, taking a deep breath, "had come for me. He used to make me carry them across border checkpoints in my hair. Anyway, that's how I knew what it was. I knew he was watching us and that's why I yelled at you. He hated anything not completely human and I was afraid he would try to torture you. I was so scared.

And you don't repulse me and I don't care that you shift--in fact it was kind of … oh," she blushed, but hastened on. "So what happened with King Attor, was anyone hurt? Why were you gone so long?"

Nadja stopped, looking expectantly at him. She blinked, looking up at him through the veil of her lashes.

Through her whole babbling tirade, Olek managed to piece her story together. His wife was so beautiful, her wide eyes searching him as if her whole life depended on what he would say next. Gone was his reserved Nadja who always had a calm answer. He found he liked the babbling woman before him.

"We all are fine. Attor is dead. I've been negotiating peace with his son, the new Var King. It looks promising--" he couldn't finish his answer.

"So you know I'm pregnant?" Nadja rushed, breaking into his words.

Olek was going to say that peace looked promising. That it would be slow going, but could be achieved. Some of the older nobles would protest on both sides. However, in the end, they would bow to the decision of their leaders.

"Yes, I heard your father mention it in the forest and you told me in the medical ward before you spoke to Olena."

"I did?" she asked, surprised. It had all been such a blur.

"Yes, you did," Olek replied. He was about to say more, when she broke in again at a furious pace.

"Do you hate me?" Nadja looked like she wanted to rush forward into his arms. She hesitated. "I never killed anyone, I swear. Well, no one but my father. I never did the things he did. I understand if you want me to leave. I know this has to be an embarrassment to your family. So, do you hate me?"

Olek swept forward to her, gracefully wrapping his arms about her waist. "How could I even think of hating you, Nadja, when I have loved you since first seeing you?"

Nadja trembled. Tears began pouring down her face and she jumped up and back around his waist. "You love me, you really do?"

A rush of feeling poured out of him, connecting her to him and him to her. This connection was strong and free. It would never be severed. Nadja shivered feeling the truth of his words and finally understanding what King Llyr had been trying to tell her in his gruff warrior way.

"Y--"

Olek couldn't even get the word out. Nadja was kissing his face.

"I love you. I love you," she said into him, panting her words between her light, scattered kisses. "I love our baby. I love our life. I love this. I love you, Olek. I love y--"

Olek captured her lips to his, chuckling happily into her. Nadja instantly melted, moaning against his warmth. His arms pressed her to him. Suddenly, Nadja pulled away, her eyes shining with mischief though her face was serious.

"What?" he asked, his lips curling with his perfect smile.

Nadja licked her lips and squirmed naughtily against him. Softly, she answered, "I think your sword is poking me again."

Olek growled, "Keep moving like that wife, and it will be sure to impale you."

Nadja's laughter was cut off by her Prince's kiss. She clung onto him, taking everything he gave her. Her life was perfect. He was perfect. And, as he carted her off to his bed, she hoped he never let her go.

THE END

To learn more about the Dragon Lords series, or Michelle M Pillow's other titles, please visit her website (www.michellepillow.com).

Printed in the United States
40803LVS00001B/41

9 781586 086909